J. F. STRAKER

HELL IS EMPTY

Complete and Unabridged

LINFORD
Leicester

First published in Great Britain

First Linford Edition
published 2009

British Library CIP Data

Straker, J. F. (John Foster)
Hell is empty.—Large print ed.—
Linford mystery library
1. Gangsters—Fiction 2. Fugitives from
justice—Fiction 3. Scotland—Fiction
4. Suspense fiction 5. Large type books
I. Title
823.9′14 [F]

ISBN 978–1–84782–525–4

Published by
F. A. Thorpe (Publishing)
Anstey, Leicestershire

Set by Words & Graphics Ltd.
Anstey, Leicestershire
Printed and bound in Great Britain by
T. J. International Ltd., Padstow, Cornwall

This book is printed on acid-free paper

Hell is empty,
And all the devils are here.

The Tempest, Act 1, Scene 2

1

He is as disproportion'd in his manners
As in his shape.

The Tempest, Act V, Scene 1

Tyres screeched in protest as the Zephyr took the bend a little too fast, a little too wide. For a few seconds the car sagged to the right, as though weight had suddenly been added to that side. Then it shook itself on to an even keel and, after a moment's hesitation during which the front wheels wobbled alarmingly, shot off down the hill.

Donald Grant's grip on the near-side door slackened, his feet relaxed their pressure on the floorboards. 'You took that bend a damned sight too fast,' he said sharply. 'Don't be a fool, Kay. A flaming bad temper is no reason for trying to put us both in the ditch.'

His wife's lips set defiantly.

'I am *not* in a bad temper,' she

snapped. 'Though with all your carping and criticism it's a wonder that I'm not. You've done nothing but find fault with me the whole day, and I'm sick of it.'

She made no reference to her driving because she knew he had been right. She *had* taken that bend too fast; there had been a sickening moment when she had had to fight the car for control, when it had seemed that the car was winning. Had he not spoken she would have lifted her foot from the accelerator and relaxed, thankful to be still on the road. But because of her anger, and because she was young and sufficiently inexperienced to resent fiercely any criticism of her skill as a driver, she took a firmer grip on the steering-wheel and depressed the pedal still farther.

Donald glanced at her, opened his lips to speak, and then thought better of it. He had seen that look on her face too often during the eight years of their marriage to mistake it. Any further protest from him and her angry pride would blaze up into an inferno that neither of them could check. In such a mood she would be liable to drive even more recklessly.

Stubborn little fool! he thought bitterly. Why did she always have to climb on to her high horse whenever they had a difference of opinion? Why did every argument have to disintegrate into a display of verbal fireworks, in which both of them said more than they intended, and which invariably stagnated into a period of sullen hostility that ended only when he decided to apologize? For, right or wrong, it was always he who was the first to surrender; he could match neither her pride nor her irritating aloofness. And though surrender was sweet, culminating in bouts of passion and self-abasement, he was left sometimes with the uneasy wonder of what would happen when her physical attraction for him began to wane, when the incentive to surrender was no longer so compelling.

Another bend, and no slackening of speed. The muscles in his legs tightened involuntarily. But this time she had the car well under control, and he relaxed once more into sullen, resentful brooding.

It was a warm evening, after a morning of rain and mist. Ahead of them the tarmac, caught in the westering sun, shimmered and danced or lay like a gleaming pool of water across their path. The air was filled with insects, that flattened themselves against the windscreen in untidy splodges of grey and brown. A wandering bee smacked heavily into the glass, causing them to duck involuntarily.

They were approaching the mountains now. There were still ten miles to go before they would sight the loch, but already the long ridge that flanked the eastern shore was beginning to rear its boulder-strewn hump above the trees to their right. Far to the north the Malloch Hills showed as a purple barrier across the valley; to the north-west towered Ben Carne, its white bonnet lost in filmy cloud. The green fields on their left rose gently upward, gave way to bracken, and then were lost in the heather that covered the lower slopes of burn-ribbed Grean Muir.

A man came out from the trees ahead

and crossed the road, to stand, one hand hopefully upraised, awaiting them. Instinctively Kay released the pressure of her foot on the pedal.

'Don't stop,' Donald said. 'We're late already.'

His imperative tone decided her. Her right foot switched from accelerator to brake, her left foot came down hard on the clutch. She had been driving too fast for her own peace of mind, but to have slowed before would have been to admit the justice of his criticism. The hitch-hiker enabled her to do so without loss of face. Nor was that her only reason for stopping. That Donald was against it meant, in her present mood, that she was for it. It was yet another opportunity to defy his assumption of marital authority.

As the Zephyr slowed to a halt beside him the hitch-hiker, after a quick look at the scowling Donald, skipped nimbly round the bonnet to smile ingratiatingly through the open window at the young woman.

'Thanks,' he said. 'Nice of you to stop.

Not much doing on the road this evening.'

Kay was not impressed by his appearance. He was slightly built, with dank-looking hair that grew long over the back of a dirty collar and too far down his cheeks. His blue suit was ill-fitting and badly stained, and the loud American tie (bright yellow, adorned with a nude woman all bosom and hips) caused her to shudder inwardly. But it was his eyes that she mistrusted most. They roved over her boldly, appraisingly, from her blonde hair to where the V of her breasts showed above the low-cut summer blouse. She was used to bold, appraising glances from men, had come to accept them as her due. Yet this man's eyes did not stimulate her female ego, they made her feel mean and dirty. Temporarily forgetful of their quarrel, she was suddenly glad of her husband's presence beside her.

'We're not going far,' she said doubtfully. 'Only to the loch. We turn off there.'

'That'll do fine,' the man said. 'Ta.'

As he backed away from the window, still smiling, his eyes still appraising her,

Donald said angrily, 'Here, what the hell!'

Kay turned quickly. Two men were at the near-side of the car. She could not see them clearly, for they were big men, and the roof hid their faces from her. But as Donald struggled round in his seat to confront them the rear-door handle snapped down. For a brief moment she was aware of bloodshot eyes peering at her from an enormous and bewhiskered head, on which an ancient cloth cap rested insecurely; then the cap was snatched off, and the head moved forward into the interior of the car, to be followed by its equally outsize body. As the man settled himself on the back seat with a *plop* that caused the Zephyr to sag protestingly the third man clambered in hastily after him.

Donald Grant swore blasphemously. Kay clutched his arm. She was really frightened now.

The first man, the man who had stopped them, opened the off-side door and squeezed himself into what little room his two companions had left him on the back seat.

'No call to get shirty, folks,' he said, his voice smoothly amiable. 'It's a dodge, see? Drivers won't stop for the three of us — either they're scared, or they think there isn't room. So my two mates here keep out of sight while I do the bumming; me being the smallest, folks'll stop for me where they wouldn't for one of them. And when they've stopped — well, they can't say no to the others, can they? Not if there's room.' Kay could see him grinning at her through the driving-mirror. 'No offence, eh? It's just a dodge, like I said.'

'Of all the bloody nerve!' Donald's face was purple with rage. 'Get out, the three of you! And look slippy! I've a damned good mind to report you to the police for — for — '

He stopped — not through any inability to express himself, but because he had suddenly become aware of the look on the big man's face. The thick lips, their redness accentuated by the dark hair that surrounded them, had parted in a snarl to reveal blackened, disfigured teeth. There was an ugly glint in the bloodshot eyes that cowed him.

Kay too had seen the look. Her grip on her husband's arm tightened warningly.

'It — it wasn't very polite,' she said, trying to keep her voice steady. 'But now you're in you may as well stay. I told you, we're not going far.'

'That's the ticket,' the first man said cheerfully. 'And no hard feelings, eh?'

Neither of them answered. Kay stretched out a shaking hand to switch on the ignition.

Her grip on the steering-wheel was a little tighter than usual, the gears slipped less surely into position; but it was a relief to be driving again, to have something to distract her mind from the men in the back. Yet she could not be rid entirely of her fear; whenever she glanced at the driving-mirror the bearded face was there to remind her of it, staring at her reflection with an unwinking intensity, the threatening look gone but the expression somehow no less unnerving. The first man, the one who had stopped them, leaned uncomfortably in his corner, jammed into it by the bulk of his neighbour; his eyes were closed, but she did not think he slept. The third man's face was turned away from her, but his body was tall and gave an impression of youth.

Donald Grant sat rigidly in his seat, an angry frown on his face, his eyes fixed on the road ahead. Once he pulled a packet of cigarettes from his pocket and lit one, inhaling deeply. As the smoke drifted back the first man opened his eyes and said, 'I could use one of them, mister, if you've any to spare.' Donald handed him the packet over his left shoulder without looking round. He made no protest when the packet was not returned, but the creases in his forehead deepened, and he puffed more furiously at his cigarette.

Kay began to find the silence almost unbearably oppressive; yet she had nothing to say, and small-talk seemed inappropriate. It was with an infinite relief that, as they crested a hill, the first gleam of sunlight on water showed across the tops of the trees to their right. She said, clearing her throat noisily first, so that the sudden sound of her own voice might not cut too abruptly into the heavy silence, 'There's the loch. That's as far as we go.'

The men made no immediate comment. Glancing into the mirror, she saw the two directly behind her exchange a quick look. The big man nodded slightly, and then once more his bloodshot eyes were featured in the mirror.

Kay found herself trembling.

Presently the first man said, 'That's quite a lot of water. You live up this end?'

She swallowed and nodded. But the easy, normal manner in which he had spoken helped to calm her fears. After all, the men had said nothing, done nothing, which could be interpreted as intimidating. There had been only that one baleful look from the big man for her unquiet mind to feed on.

Only that. And yet, recalling the look, she could not believe her fear unjustified.

'Yes,' she said, realizing that her nod might have gone unnoticed, and anxious not to anger them. And it was better to talk than be silent; in silence her fears had time and space in which to multiply. 'On an island. At least, we're staying there. It's called Garra. We'll be able to see it in a few minutes.'

The sound of her own voice, the commonplace words, helped to reassure her. She was even able to feel anger against her husband. Why didn't he say something, try to help her out? Why leave it all to her ? She gave him a sharp glance, but he was too preoccupied with his thoughts to notice it. He was leaning forward now, his shoulders hunched, his lean fingers gripping his knees. He's angry too, she thought. With me? Or with the men?

'There it is,' she said. 'There's the island.'

It was a dark green cone in the distance, visible for only a few moments above the trees. Then the road dipped, and it was lost.

'Bit lonely, ain't it?' the first man commented. 'Was that a house down by the water?'

'Yes. A bungalow. It's the only building on the island. The only habitable building, anyway.'

It would not be long now. When they

saw the island again, over the next rise, it would stay in view until they turned off through the woods to the jetty. They would drop the men off at the corner and then . . .

'How many people live on the island?'

It was the first time the big man had spoken. His voice was rough, but with a loose resonance to it, as though his vocal cords were the bass strings of an old piano. It had a transatlantic twang.

Startled by the unexpected sound, Kay momentarily lost control of the car. 'Look where you're going,' Donald said sharply, as it veered towards the grass verge. 'You'll have us in the ditch.'

She had not needed the warning; even as he spoke she had swung the wheel over. It merely increased her anger against him, and she said tartly, 'Quite the conversationalist, aren't you? Real matey.'

The big man said again, 'How many people live on the island?'

'Only my husband's aunt and uncle and their daughter,' she told him, already slightly ashamed of her show of temper. Donald's nerves must be as much on edge as were hers; neither of them could be expected to behave normally under such conditions. 'The three of us are spending our holidays with them.'

'Three?'

'We have a small son,' she said.

That seemed to exhaust the conversation. No one spoke again until Kay swung the car off the road on to a track that led through the woods to the side of the loch. A few yards along it she brought the car to a stop.

'This as far as you go?' said the first man.

'I'm afraid so. This leads down to the jetty. But I don't suppose you'll have to wait long for another lift.'

She waited expectantly for the men to get out. No one moved. Donald turned. As she saw his face Kay realized that her own anger had been as nothing to his; he was very pale, and his lips were drawn back over the tightly set jaws. Yet he had his voice under control as he said, more calmly than she had expected, 'Didn't you hear what my wife said? This is where you get out.'

Slowly the big man heaved himself forward on the seat.

'About this island of yours, mister. Sounds a nice, quiet place for a holiday. Now, me and my mates here, we've been on the hoof for quite a spell. We're tired, see? I reckon we could do with a few days' lay-up.' The red lips pursed, as though about to spit. 'How about inviting us over, mister?'

Donald stared at him incredulously, wondering if he had heard aright. Kay said quickly, her voice unnaturally shrill, 'We can't do that. It isn't our island, you see; we're only guests there ourselves. And the bungalow is small — there wouldn't be room for — '

'Get out,' Donald said unsteadily. 'Get out, or — '

Kay turned sharply to see what had caused him to stop. She found herself looking at the business-end of a gun.

'We've tried to talk pleasant,' the big man said. His voice was steely, as though the strings had been tightened. 'Now this'll do the talking.' He patted the gun with his left hand. The exposed wrist and the back of his hand were covered with black hair. 'Turn round, mister, and keep your hands in your lap. And don't try any funny business. Guns talk easy.'

For a fraction of a second Donald hesitated, wondering whether the other was bluffing. Too terrified to speak, Kay implored him in her heart to obey. She had no doubt about the determination behind the threat. Neither, after that momentary hesitation, had her husband. He did as the man ordered, not looking at her.

'That's better.' The bloodshot eyes shifted to the girl, but the gun was within inches of Donald's neck. 'Is there a boat at the jetty?'

'Yes.' Her lips formed the word, but there was no sound from them. She nodded.

'Belongs to the island, does it?' And, when she nodded again, 'Any folks likely to be around?'

Kay took a grip on herself; she was beginning to be annoyed at this catechism, and she could not go on jerking her head like a toy mandarin.

‘No.’ It was only a whisper, but the sound of her own voice restored a little of her lost pride. She even, after clearing her throat, ventured a mild protest. ‘You can’t do this. It isn’t — ’

‘Get going, lady.’ He did not raise his voice, but the curt words and tone were enough to silence her. ‘And take it steady. You wouldn’t want to jerk my trigger-finger, would you? It’d come kinda hard on your old man.’

Like Donald, she did not obey at once; there was something about the man’s eyes that mesmerized her, so that it was impossible to turn her own away from them. Then out of the corner of her eye she saw the gun move. The spell was broken, and she turned, reaching for the ignition key.

She took it ‘steady’ — not only because he had so directed, but because the rough, winding track allowed of no other rate of progress. After a few yards the trees closed in on them, shutting them off from the road. No help could come now from that direction.

Kay pondered uneasily on the men’s

intentions. She had no doubt that they were wanted by the police — but what had they done? And if they were on the run why had they not taken the car? Surely that would have offered a better chance of escape than the island? They could not stay on Garra indefinitely. A few days, the big man had said. But what then?

Preoccupied with her thoughts, she took a bend too wide, and had to pull the wheel over sharply to regain the track. The car lurched sideways, throwing Donald against her. But this time there was no reproof, either from her husband or from the men in the back. She gave a swift glance into the mirror. The bearded face was still watching her, its expression unchanged.

It was a compelling face, Kay thought, her eyes once more on the track ahead. Even its ugliness fascinated. The flat, misshapen nose; the dark, bushy eyebrows that sprawled extravagantly in an almost unbroken line above those bloodshot eyes; the wide mouth, thick-lipped as a Negro's, moist and red as raw meat on a butcher's slab; the bald crown, and below it the fringe of black hair that spread downward over the weatherbeaten face, covering cheeks and upper lip and chin and neck, sprouting wildly from the too small ears that stuck out so ludicrously. The man himself might be tough and brutal, but he had an inner power that matched his physical strength and size, that gave a crude dignity to his ugliness. It was not only the gun that had made her obey him. He had not even had to raise his voice. It was his complete confidence in his might, in his own right to authority, that had tamed her pride as Donald had never tamed it.

Kay shuddered. What would the next few days be like? How would the men treat them? Yet her shudder was not born entirely of fear; added to it was a new and rather delicious feeling of anticipation, tingling in its possibilities. Already after a week she was bored with the island; fishing and bathing were not her idea of a holiday. She wanted excitement and gaiety — it was these that made her sparkle and feel that life was good, that lifted her impatient ego out of the dullness of being married to Donald. And these men could do that for her. There might not be gaiety, but at least there would be excitement.

The wood was thinner now. Through the gaps in the trees they could see the loch, its unruffled surface a deep blue in the sunlight. As they turned the final bend they were confronted by a low wooden building, felt-roofed. Behind it the ground dropped steeply to the water's edge.

'What's that?' the big man said, as the car slowed.

'The garage.' Kay put on the hand-brake and turned to look at him. 'The jetty is down there to the right. You'll have to walk from here.'

She was surprised and delighted at her own composure.

The big man grunted at his companions, who scrambled clumsily from the car; they were wedged so tightly into their respective corners by his bulk that it was only with difficulty that they were able to lever themselves clear of it. As the first man — the one who had stopped them on the road — moved round the front of the car Kay saw that he too carried a gun. She wondered why she had not noticed before that he walked with a limp.

With the barrel of his gun the big man prodded Donald gently in the back of the neck. Donald shivered at the cold contact.

'Get out, mister,' the man said. 'Stand over by my mate there until we're ready for you.' The barrel pressed a little harder against the skin. 'And no funny business, see, or there might be an accident. Fred there ain't all that steady with a gun. It's liable to go off when folks move as didn't ought to.'

Donald hesitated. He did not look at the man, but at Kay.

'Do as he says, darling,' she said, concealing her impatience. She knew that his reluctance to leave her was due to a desire to protect her, but a show of heroism now would harm rather than help. 'I'll be all right.'

'You'll both be all right if you act

sensible,' the big man said. 'Get going, mister.'

Without a word Donald obeyed.

The third man had gone over to the garage to open the doors. Now he stood facing the car, and for the first time Kay was able to see him clearly. He was a tall, lean young man in the middle twenties, with a mop of unruly fair hair adorning a white face. He wore a green sports-jacket and dark flannel trousers, both of which garments were several sizes too small for him.

He looks like an unhappy scarecrow, thought Kay. But he's good-looking. She wondered at his unhappiness.

The big man heaved his bulk off the seat and got out of the car; Kay felt the body sag to one side and then, relieved of his weight, spring joyously back to an even keel.

'Put the car away,' the man said curtly, slamming the door shut.

She put the car away. When she came out of the garage the blond young man closed the doors after her, and she smiled at him and thanked him. She felt grateful for his presence, though he did not return the smile; there was something reassuring about his youth and his sad expression. She had the impression that he did not like the business on which he and his companions were engaged. He might be worth cultivating; a friend in the enemy's camp could be useful. And he certainly was good-looking.

Donald was standing against a tree, with the one they called Fred beside him. The big man waited for her in the middle of the clearing. He was tall, though not so tall as she had thought, and the breadth of his shoulders was enormous. His hairy hands and face, and his unusually long arms, gave him a gorilla-like appearance which was heightened by the suspicion of a paunch revealed by the tight denim trousers. Above these he wore an open-necked khaki shirt and a frayed and tattered waistcoat; a haversack was slung across his shoulders. With the cloth cap perched on top of his large head, any other man would have looked ridiculous. Yet Kay felt no inclination to smile at the figure he presented. There was that look in his eyes which forbade it.

At his direction she led the way down the steep path to the jetty. Behind her came the blond young man, and behind him Donald. Fred and the big man, the guns still in their hands, brought up the rear.

It was not a long walk. As they emerged from the trees on to the low ground at water-level the grass was wet under their feet. The grass gave way to rushes, which concealed the water in which they grew. Kay skipped nimbly from one dry mound to another until she reached the long wooden jetty. Most of its planks were rotten, and some were missing. Behind her the big man cursed as he withdrew his boot from a wet patch. She wondered if she should warn him about the jetty. It would be amusing to see one of the planks give way beneath his weight, but he might see to it that her amusement was short-lived. She suspected that he lacked both a sense of humour and the natural chivalry of a man towards a woman.

He was beside her before she could

resolve that problem; the planks sagged under his weight, but they did not give. For a moment he stood staring across the loch at the island, some three-quarters of a mile distant; from the jetty it looked neither so high nor so dark, and the green-and-white bungalow on the hillside gleamed cheerfully in the sun. Then with a grunt, and more nimbly than Kay would have expected, he stepped down into the boat and turned to Donald.

'Who runs this thing? You or your missus?'

'I do,' Donald said.

'Start her up, then.'

The *Stella* was a small cabin cruiser, elderly but well-cared-for, with an open cockpit and a high deck forward. She carried no mast. Over the fresh white paint on her sides rope fenders were suspended; her mooring-lines looked new. The brasswork shone in the sun, and there were gay chintz curtains at her portholes. The woodwork in cabin and cockpit, the mahogany deck, glowed from recent varnishing.

Donald went over to the switchboard.

'Watch him, Joe,' said the big man. 'Find out how she works. We may want to use her ourselves.'

The blond man nodded and joined them in the boat. 'What's the power?' he asked, examining the instruments with interest. His voice was flat, and he mumbled his words. Kay was disappointed. He did not sound as interesting as his melancholy but youthful good looks had promised.

'Ford V-Eight,' Donald told him, pressing the self-starter. There was nothing to be gained by withholding information, and a show of co-operation might make their lot easier. The men had threatened force, but he did not think they would use it unless deliberately thwarted.

He pressed the starter again. The engine fired unevenly, so that the *Stella* throbbed under their feet. Joe climbed up on to the deck, his rubber-soled shoes squeaking on the mahogany, and began to unfasten the mooring-rope. Kay stood uncertainly on the jetty, unpleasantly aware of Fred's proximity, of his hot eyes gazing at her back.

'Get in,' the big man told her. 'Undo that rope at the back, Fred, and let's get started.'

Fred did not immediately obey the instruction. At the first words, before Kay could move, his left hand had grasped hers, his right had moved caressingly up her bare arm to hold it firmly just below the armpit. 'I'll give you a hand, lady,' he said, his voice genial but thicker than before. 'Mind the step.'

Kay moved aside, wrenching herself free. She did not have to struggle; the man let her go willingly enough. But she was glad that Donald had not witnessed the episode. Donald was fiercely possessive. For a man like Fred to lay hands on her was to invite trouble.

Fred grinned at her and went to undo the rope.

Seething with rage, Kay glanced down at the gently rocking boat. She was not used to boats, and the descent into the *Stella* looked tricky in high-heeled shoes; she would probably stumble and fall, and in front of these men it seemed to her imperative that she should preserve her dignity. That and her pride were all she had to combat them with.

Hesitating, she looked up. The big man was staring at her impassively from the cockpit. 'Cold feet, eh?' he said. 'Give the lady a shove, Fred, or we'll be here all night.'

As Fred moved eagerly towards her Kay jumped. It was better to fall than to have him touch her again.

But she did not fall. The big man made no move to help her as she stumbled; it was Joe who caught her. His grip was firm but impersonal, and he released her almost immediately.

Kay rounded furiously on the big man. In the car she had been mesmerized into obedience by those eyes of his, by the gun. But she wasn't mesmerized now, and hurt pride had ousted fear. That this — this ape-like oaf should treat her so casually . . . as though she were a sack of merchandise to be bundled unceremoniously aboard . . .

'You — you — ' She wanted to hurt him, but she could think of no taunt sufficiently savage. He looked impregnable to words. Trembling, she said, 'What a pity they have abolished public hangings. Yours is one I certainly would not have missed.'

The bloodshot eyes narrowed slightly. Then he turned to Donald. 'Get going, mister,' he said.

2

You are three men of sin, whom Destiny,
That hath to instrument this lower world
And what is in't, the never-surfeited sea
Hath caus'd to belch up you; and on this island . . .

The Tempest, Act III, Scene 3

Janet Traynor sat on the steps of the island bungalow idly skimming through the pages of *Vogue*. The world of fashion affected her little (life on Garra was too remote for that), and her interest in the magazine was almost impersonal. Almost, but not quite. Garra was her home, she was part of it and it of her; but there were times when she allowed herself to dream of another world, in which wealth and fashion and romance predominated, in which household and farmyard and agricultural chores were non-existent, in which ocean liners and the gay, exciting cities of a cosmopolitan world took the place of a trip across the loch in the *Stella*.

She was dreaming now. It had been a long and tiring day. Since ten o'clock that morning, when Donald and Kay had departed, she had had her nephew on her hands. She was fond of Bobby, and he was no more difficult to manage than any other six-year-old; but she was not used to children, and she had found the task of entertaining him for a whole day an exhausting one. It had been a relief to get him to bed, to sit down for a few minutes before helping her mother prepare the evening meal.

She looked up from the magazine to gaze across the loch. The sun beat a flarepath over the water, and she shaded her eyes with her hand. The jetty was partly in shadow now, but she could see the *Stella* clearly. No sign of movement there yet. She hoped her cousins would not be late. It always put her father in a bad temper if he had to wait for a meal.

Mrs Traynor came round the corner of the bungalow, a battered pail in one hand. Feeding the chickens was practically the only outside chore she permitted herself. Despite sixteen years on Garra, she was still essentially urban in outlook.

She frowned when she saw her daughter. 'I've told you before, Janet, those shorts aren't decent. They are far too skimpy for a girl of your age.'

My age, thought Janet. Twenty-nine — so soon to be thirty. She looked down at her long legs, tanned, as was the rest of her body, to a rich bronze. There had been a time when she had been proud of that tan; now it was just one more thing that went with the island. She did not think of it, except occasionally to regret, in those moments of day-dreaming, the leathery texture of her skin.

'There's no one to see that matters,' she said, somewhat regretfully. Men on Garra were almost a novelty.

'There's Donald,' Mrs Traynor reminded her, pausing for a moment at the foot of the steps to look across at the *Stella*. She was a small, thick-set woman, with a complexion finer than her daughter's and an abundance of rich brown hair (still, at fifty-five, only faintly streaked with grey) that was her sole personal vanity. She had no other claim to beauty. A faint moustache adorned her upper lip; tufts of hair sprouted from her chin. 'Are you coming in to help me get the meal?'

'In a minute.'

'I hope those two won't be late,' her mother said, beginning to mount the steps. 'You know how it annoys your father. Where is he, dear?'

'In the living-room, listening to the news.'

'Well, don't be long. We'll need another lettuce for the salad. And don't forget the paraffin.'

When her mother had gone indoors Janet resumed contemplation of her legs. Certainly the shorts were brief — they had been longer once; she had taken them up when the hems became frayed — but they were not as brief as Kay's. Nor was her blouse as revealing as those Kay usually wore on the island — although I suppose I haven't much to reveal, she thought, glancing down at her flat chest. Compared with Kay, I suppose I've no statistics at all. And they're certainly not vital.

She stood up reluctantly, fetched the paraffin can from the shed at the back, and sauntered down the gravel path to the little bay which formed the only notable indentation in the island's perimeter. The path was picked out in red granite, hewn from the hillside and carefully shaped by her father. In the wide flower-beds on either side were hydrangeas, dahlias, and gladioli, and behind them climbing roses and sweet-peas clung to the lattice fencing. The bungalow itself stood on the side of the hill which formed the central core of the island; its white paint, with the green window-frames and door, shone freshly in the sunlight. Behind it the trees, mostly larch and rowan, were massed to within a few feet of the crown of the hill; in front the ground had been cleared to form a gently sloping garden, V-shaped, with the bungalow at its apex and widening near the shore into a well-trimmed lawn that ran down to the gravel beach and the jetty.

Janet paused at the jetty to gaze once more across the loch. There was no sign of Donald and Kay, and she turned left and followed the shore until the lawn gave way to trees — spruce and rowan and an occasional oak, thinned out, and with the ground well cleared. A track led through the wood, and at the end of it was the kitchen-garden. It was typical of Robert Traynor, a martinet and a keen horticulturalist, that he would have no vegetables growing within sight of the bungalow. He acknowledged their necessity, but he would not allow their mundane presence to spoil his view. That this entailed unnecessary physical exertion on the part of his womenfolk had not occurred to him. Had it done so he would not have considered it a sufficient reason to change his opinion.

Janet cut the lettuces and laid them in a heap near the path; then she went on and up. The ground was pasture here, wired in and undulating, and dotted with patches of rush and bracken and an occasional bush; grazing-land for the two Friesians. These and the chickens were the only livestock on the island. Janet and her mother would have welcomed a dog; but

Robert Traynor did not like dogs, and nothing was done about it.

The fuel-store was a natural cave in the hillside, ventilated and well-shored and protected by a stout wooden door. This was another instance of Traynor's insistence on 'everything in its place.' There was petrol for the boat, paraffin for the stoves and the lamps — dangerous stuff, Traynor insisted, to have anywhere near a wooden bungalow. His wife's protest that she should not be expected to go so far for fuel, at all times and in all weathers, was brushed impatiently aside with the retort that there would be no need for her to do so; he would do the fetching and carrying himself. He seldom did; he was usually employed on some other task when fuel was urgently needed. Rose Traynor kept her own secret store of paraffin near the house, but even that needed frequent replenishing.

As she reached the lawn on her return Janet saw that the *Stella* had left the far shore and was on her way across. For a few moments she watched it. Then, as the boat veered momentarily from its course and she saw it broadside-on, she gave an exclamation of dismay and hurried back to the bungalow.

Robert Traynor was in the living-room, busy at his typewriter. He frowned at his daughter's noisy entrance, his train of thought disrupted. But in a rather detached way he was fond of her, and his spoken reproof was mild.

Janet brushed it away with a vague gesture. She recognized his right to authority, but she did not share her mother's awe of him.

'We've got visitors,' she said. 'Where's Mummy?'

'In the kitchen, I hope.' The frown returned. Visitors at this late hour would result in the evening meal being delayed. (He always referred to it as the 'evening meal': 'dinner' was too grand a term for such a modest repast, and 'supper' a word he could not abide.) 'Who are our visitors?'

'I don't know. But there are at least four or five people on the *Stella*, and they will be here in a few minutes. I must warn Mummy.'

She picked up the paraffin can, which she had temporarily deposited on the floor, and made for the kitchen. With a sigh her father abandoned his typewriter and followed her. He was by nature a hospitable man, and if there were to be visitors they must be met and welcomed and, if necessary, nourished. But he preferred his hospitality to be dispensed at his own choosing. The unexpected guest unsettled him.

Not so his wife. She was at home in the kitchen, and the thought of company excited her. 'There's omelettes and a salad,' she said. 'And cheese. They can't sniff at that, can they?'

'It depends on the cheese,' Traynor said.

'Cheddar, dear. You had some for lunch yesterday.'

Janet smiled, her father frowned. One had to hammer a joke home for Rose to see it. He said, 'I'll go down to the jetty. Coming, Janet?'

'Take your shorts off before you go, dear,' Mrs Traynor called after her daughter. 'Donald might not like your meeting his friends in them.'

'He'd disapprove still more if I were out of them,' Janet said, laughing. 'Anyway, there isn't time to change.'

The *Stella* came in too quickly, bumped against the jetty, and veered away. Traynor, standing on the jetty with Janet beside him, frowned. Mentally he chalked up yet another black mark against his nephew, and watched with anxiety as Donald put the boat into reverse, backed away, and came in again. He sighed with relief as the fenders rubbed gently against the wooden piles, and grabbed the rope that was thrown to him.

Only then did he notice the thrower — a tall, blond young man who had apparently outgrown his apparel. Perplexed, his eyes roved over the *Stella*'s other passengers, until they came to rest in startled fascination on a bearded, hairy face that gazed fixedly up at him from beneath a grimy cloth cap.

Janet was quicker than her father to realize that something was wrong. She had always been scornful of her cousin's handling of the *Stella*, and his inability to lay the boat alongside the jetty at the first attempt had occasioned her no surprise. While her father's concern had been all for the *Stella*, her interest had been concentrated on the passengers. And the odd group that met her gaze was very different to what she had expected.

Perplexed and troubled, she turned to look at her father. He still stood with the rope in his hand, frowning in angry bewilderment at the boat.

'What a crew!' she said. 'Where on earth did Donald pick that lot up?'

Traynor shook his head, and watched grimly as his nephew scrambled rather awkwardly on to the jetty and came to meet them. Behind Donald came the man with the beard.

'Brought you a boatload of trouble, I'm afraid.' Donald spoke curtly, angry with himself. At the back of his mind was the uncomfortable suspicion that he had been too timid, that he should have taken some bold step to prevent this invasion. He jerked his thumb to indicate the men behind him. 'These toughs held us up and forced us to bring them across. They want to lay up here for a few days.' Seeing the look in Traynor's eyes he added hastily, 'Take it easy, Uncle. They're armed.'

In proof of this statement the big man produced his gun, slapping the barrel noisily into the palm of his left hand.

'He's dead right there, mister. You just take it easy, like he said, and everything'll be fine. We don't aim to cause no trouble, but we ain't scared of it.'

Donald took the rope from Traynor's hand and bent to tie up the *Stella*. He moved slowly and deliberately. The big man had not hitherto shown himself possessed of nerves, but with his finger on the trigger it was safer not to startle him into activity.

Kay walked down the jetty towards them, Fred and Joe behind her. She nodded casually to Janet.

'Sorry about this, Uncle Robert,' she said, her smile a brave attempt at nonchalance. 'We stopped to give these — er — gentlemen a lift, and now we're stuck with them. They haven't been very communicative so far, but one gets the impression that the mainland isn't particularly healthy for them at present. They hope you may prove more hospitable. Oh — let me introduce you. This is Joe, and this is Fred.' She did not look at the latter, indicating him with a sideways nod of her head. 'The one in the heavy disguise hasn't so far disclosed his identity.'

The big man did not take his eyes off Traynor. 'Call me Bull,' he said shortly. ''Tain't my real name, but it'll do.'

'It'll do very well,' Kay agreed. He had ignored her on the trip across, and this had increased her anger against him. She was not used to being ignored, least of all by such as he. But she had her anger under better control now. Somehow, some time, she would get even with him; until that time came she must content herself with pinpricks. He might not feel them, but they would help to heal her wounded self-esteem. 'Most appropriate, apart from the fungus.'

Donald frowned. Baiting their captors could only make their lot worse. But it was typical of Kay; put her in an ill humour and she would let fly, without pausing to consider the possible consequences. Why the devil couldn't she curb that damned tongue of hers?

Janet was suddenly aware that her mouth was open. She shut it hastily. So far the newcomers had taken little notice of her. The one called Fred had looked her over, his eyes lingering on her long, bare legs, and had then returned his gaze to her father. They were all watching her father, she realized, waiting to see what he would do. Alarmed, she watched him too.

Robert Traynor's anger was so intense that for once he had been unable to find words with which to express it. Apart from his family there were two great loves in his life — his boat and his island. That these toughs should commandeer the one and invade the other — that they should actually threaten him — here, on Garra . . .

Joe licked his lips nervously. Fred said brightly, 'Come on, guv. Let's get the reception over and bring on the eats. I'm starving.'

Traynor took a short pace forward. Standing very upright, shoulders squared, his thick grey hair shining almost white in the westering sun, he looked steadily from one to the other of the three men. The nails of his fingers bit into the palms of his hands, so tightly were his fists clenched. With a supreme effort at control he said, 'My nephew will take you back. Now. We don't want your sort on Garra.' Fred's gun came up menacingly, but Traynor did not flinch. 'And don't wave your gun at me, my man. You won't frighten me that way.'

Bull's eyes contracted. He stepped forward so that his hairy face was only a few inches from Traynor's.

'You've got the wrong idea, mister.' His voice was a growl. 'We're here and we're staying, and there ain't nothing you can do about it, see? Now you go back to the house and tell your missus to get a meal ready.' He turned to Janet. 'You too, miss. We — '

It was too much for Robert Traynor; he was used to giving orders, not receiving them. Heedless of the consequences, and with no thought in his mind other than the need to protect his beloved island from the threatened invasion, he aimed a wild blow at Bull's head. But Bull, although he had turned to speak to Janet, had kept a wary eye on the old man. He saw the blow coming, and ducked. Then his own fist came up. It exploded on Traynor's chin, and the old man went down, knees sagging, to lie in a crumpled heap on the jetty.

Janet screamed. Donald had started impetuously forward, only to be brought up sharply as Fred dug a gun-barrel viciously into his side. At the sight of the gun Janet intensified her screaming. Bull wheeled on her, his hand slapping across her cheek with a stinging blow. She stumbled away from him, and would have fallen had not Joe caught her arm.

One hand to her smarting cheek, she stared incredulously at the man who had hit her. But she had stopped screaming.

Kay said, 'Aren't you getting a little rough, Mr Bull? Or is that just to impress us? An old man and a girl! Quite a tough guy, aren't you?'

The big man turned on her.

'Shut up, you! Any more of your lip and you'll get what I gave the other dame.' He stirred the prostrate Traynor with his foot. 'The old fool!' he said wonderingly. 'What the hell did he want to do that for? Hey, mister!' The foot prodded deeper. 'Get up!'

Traynor stirred and groaned. Joe bent and hauled him to his feet, holding him firmly. The old man's eyes were still glazed, and he looked about him uncomprehendingly. Janet went to him, taking his arm, her own fear forgotten in her concern. She even managed a weak smile of gratitude for Joe.

The young man flushed. He did not return the smile.

Mrs Traynor came out of the bungalow and stood on the steps, shading her eyes with her hand. She had heard Janet's scream. 'What is it?' she called to them. 'What's wrong with your father, Janet?'

She began to bustle down the steps. Bull swore. 'Head her off, you,' he said to Kay. 'I don't want any more bloody females treading on my toes. Take her back to the house and tell her to get cracking with the eats. You go with 'em, Fred. Joe and I can deal with this bunch.'

Kay hesitated. She did not want to obey him, and she did not want Fred as a companion. She looked inquiringly at Donald.

He nodded. 'Better do as he says, Kay,' he said quietly, determined that since heroism was beyond him he would at least be dignified. 'Some one has to tell Aunt Rose.'

Kay went, her head high. She walked sedately, not hurrying, ignoring the limping Fred at her side. Bull and Donald watched them go.

'Quite a game one, your missus,' Bull said dispassionately. 'It'll be a pleasure taking the stuffing out of her.'

* * *

There was little conversation at the meal, but it was not a silent one. Bull ate ravenously, wolfing his food, knife and fork and spoon plying noisily; the sound of his champing jaws, the curious sucking noise with which he completed each enormous mouthful, made Janet feel sick. She sat opposite to him, but she could not bear to watch him; he kept his mouth open as he ate, pushing the food forward with his tongue, rolling it round and round until it was crushed by the black, disfigured teeth and swallowed with a noisy gulp. The way his lower jaw swung from side to side reminded her or a cow. She preferred to look at Joe, who sat next to him. Joe ate as eagerly as Bull, but more quietly, and with only a slight movement of his jaws. He seemed to swallow the food without chewing it. Mouthful after mouthful was shovelled in, to slide easily down his gullet, his prominent Adam's apple working overtime.

Fred caught the direction of her glance, the surprise and disgust on her face, and grinned at her. 'Last meal we had was midday yesterday,' he said. 'Tin o' beans between the three of us.'

Though he had been the most vociferous in his demand for food, he ate sparingly; he had a weak stomach, and the excitement of sitting next to Kay Grant (into which position he had adroitly manœuvred himself) had dulled his appetite. The scent of her in his nostrils, the occasional contrived contact (a contact Kay could not avoid, for they were tightly packed round a table designed to seat six), put butterflies into his stomach. His mind was tormented by erotic fancies. The only women he had known hitherto had been the occasional prostitute, bought and clumsily possessed in some dark alley. To be seated next to this disdainful, beautiful creature . . . to have her to some extent in his power . . . to gloat on the victory that might be his if only that power could be made absolute was to drive from Fred's sex-ridden mind all thought of food.

Kay too ate little. Fred's nearness disgusted her; each moment of contact filled her with loathing. Once she made to get up, to insist that Donald should change places with her. As her chair scraped back over the carpet Fred's hand came down hard on her thigh, the long, thin lingers biting into the soft flesh so that she nearly cried out with the pain. But she did not cry out, nor did she again try to move. Neither Donald nor her uncle could help her now. It was to Bull she would have to appeal; and rather than ask the help of that hairy-faced monster she preferred to suffer in silence the indignities Fred forced on her. Her anger against Bull was even greater than her loathing for Fred. Had Fred been of her own kind and a reasonably personable male she might even, while outwardly reproving him, have accepted his advances as evidence of yet another desirable conquest.

Like Janet, she too watched Bull. But his gluttony and pig-sty manners did not sicken her as they sickened her cousin; they added to her anger against him, but they did not repel her. Rather they fascinated her. Bull was an elemental, an animal; it was in keeping with his other animalisms that he should also eat like one.

She turned to look at Donald. He was eating steadily, his eyes fixed on his plate.

It annoyed her that he should remain so unconcerned. Unreasonably, her annoyance grew with every mouthful he ate, becoming part of her hatred of Bull and her loathing for Fred, so that she could hardly wait for the meal to finish and a chance to vent her spleen on him. If she could do little as yet about the others, at least Donald should not escape her wrath.

Donald was unaware of her mounting annoyance. He had a good appetite, and he ate mechanically, from habit. His thoughts were concentrated on the catastrophe that had befallen them, and his own part in it. Eight years of marriage to Kay had made him even more of an introvert than before, had blunted his self-confidence; now he searched frantically for an excuse to shift, to his own satisfaction if not to theirs, the blame which he believed the others must attach to him. Yet where else could he place it? On Kay? She had stopped the car against his advice. But to hide behind Kay would only highlight the fact that it was she who wore the trousers, who was the dominant partner in their relationship. To Donald, anxious above all to appear in a heroic light, this was not an attractive alternative. Even to himself he would not admit it.

He paused in his eating to look round the table, prepared to answer an accusing look with defiance. In particular he looked at his uncle, who must resent this invasion more than anyone. His uncle had never liked him, he knew that. It was Kay who was the favourite, who was responsible for their presence there on Garra. Without Kay he would never have been invited.

No one was watching him, not even Uncle Robert, who, slumped back in his chair, his food untasted, was staring fixedly at the centre of the table. Relieved, Donald returned to his eggs and bacon.

Eggs and bacon were what the men had demanded. Three eggs and three rashers apiece, with thick slices of fried bread. When Rose had mentioned the salad already prepared Bull had said that would be okay, they would have it with the cheese. Privately she had thought that they would have no room for cheese; now, having seen with what speed the bacon and eggs had been dispatched, she began to wonder anxiously about further supplies. They would be all right for milk and eggs, and Janet and she baked some of the bread; but for the rest it would mean Janet must go shopping on the mainland. Or some one must. Their normal weekly supply would not last long at this rate.

With a piece of bread clutched between thumb and fingers Bull wiped the last traces of egg and bacon fat from his plate. He thrust the bread into his mouth and immediately reached for the cheese, cutting himself a large wedge.

As he speared it with his knife Rose said sharply, 'That's all the cheese we have.'

'No more outside?' he asked.

'No. No more cheese and no more bacon. And at this rate there will be no more of anything by this time to-morrow. This isn't an hotel.'

He shrugged. 'There's shops, ain't there?' he said, and went on with his meal.

Yes, she thought, there are shops. And

with the thought came a gleam of hope. Even if the men did the shopping themselves their presence in the village would evoke surprise and comment. Inquiries might be made . . . they would be watched, perhaps followed . . . She glanced across at her husband, hoping that the same thought might have occurred to him. His present apathy worried her far more than the presence of the three men. She had never seen Robert like this before. For over thirty years it had been Robert who had made the decisions, had given the orders; she who had abided by them. Even when the greatest decision of all had been taken — to buy Garra and make it their home, to cut themselves off from their old life and friends so that he might write his books in peace and solitude — she had not questioned it. Garra meant a way of life completely alien to her nature and upbringing, but she had accepted it uncomplainingly. Robert always knew what was best; he did not make mistakes, he was never at a loss. He was omniscient, impregnable.

So she had thought. Now, disillusioned and sad, she watched him covertly. She had been both proud and dismayed when they had told her what had happened on the jetty. Robert was over sixty, too old to tackle men like these; it had been inevitable that he should get the worst of it. But she had not thought that they could defeat his spirit.

'Eat something, dear,' she said. 'It's after nine. You must be hungry.'

He looked at her vaguely. His spirit was not defeated, merely dormant; he had not yet recovered from the effects of the blow Bull had landed on his chin. The events that had followed it were like the events in a dream, nebulous and unconnected. The men were there at his table, eating his food; but he could not remember why they were there. He knew that they displeased him, the one with the hair on his face in particular; but he was not greatly concerned. At any moment they might change or vanish. In a dream nothing logical happened. It was not happening now.

Rose thought he had not heard her.

'Eat something, Robert,' she said again. 'It's after nine o'clock.'

That reached him. Nine o'clock meant the news, a ritual he never missed. He pushed his chair back and rose.

They all looked at him. Joe and Bull stopped eating. 'Siddown, mister,' the big man said, a piece of Cheddar balanced on the knife before his mouth.

Traynor took no notice. He walked across to the radio and switched it on. Fred half rose from his chair, reaching for his gun.

Bull shook his head. 'Let him be,' he growled, and snapped at the cheese. There was a click as his teeth scraped the knife. 'He can have the radio if he wants it. But watch him. He's an obstreperous old bastard.'

Traynor turned to look at them. The haze was beginning to clear; perhaps he could have shaken it off earlier had he so willed. But in his subconscious mind had been the unpleasant thought that once he was rid of the dream he would have to take action. And he was not ready to act, to make decisions.

Into the silence came the voice of the announcer.

'. . . are believed to have got away with about three thousand pounds in cash. The police have so far been unable to question Howard Kemp, the man who was shot. His condition is said to be critical.

'A woman who lives opposite the factory, and who heard the shot and saw the two men leave, said this morning that she thought there was a third man in the waiting car. The car, a Rover saloon, was later found abandoned on the outskirts of the town. It had been stolen from outside a doctor's surgery.

'The police have issued the following descriptions of the two wanted men. One is just over six feet in height, massively built and with broad shoulders, and when last seen had a thick growth of hair on his face. He was wearing trousers and waistcoat, with no jacket. The — '

Bull shouted angrily, 'Turn that damned thing off!'

Traynor stared at him, his arms limp by his sides, motionless save for a slight twitching of the fingers.

' — about five feet seven inches in height. He was wearing a blue suit and walks with a slight limp.

'At least one of the men is armed. The public are — '

It was Joe who switched it off, moving across the room in great loping strides. He stood by the set, beads of sweat on his forehead, and glared at them in ashamed defiance.

No one else moved. Kay said acidly, 'So that's who you are!'

Bull shifted a wad of bread to one side of his mouth, so that his cheek bulged ludicrously. 'That's who we are, lady. And that's why we're here.' With his tongue he hooked the bread back for further mastication.

'I've no doubt this Mr Kemp was elderly, and unarmed.' Kay's voice was smoother now. The opportunity to lash him with her tongue delighted her. 'Which of you was brave enough to shoot him?' She felt rather than saw the frown on her husband's face, felt Fred wriggle uncomfortably on his chair as he placed a warning hand on her thigh. She brushed the hand away. 'Well?' she demanded, staring accusingly at the bearded face opposite. 'Don't you want to boast about it, now that your secret's out?'

Bull mashed a piece of bread in the sauce from the pickles on his plate, and popped it into his mouth. 'You got a wide mouth, lady,' he said, chewing rhythmically as he leaned forward across the table. His gaze shifted to the anxious Donald and back to her. 'Your old man should have done something about that. Or maybe he don't know how? I'll have to learn him.'

Slowly he pushed himself up from the table. With a dirty fingernail he began to prise particles of food from between his teeth, his bloodshot eyes fixed reflectively on her. Then he belched — an enormous, reverberating belch, that started in the pit of his stomach and rumbled noisily upward. It seemed to startle him. He said, with the first trace of humour he had so far shown, 'Seems like you and me both suffer from wind, lady.'

If he had slapped her he could not have

angered her more; her dignity was more easily hurt than her body. To be spoken to in such a manner — and by such a man! Seething with impotent fury (impotent because she could think of no biting rejoinder), she watched him turn heavily away and walk across the room to her uncle. Her mind was nothing but a receptacle for anger, her whole frame quivered with it. Had Donald chosen that moment to reprove her, or Fred to touch her, she would have struck them — blindly, furiously, forgetful of sex and dignity, venting on them the anger she could not vent on the man who had aroused it.

Bull said, hitching up his denims, 'I told you to switch that bleeding thing off, mister.' He lit a cigarette from the packet Donald had handed over in the car. There was a rougher twang to his voice as he added, 'Better do as I say next time, or you and me ain't going to get on so good.'

I mustn't let him score off me so easily, Kay told herself. That's what he wants. I mustn't let him see when he gets me rattled with his rudeness and his brutishness. I've got to be cool and collected and disdainful, ignore him unless I have something really cutting to say, something that will penetrate even his thick hide. I can only fight him with words — I can't use my sex, he isn't a man, he's just a brute beast. But I'll beat him somehow.

She remembered the slap across the face with which he had silenced the screaming Janet, and her enthusiasm for the fight was momentarily chilled.

If Traynor heard the warning he did not need it. He was staring wide-eyed at Bull and Joe. 'Gunmen and murderers!' His voice was a whisper. 'In my house — at my table. Good God!'

Bull scowled. It seemed that the old man could get under his skin more easily than could Kay — perhaps because his indignation was more honest.

'He ain't dead yet,' he said harshly. 'Don't wish it on him.'

Rose glanced anxiously across at her husband. It was a relief to know that he had come out of his stupor, that he was himself again, but she did not want him to start another fight. She said, hoping to ease the tension by a return to normality, 'If you've all finished eating, Janet and I would like to get on with the washing-up. There's a lot to do.'

They stood up. Janet began stacking the plates, eyeing with disgust the scraps of food on the table where Bull had sat. Bull said, 'Give 'em a hand, Joe, but see that they stay in the kitchen. I don't want no one wandering around. Fred, you stay here and keep an eye on the two men. I'll take the blonde.' He turned to Kay. 'Come on, lady. You and me'll go fix the sleeping-quarters.'

Kay's grip tightened on the back of her chair; her knees felt wobbly, her eyes were not focusing properly. It was one thing to bait him in public, but how brave could she be when she was alone with him? To fix the sleeping-quarters, he had said. But why pick on her? Why not Janet, or Aunt Rose? Had she summed him up wrongly? Was he another, but less subtle, Fred? Not that Fred was subtle in his approach. But she could handle Fred, she thought; Fred was the slimy, insinuating kind, he would not seek to rely on force. But Bull . . .

She said faintly, trying to appear unconcerned, 'You had better take Aunt Rose or my uncle. It's their home, not mine.'

He walked slowly across the room, passing close to her without looking at her. At the door he turned.

'You folks don't catch on so quick,' he said. 'Listen — I'm giving the orders, see, and you do the jumping. And if you don't jump good and smart — ' He licked his red lips. 'But that ain't nice to talk about. Coming, lady?'

As Kay still hesitated, reluctant to leave the comparative safety of the room, Donald stepped forward.

'Now see here, Mr Bull — '

'Bull,' the big man said. 'You can cut out the mister.'

'All right. Now, you've got the whip-hand at present, and we're not denying it. We can't. We must do as you say, whether we like it or not. But you can drive us too far, you know. I'm damned if I'll sit tight and let you walk out of here with my wife.

If she goes I go.'

Bull's eyes narrowed; his lips were drawn back over the blackened teeth in a snarl. He took a step towards Donald.

'You do, do you? Listen, mister — ' He paused. A look of astonishment appeared on his hairy face, to be followed by a broad grin. He began to laugh, a deep rumble that shook his whole frame. 'Jesus! You think I got hot pants for that wife of yours? Mister, all I want right now is to hit the hay. I don't aim to get tangled up with no woman. And if I did . . . ' He bowed mockingly to Kay. 'Lady, if you're hugging the same idea as your old man, forget it. You ain't got a chance. Not with me you ain't. I'm choosey about dames.'

Kay's cheeks flamed. They could not have been redder if he had slapped her across the face with his hand. The beast! she thought. The filthy, mocking beast! Now I know how people can be driven to murder. If I had a gun I'd shoot him without the least compunction.

'Get moving, lady. We ain't got all night.'

Without looking at him, she walked

past him into the hall.

The bungalow was built in the shape of an L, with the kitchen and the large living-room in one arm, the bedrooms and bathroom in the other. At the far end of the latter was the guest-room, with twin beds and gaily painted walls and furniture. Its windows faced north and west, overlooking the loch.

'My husband and I are sleeping in here,' Kay said. And added, 'With your permission, of course.'

He grunted non-committally and walked out into the passage, pausing outside the door of the middle bedroom.

'Bobby's in there. He's sharing it with my cousin Janet.' For a moment she forgot her dignity and her anger, and was her natural self. 'Don't go in, please. He's asleep, and I don't want him woken up.'

He pushed her aside, opened the door, and went in.

It was a small room, with a single window facing north. Bobby, plump-cheeked and with fair curly hair, lay in one of the two iron bedsteads. He slept on his side, one fat little arm outside the coverlet, the other tucked under his pillow. On a chair beside the bed, on top of an untidy pile of clothing, was a toy revolver and an imitation leather holster and belt. A wide-brimmed stetson hung by its strap from the chair-back.

Bull looked at the boy. Then he rejoined Kay in the passage, closing the door quietly.

They went into the last and biggest of the three bedrooms.

'The old couple sleep in here, eh?'

'Yes.'

'And that's the lot?'

'Yes.'

'Okay. You and your old man can stay put. The girl can move in here with her folks, and I'll sleep with the kid. My mates can doss down in the living-room.'

She said hotly, 'You can't sleep in the same room as Bobby. He'd be scared stiff if he woke up in the night and saw you there. I'll move him into my room.'

He shook his head. 'The kid stays where he is. He'll be a hostage for the rest of you. You start something, and I take it out on the kid. Get me?' She nodded, knowing that this was no idle threat. But he had lost interest in her and the boy. He said, frowning, 'I'll have one of my mates sleep in the boat, just in case some one ain't all that fond of the kid and thinks of taking a trip.' And added, speaking his thoughts aloud, 'It'd better be Fred. Fred don't know about boats or engines.'

She wondered what was in his mind.

As they turned the corner into the hall they heard Robert Traynor say, 'Keep them up. High. Donald, lock the kitchen door and then take his gun. Don't get between me and him. If he moves at all I'll let him have it.'

He was standing just inside the room, a shotgun under his arm. Its muzzle pointed at the scowling Fred. Impetuously Kay started forward, only to be brought up short as Bull's hand closed round the back of her neck and gripped it. A choked scream escaped her. Bull threw her backward and dug his gun hard into Traynor's back.

'Drop that gun, mister. Put it on the floor quick if you know what's good for you. My finger's itching.'

Only for a second did the old man hesitate. Then he bent slowly and placed the gun at his feet.

'Pick it up, Fred.'

With a sigh of relief Fred lowered his arms. He walked across the room and hit Traynor hard on the cheek with his open hand. Traynor just looked at him, deigning neither to duck nor to move.

Fred said viciously, his eyes bright, 'You try any more tricks like that, guv, and you'll get more than a slap in the face.' He brought his gun from his inside breast-pocket and dug it into his victim's stomach. Traynor groaned, bending forward involuntarily — only to be straightened up by Fred's cupped hand hard under his chin. 'I don't carry this here gun for fun, guv. Ask that chap at the factory — if he's still breathing. He'll tell you.'

'Shut up, damn you!' Bull roared. 'Pick that bloody gun up, like I said.' He prodded Traynor with his own gun. 'Get over there and sit down, mister. You too, Grant. And keep your fannies glued tight to them seats if you don't want a bellyful of lead.'

Without a word they did as he ordered — Donald in a flurry of obedience, the older man more calmly, without haste. Bull turned on Fred, his face suffused with anger.

'How did he get hold of that gun? I thought I told you to watch the bastards?'

'He said he wanted to go to the lav.' Fred's eyes were wary. Bull in a temper was a man to be feared. 'How the hell was I to know he kept a gun in there?'

Bull stepped closer to him. 'You got eyes, haven't you? Why the hell didn't you search it first?'

'I didn't think.'

The big man spat in disgust.

'You didn't think! Smart, ain't you? You'd better start using your loaf, mate, if you want to stay alive in this racket.' But it was plain that his anger was cooling. He said wearily, 'You're sleeping on the boat to-night, in case some one tries to pinch it. Better get down there now.'

Fred said sullenly, 'Why me? Why not you or Joe?' And then, as the bloodshot eyes narrowed, 'Okay, okay. What do I use for blankets ?'

'There are blankets in the lockers under the bunks,' Donald said.

Without further argument Fred went into the hall and out through the front door, slamming it shut behind him. He did not see Kay. Earlier in the evening she had thought that they might be able to make use of Joe, sensing that he had no liking for the business afoot. Now, seeing the wrathful look on Fred's face, she began to wonder whether Fred might not prove the more willing ally. She realized, too, why Bull had chosen Fred to sleep on the *Stella*. He trusted his confederates no more than they liked or trusted him or each other. Either of them, he knew, might rat on the other two if they thought it would pay them and if the opportunity offered.

But Joe knew about boats, Bull had said, and Fred did not. So Fred slept on the *Stella*. He wasn't giving them that opportunity.

3

He is not valiant.
The Tempest, Act III, Scene 2

Kay's prediction that Bobby would be terrified at the unexpected sight of Bull in the bed formerly occupied by Janet had been proved wrong; the boy had, in fact, been fascinated by his new room-mate. But his fascination had been tempered with discretion. Even to Bobby's immature mind it had been apparent that this bewhiskered stranger was some one to be handled with care. His friendship could not be attacked with the same abandon as that of more ordinary mortals.

Bull looked up from putting on his boots (apart from these he had slept fully dressed, with door and window locked, and the haversack and pistol under his pillow) to see the boy regarding him wide-eyed. He nodded and stood up. Encouraged by the nod, Bobby wished him a polite good-morning.

'Morning,' said Bull. He was unaccustomed to politeness. He fished a crumpled cigarette from a waistcoat pocket and lit it, bursting into a noisy cough as the smoke hit his lungs.

'Did you come back with my daddy?' Bobby asked.

'Yep.'

'Where's Aunt Janet?'

'In one of the other rooms.'

The boy pushed back the bedclothes and sat up. Ignoring his evident desire to be friendly, Bull turned and reached under the pillow. At sight of the gun Bobby drew in his breath sharply.

'Gosh! Is that a *real* pistol?'

The man nodded absently. He stuck the gun in his hip-pocket and opened the haversack. It was stacked with bundles of five-and one-pound notes, but the sight of so much money did not bring immediate joy to his face. His mouth was shut in as near to a straight line as the full lips would allow, his brow furrowed in thought. With a dirty forefinger he began to pick his nose.

It was all his. Fred and Joe, they thought they had a share coming. They hadn't worked with him before, the suckers, they didn't know that letting him take charge of the dough was as good a way as any of saying good-bye to it. They would catch on eventually, of course, when it was too late. Joe wouldn't make trouble; Joe was soft, this was his first snatch, he didn't know his way around. And Fred? Fred had a gun, but he lacked guts; he wouldn't face a showdown — not with a man whom he knew to be the better shot. A slug in the back was what he had to fear from Fred. And if I'm mug enough to give the bastard the chance, Bull thought grimly, that'll be what I deserve.

He took a bundle of one-pound notes from the haversack. Would the old man have enough dough handy for the shopping that had to be done? The woman had said . . .

'Stick 'em up!'

With an oath Bull dropped the money and swung round, his right hand going instinctively to his hip. Bobby, his blue eyes dancing gleefully, stood on the floor in his pyjamas, his toy revolver pointing at the man's stomach. His stetson was perched crookedly on the back of his head.

Bull took a deep breath. Elbow bent, he raised his arm. But Bobby did not recognize the threat in the gesture, and he did not flinch. The revolver was steady in his fist.

For a few seconds the man and the boy stared at each other, a faint bewilderment in Bobby's eyes that his victim should look and act so oddly. Then Bull's arm dropped slowly to his side.

'Don't you ever do that again, son,' he said hoarsely.

⋆ ⋆ ⋆

Once they were away from the jetty and well out into the loch Janet said, 'Do you want to take over?'

Joe nodded.

'Ever handled a boat like this before?'

'Yes.'

She made way for him at the wheel.

‘It’s choppy out in the middle to-day. Quite a breeze. I should take her down past the point there’ — she stood beside him, indicating the landmark — ‘before you go across. It’s more sheltered there. It means doubling back, but she’d ship a lot of water if she took that chop beam-on.’

It was good to be away from the island, she thought, turning to watch the *Stella*’s wake boiling and creaming behind them. The stiff breeze cooled the sun’s rays and gave lift and life to the loch’s surface. Above them seagulls swooped and chattered, flapping their wings madly as they hovered low over the water, then beating powerfully away, their pink legs trailing behind them.

Joe handled the boat well. For a few minutes she watched him, then went into the cabin to fold and stow away the blankets that Fred had slept in. When she came out they were well down the loch.

She settled herself in the stern, noting with approval how Joe held the *Stella* firmly on course, cutting the throttle to prevent the engine from racing as they hit the crests. He stood very erect, the breeze ruffling his fair hair, seemingly oblivious of the occasional bursts of spray that enveloped him. Once or twice he turned to look, not at her, but at the fast-receding island and the long vista of the loch. Water dripped from his face and hair, and the green jacket had assumed a darker hue. But his grey eyes no longer had the dull, lost look she had hitherto seen in them. They were alert and shining.

She could guess the reason for the transformation. He's like Daddy and me, she thought. He may be a common crook, a thief, a tough, but put him in a boat and he isn't any of those things. He's just — well, he's just a person who's happy because he's where he wants to be.

She began to wonder about him. How did he come to be a thief, an associate of men like Bull and Fred? He didn't look right in their company, yet she could not doubt that he was there from choice. Why had he made that choice?

They were in smoother water now. Reluctantly she stood up and walked across to him, tapping him on the shoulder.

'Better take her in now.'

He nodded, gave her a quick look, and brought the *Stella* round in an easy curve. Janet stood by him, noting how his hands fondled the wheel. He knew, as did she, that a boat wasn't just an inanimate mass of wood and metal; it had life and character, it had to be handled sensitively if one wanted it to respond.

What else, she wondered, have we in common?

A tinge of sadness touched her. Why did he have to be what he was? Had he come to Garra as friend or employee how eagerly she would have welcomed him! Youth was leaving her fast, the simple pleasures of life on the island were losing their savour; pleasures did if one tasted them alone. With some one of her own generation (Joe, she thought, was younger than herself by two or three years) to share them, Garra for her would be a more cheerful, more satisfying home.

They had turned back and were approaching the mainland jetty. As always

Janet experienced a feeling of regret that the journey across the loch was over; she was happiest on the *Stella*. But on this occasion her regret went deeper than usual. Out on the loch they had both become detached for a short while from their respective rôles of captor and captive; they had been as they wanted to be, not as they were. Now they must return to an unkind reality.

In silence they made the *Stella* fast; it seemed that Joe was as reluctant as she to leave the boat. But as Janet started to pick her way along the jetty he caught her arm.

'Just a minute, miss. You got it straight, what Bull told you?'

'Yes,' she said.

Why had Bull chosen Joe as her guardian for this expedition? She had thought it would be Fred, since Fred was obviously a more accomplished, dyed-in-the-wool villain than Joe, and could be expected to handle her more firmly. Was it because Joe looked nearer the part he had to play — that of a handyman newly employed by her father? Or was Joe the more trusted accomplice?

'It'll be your folks on the island as'll suffer, you see,' he warned her.

She nodded. Bull had made that very clear. 'We gotta eat,' he had said, his eyes, slightly less bloodshot after a night's sleep, boring into hers. 'You do the shopping, miss. But no tricks, see? No passing notes to your shopkeeper pals, or trying to give Joe the slip. You go making trouble for us, and we'll make trouble for you and your folks here.'

It had not needed the slap of a hand on the gun at his hip to impress his meaning on her.

Joe released her arm. 'All right,' he said. His voice was once more flat and impersonal. 'Let's go, miss.'

* * *

With Traynor and Donald beside him, Bull watched the *Stella* until she was well down the loch. Not that he was greatly interested in her progress, or perturbed about the outcome of the expedition; the Traynor girl was the least spirited of the bunch — she wouldn't give Joe any trouble. But he knew that Traynor was watching him, was waiting for his next move. And he had not yet decided what that move should be.

Their coming to the island had been on impulse, born of fatigue and indecision. Now only indecision remained — and that too must go. They could not stay indefinitely on Garra, or eventual discovery would be inevitable. Nor had he risked freedom merely to vegetate on an obscure island. Money was for spending — on liquor, on gambling, on anything that took his fancy. Why hoard it for a future that might never materialize? There was always the present. And with that kind of dough the present could be full of interest.

So he had to make plans. But the immediate problem was how to safeguard the money while they were still on the island. The haversack was both bulky and heavy, and its presence on his back was a constant reminder to Fred and Joe that they had not yet had their cut. Better to dump it in some hiding-place which he alone knew of, where only he could get at it. Fred and Joe might be suspicious of his motive, but short of open warfare there was little they could do about it. If they demanded to be paid now he could talk them out of it. Money was of no use to them on the island; provided they left Garra with him they were risking no more than when they had originally agreed (reluctantly on Fred's part) that he should be its custodian during their getaway.

If they left with him. That was something he still had to decide. It might be better for him to go alone.

Ponderously he turned to his two companions. His movements were seldom brisk without cause. 'We'll take a look-see round the island,' he announced. 'The three of us. Fred can stay with the women.'

'The two of you,' Traynor said curtly. 'Count me out. My nephew must do as he pleases, but I'm staying put. I have work to do.'

Bull's eyes narrowed, the way they always did when some one openly defied him. He rubbed the back of his hand against his bearded chin.

'I said the three of us,' he growled.

'I know. I heard you. But I don't take orders from every unwashed scoundrel who chooses to give them.'

Donald glanced anxiously from one to the other of the two men. At that moment he hated them both. They were bigger than he, both in physique and strength of will. He hated them for that. But even more he hated them for the knowledge that whenever, as now, they came up against another of their calibre there was bound to be trouble — not only for themselves, but for those around them. And Donald had had enough of trouble.

Not for the first time, he reflected that Robert Traynor should have been Kay's uncle, not his. Kay was another of the same stamp — selfish and strong-willed, puffed up with pride and self-esteem, careless of the harm they might do so long as their own wretched, inflated ego were not pricked.

'You asking for another poke on the chin, mister?' Bull said.

For answer Robert Traynor sniffed derisively, turned smartly on his heel, and walked off towards the bungalow.

Now for it, thought Donald.

But Bull made no move to follow. He hitched the haversack more comfortably over his shoulder and stared thoughtfully after the retreating Traynor, pounding his nose with a battered knuckle.

'Tough old bird, your uncle,' he said. 'All right, mister — you'n me'll take a walk on our own. We ain't likely to get lost without him. Not on this little island.'

When Bobby heard of the proposed tour he announced his firm intention of accompanying them. In the few hours he had known him he had conceived a fierce admiration for his new room-mate — much to the latter's discomfiture. Bull had no experience of children, and no great liking for them.

'I ain't taking the kid along,' he growled.

Donald was of the same opinion. But his son, although normally a polite child, had his mother's stubbornness. He took a lot of wearing down.

'I want to see him fire his pistol,' he protested eventually, after other arguments had failed.

'But he isn't going to shoot anything, darling,' Kay said. 'Not this morning. He and Daddy are just going for a walk. A long walk. If you went with them you'd come back so tired you'd have to go straight to bed. You wouldn't like that, would you?'

No, Bobby agreed, he wouldn't like that. But he was not entirely satisfied. 'What's he got a pistol for if he doesn't use it?' he demanded.

'Perhaps he does, sometimes. But not this morning.'

'I bet he will,' Bobby said. 'If he sees anything he will. Won't you, Mr Bull?'

The big man muttered an oath and turned to Donald.

'Come on, mister, let's you and me be going. His ma can sort the kid out. I ain't no nursemaid.'

Donald followed him from the room. As he went down the bungalow steps he could hear his son's now tearful voice raised in angry protest. Kay spoils him, he thought. And if she isn't spoiling him she neglects him.

He was overflowing with bitterness and self-pity. He had never found it easy to be on good terms with others, and not always with himself. He had had to fight for recognition and acceptance, both within the family and outside it. It seemed to him now that any progress he had made — with Kay, with his aunt and uncle and Janet — had been neutralized by the advent of Bull and his companions. Bull had presented him with a problem which he was ill equipped — physically, morally, and by experience — to solve. Bull had made his family see him as an incompetent and a coward, a man of straw, a man who took the easy way, who chose to consort with evil rather than fight it. He could not forget the look on his uncle's face when he had said, hoping to forestall and confound criticism, 'I suppose I had better go with him on this damned hike? We want to know what he gets up to, don't we?' And Uncle Robert had said curtly, turning away, 'You do as you please, Donald.'

Kay too had had something to say. 'Enjoy your walk, Donald. I'm sure you and your friend will have plenty to talk about. You have so much in common.'

Damn them! he thought savagely. It's easy for them to criticize me. An old man and a woman! Even these toughs wouldn't treat them the same as they'd treat me if I defied them. What do they expect me to do? One against three — and two of them with guns. What the hell *could* I do?

'How far is it?' Bull asked.

'I don't know. I've never walked it. About three miles, I think.'

Three miles was nothing to Bull; he had tramped across most of Canada in his younger days. But here the going was treacherous. Paths were few, and what appeared to be good lush grass often turned out to be bog. The ground was uneven and undulating; they were constantly stumbling, or climbing steep, boulder-strewn slopes that descended as sharply as they had ascended. By the time they had struggled half-way round the island they both felt in need of a rest.

Bull seated himself on a large boulder among the bracken, unbuttoned his waistcoat, and produced a packet of cigarettes he had taken from Rose Traynor's store. He did not offer one to Donald.

'What's them mountains over there?' he asked.

'Moorland, not mountains.' Donald's ill-temper was not lessened by the fact that his companion had appropriated the only available resting-place. 'Pretty wild country.'

Bull made no comment. He continued to sit, legs apart, his paunch accentuated by his posture. But his eyes were thoughtful as he gazed across the loch to the tree-lined shore, with the purple hills rising above the trees, fading into blues and browns and blacks as the heather gave out and the boulders and scrub took over.

Wild country. The sort of country in which a man might lose himself. Not from the police — they would be as well equipped as he to use it — but from townsmen like Fred and Joe. Go that way

— and let Fred and Joe go after him . . .

They wouldn't last long. Either the moor or the police would take care of them. As far as he was concerned they would cease to be a threat. His eyes dropped from the hills to the loch. Quite a tidy stretch of water, that. If he intended to leave the island on his own he'd have to learn how to handle the boat.

'What's that?' he asked abruptly, pointing. 'Down there. Looks like a hut.'

They were high up on a bracken-crested knoll. Donald looked down through the trees to the loch. 'The old boat-house,' he said. 'There's a jetty too, but you can't see it from here.'

'Anyone use it?'

'Not now. My uncle used to let holiday-makers camp there when he first came to the island. But he found they destroyed his privacy, so he stopped it.'

Bull's huge face creased into a chuckle. 'He don't like trespassers, eh? Maybe that's why he don't take to me and my mates.'

Encouraged by this unusual show of amiability, Donald said, 'Did you expect him to? You invade his island by force, take over his bungalow, order him about as though you owned the ruddy place. Why, you're not even his own kind — a bunch of crooks on the run!' He paused, wondering if he had gone too far. But there was no sign of resentment on the other's face, and he added, greatly daring, 'If you're not already wise to the fact that he hates your guts you must be deaf and blind. We all hate you — we only suffer you because we must. That doesn't surprise you, does it?'

'Of course it don't.' The creases were fading. 'I don't surprise easy, mister. And I don't expect nothing I can't take with me own hands.'

'And a gun.'

Bull nodded. 'The gun helps,' he agreed mildly.

Donald stared at him, suspicious of this surprising placidity. Yet he wanted desperately to take advantage of it, to assert himself — to rebel, not only against his captor, but against his own acceptance of captivity.

He said — harshly, because he was

afraid, 'I'll say it helps! Without a gun you would never have set foot on this island. Stick a gun in a fellow's back and you're the boss. Without it, one man's as good as another. You know that.'

If Bull knew it he did not say so. He had twisted round on his perch and was staring thoughtfully up at the rocky pinnacle of the hill behind them, the hill that dominated the island. Donald, stung by his indifference, said sharply, 'What's more, you know damned well that if you hadn't produced a gun in the car you wouldn't be here now. Either you'd have got out when I told you to, or we'd have taken you on to the police-station.'

Maybe it was the word 'police' that jarred Bull out of his tranquillity. He shifted his gaze from the hill to the speaker. For a few seconds he contemplated him. Then he said slowly, 'That's what you'd have done, is it?'

'It is. And you couldn't have stopped us. You try struggling with the driver of a fast-moving car and see where it gets you.'

'And without a gun one man's as good as another, eh?'

'More or less.' Donald was hedging. The thick underlip on the bearded face was thrust out aggressively, the huge torso was suddenly more erect. 'In guts, anyway, if not in physique.'

Bull smacked his lips, as though savouring this pronouncement, and heaved his bulk off the boulder. He took his gun from his hip-pocket and, after weighing it reflectively in the palm of his hand, placed it carefully on top of the boulder.

'You wouldn't want to prove that, mister, would you?' he said hopefully, taking a pace forward. 'There's the gun; you only got to knock me cold and it's yours.' Another pace nearer. 'Fred and Joe wouldn't be no trouble; not if you was to surprise them. Fred's yellow, and Joe ain't got no gun.' He was almost pleading now. 'It'd be dead easy, mister.'

Donald stared at him as though mesmerized. The strength drained out of him, so that his body became merely a fluttering stomach and buckling knees. He could not move, either to run or to accept the challenge. And he wanted to do both. Emotion urged him to lash out at the bearded, sneering face so close to his own, to destroy with one desperate blow the other's confident superiority and his own subservience to it. But mind and body told him otherwise — that he stood no chance, that it was his own face that would be battered. Better to be a whole coward than a broken hero.

Mind and body won. 'I — I said equal in guts,' he mumbled. 'There's no sense in fighting if one hasn't a chance of winning.'

The other sighed. 'Even a rat'd die of starvation if it had to feed on your guts, mister.' He picked up his gun and once more turned to look up at the top of the hill. 'What's up there?'

'Nothing,' Donald said sullenly.

'Steep, ain't it? Can one get up from this side?'

'I don't know. I've never tried.'

'Then start trying now, mister,' Bull said. 'That's the way we're going.'

* * *

Bobby had not been easily consoled at the sudden desertion of Bull and his father. It was Fred who unexpectedly tried to come to Kay's rescue.

'I've got a pistol too,' he said, producing it with a flourish.

The boy stared at it. Pistols, it seemed, were suddenly plentiful on Garra. But, although one pistol was as good as another, in Fred's hand it lost much of its glamour. For Bobby the enormous, bearded Bull typified the fictional gunman and desperado. Fred did not.

'I don't care,' he said stubbornly. 'I still want to go with Mr Bull.'

Fred scowled. His action had been prompted by the hope that he might gain the mother through the child. It was not a promising start.

'Well, you can't,' Kay said crossly. And then, to appease him, 'If you're a good boy we'll go for a bathe instead.'

It was a poor second best, but he accepted it. There was always Fred and his gun if he got bored with the water.

Kay was a strong but not a keen swimmer; an hour later, as she slipped off her wrap on the lawn and followed the eager Bobby across the pebbly beach, she was already regretting her suggestion. Despite the warmth of the sun, she knew from experience how cold the loch could be.

It *was* cold. Most of the island coastline shelved steeply, but here in the little bay by the jetty the water was shallow. It reached barely half-way up her thighs; there was insufficient depth for swimming, even had she been allowed to swim. Since Bobby could not swim himself, he insisted that she should stay with him in the shallows to splash and flounder, and her legs and feet were soon numb with the cold. When her son finally decided to exchange the pleasures of the water for those of the beach she followed him to the shore with real thankfulness.

For a while she played with him, running races and picking out the flat stones to send them skimming across the water. But he made no demands on her, and presently she left him. The exercise had restored her circulation, the sun was warm. She lay on her back on the smooth lawn and relaxed.

Kay almost worshipped the sun. She did not merely bask in its warmth, she abandoned herself to it — not, as do most women, to turn her skin a golden brown, to beautify herself, but because the feel of its rays caressing her body exalted and, in some queer, languorous way, excited her. Only the briefest of bikinis covered her; had she not known that she could be overlooked she would have discarded that too, for the wearing of even the minimum of clothing, whether swimming or sun-bathing, could not compare with the thrill of complete nudity.

As the sun's warmth crept over and through her she felt the familiar excitement stir her body, and closed her eyes in delicious abandonment to it. Were I only wealthy, she thought, pressing her hands along the length of her thighs, I would follow the sun round the world. To lie all day on a warm bed of soft, golden sand . . . to open one's eyes to a cloudless blue sky, one's ears to the murmur of surf on the beach . . . and in the evening . . .

A quiver ran through her body. A hand

other than her own had touched her warm flesh, lingered there caressingly, and then, as she jerked her leg away, been withdrawn.

She opened her eyes to see Fred sitting beside her.

Though the sun was hot he still wore his greasy blue jacket and the gaudy tie. He sat sideways, propped on one arm, the other poised above her body. His hot eyes encompassed her. He was breathing heavily; the perspiration on his face was not caused solely by the sun.

For a moment Kay lay staring up at him, too startled and outraged to move. Then she scrambled quickly to her feet.

'How dare you touch me!' she stormed. 'How dare you!'

He stood up too, licking his lips. 'A — a fly,' he said hoarsely. He moved his head, as though his collar were choking him. 'One of them horse-flies. I thought it might bite you.'

She knew he was lying; there had been no fly. But to argue with him was beneath her dignity. She turned away and picked up the wrap, welcoming the protection it gave her from his scrutiny.

'I was watching you and the kid from the window,' he said. 'Ain't no reason why I shouldn't join you, is there?'

He moved closer to her.

Kay was not unused to advances from men; she had known them crude and she had known them subtle, but she had always been able to control them. She was not afraid of this one, only disgusted, and she stood her ground. She could handle Fred.

'Every reason,' she said icily. 'The main one being that you're not wanted — though that won't deter you, I suppose. You forced your way on to the island, but that doesn't mean we have to accept you. You're not wanted by any of us — least of all by me.'

She turned to go up to the bungalow, but he caught her arm. 'I thought it was Bull as got your goat,' he said. 'Not me.'

She had been about to round on him for his effrontery in physically detaining her, but his words made her pause. She stared at him in astonishment.

'I seen the looks you give him,' he said,

grinning. He still held her arm. 'Hate his guts, don't you? Well, you ain't the only one.' He shrugged, and the collar of his jacket went up, so that his hair stood out round his neck like a dark fringe. 'Bull don't go much for women. He prefers the booze. But me' — the grip on her arm tightened; he seemed to have some difficulty in swallowing, for his head jerked forward as he did so — 'me, now, I know a good-looker when I sees one. And seeing as you ain't all that gone on your old man I — well, I been thinking — '

He paused expectantly. With her free hand Kay removed his hand from her arm, inwardly shuddering at the contact; although his skin was coarse, it had an oily feel to the touch. But she did not show her revulsion. The way in which he had spoken of Bull reminded her of the look she had seen on his face the previous night, when Bull had ordered him to sleep on the *Stella*. She had thought then that Fred should be cultivated; now she was sure of it. Yet even to revenge herself on the hated Bull she could not bring herself to unbend to this slimy, dirty-little man. Not yet. And certainly not unless she had a firm plan that promised some measure of success.

'You had better stop thinking, then,' she said coldly. 'There's nothing amiss between my husband and myself. And if there were I certainly would not discuss it with you.'

He nodded, as though that was what he had expected her to say. The dank hair fell forward over his forehead, and he pushed it back impatiently.

'Okay, okay. But Bull, now — he's different, ain't he?'

A flight of peewits swept over them and Kay looked up, following them with her eyes until they vanished down the loch.

'Yes, he's different,' she said slowly. 'Very different.'

Fred had had little experience of women, but a complete faith in his own ability to sum them up correctly nullified any uncertainty he might otherwise have felt in dealing with them. He thought he understood Kay. Yet he was not entirely a fool. He had no flattering illusions about his possible appeal to a woman of Kay's world, was even doubtful whether, given the opportunity, he could take her by force. She was young and spirited, she would certainly fight back. But he could not believe that she was in love with her husband, and he had seen the look in her eyes when he had spoken Bull's name; both could work in his favour. Right from the start he had summed her up as a 'hot piece.' I bet she's run off the rails a few times since she was married, he thought; it don't mean all that much to her. Maybe I ain't her sort; but if I was to promise her . . .

His body quivered ecstatically at the prospect his mind envisaged; his damp face shone in the sunlight. He said, the hoarseness back in his voice, 'Bull ain't no friend of mine; I got my own score to settle with that bastard. You'n me too. I ain't risking my hide for nothing — that don't make sense. But if you was to play ball with me — I wouldn't tell no tales, your old man wouldn't know nothing about it . . . '

His voice tailed off; if the words were incoherent, his meaning was plain. But

Kay did not answer. For a full half-minute she eyed him steadily, while he shuffled and blinked and ran a grimy finger round the inside of his collar, uncertain whether he had said too much or too little. Then her lips parted and a sigh escaped her, as though she had held her breath for too long. She shivered, and pulled the wrap closer about her.

'It's cold,' she said. 'I'm going in.'

He watched her go. The sun still shone as brightly as before; in the shelter of the bungalow the breeze did not even ruffle his hair. She ain't cold, he told himself gleefully, she's scared. She don't want to do it, but she will. And she's scared because she knows she will.

With a skip and a jump, like a young ram in the mating season, he limped jauntily down to the beach to join Bobby.

* * *

It was at Joe's insistence that they visited the pub. The Traynors were teetotallers — Robert through precept, Rose because he wished it — and there was no liquor on the island. 'It ain't human,' Bull had said, when this unpleasant fact was brought to his notice; he had instructed Joe to ensure that, no matter what items might be omitted from the shopping-list, the booze was not among them.

Janet wanted to stay outside in the car, but Joe would not permit this; not even if, as Janet suggested, he took the ignition key with him. 'Suppose I refuse to get out of the car?' she asked. She had no intention of attempting a trial of strength with him, but was curious to see how he would react. 'You can't use force, can you? Not with people about.'

He shrugged. 'Have to leave it, I suppose.'

'So what?'

'Bull'll be mad,' he said, in that flat, colourless voice of his. 'It was him wanted it, not me. Him and Fred.'

She shivered. She could fence and prevaricate with Joe, but not with Bull. Bull's wrath was something to be feared. He was the ogre with which, like a recalcitrant child, she could be threatened if she did not behave.

She got out of the car without further demur.

Joe drank draught beer. Janet refused a drink when he asked her. She was not teetotal from principle, but the absence of alcohol on the island had made her unused to it.

He did not press her. The bar was almost empty, and they sat at a small table from which they could look out on to Grean Muir. Joe drank his beer quickly, in silence. When he had finished it he again asked her to have a drink.

'Because it's me asking you?' he suggested, when she refused.

'No.' And that was true. 'It's just that I'm not used to alcohol. This is the first time I've been inside a pub for — oh, ages.'

'There's worse places than pubs,' he said defensively. He looked at his empty glass, hoisting it in his hand.

'I'm sure there are. And have another beer if you want to. I don't mind waiting. I'm in no great hurry to return to your unpleasant friends.'

He ignored this thrust. 'No fun in

drinking alone,' he said, still playing with the glass. 'We'd best be going.'

'All right,' Janet said. 'I'll have a sherry.'

She wondered if she should offer to pay. Was it his own money he was spending, or the proceeds of the robbery? Bull had rather reluctantly proffered money for the food that had to be bought, and had looked relieved when her father had refused it. 'I'll not have any member of my family handling dirty money,' Traynor had said, gazing with distaste at the notes in the big man's hand. 'I'd rather starve.'

Janet had thought that a short-sighted policy. It might well be that the police had the numbers of the notes, so that by circulating them in the village the presence of the thieves on the island would become known. But her father was rigid in his principles. The end could never justify the means.

'It's sweet,' Joe said, putting the glass on the table. 'Is that all right?'

'I expect so, thank you. I don't really know. I'm not a connoisseur.'

'Me neither,' he confessed. 'Don't

drink anything but beer myself. But girls like sweet things, mostly.'

She felt oddly flattered at being included among the girls.

The shopping had been easier than Janet had expected. Joe had remained steadfastly at her side without being obtrusive; he had carried the parcels, but had taken no part in the choosing or buying. There had been one awkward clash, when she had insisted on going into the chemist's alone. Only after a heated and embarrassing argument had he reluctantly compromised by accompanying her into the shop and standing as far as possible from the counter, his unseeing eyes glued to a display cabinet of perfumes. Janet had been sorely tempted to explain the situation to the girl who had served her, but she had resisted the temptation; she had given her promise to Joe that she would not, and she could not bring herself to break that promise. She knew that Bull himself would certainly not have trusted her, that Joe was risking his wrath in disobeying instructions. And Bull's wrath was something to be feared.

She did not enjoy the sherry; it had a burnt taste, she thought. But she did not want to hurt his feelings, and tried to conceal her distaste as she sipped it.

That's queer, she thought, at the third sip. Why should I worry about his feelings? I must be soft in the head.

'Do you spend most of your time on the island?' he asked presently.

'Yes.' She wondered if he was really interested, or just trying to make conversation. 'We only come to the mainland to do the shopping. We haven't many friends around here.'

They had met one of those friends that morning: Angus McFee, an elderly and not particularly distinguished man of letters with a passion for the works of Shakespeare, who had crowned his devotion to the playwright by marrying a young actress from the Stratford Repertory Theatre. Janet had introduced Joe to him as her father's new employee — an introduction that had intrigued the Scot. 'So Prospero has his Caliban at last, eh?' he had said; he always referred to her father as Prospero. 'Though he hasna the look of Caliban — and he's no Ariel. Too solid.' He chuckled, and winked at her. 'Take care he doesna turn out to be Ferdinand, lassie.' Janet had blushed, hoping Joe would not understand the allusion; but it occurred to her that McFee's reference to *The Tempest* was more apt than usual. Bull had more the appearance of Caliban than did Joe; only Caliban had been a slave, however much he had longed to lord it on the island. And Bull was no slave. Perhaps he was Antonio or Sebastian? Both had been evil men.

Joe was staring out of the window. 'I like mountains,' he said. 'Where I come from it's flat.'

'Where is that?'

'Essex. Near Chelmsford.'

'You like boats too, don't you?' she said. 'I was watching you in the *Stella*. You handled it as though — as though it were alive. One can always tell. Some people look right in a boat, and some don't. You're one who does.'

He nodded, a taint look of pleasure on his face. 'A man I worked for once had a cruiser on the estuary. Diesel she was — a beauty. He used to lend her to me week-ends.' He smiled. 'There's a lot of mud up them creeks. Many's the time I got her stuck on a mudbank and had to wait for the tide to float me off. Wait all night, sometimes. Not that I cared. The boss did, but not me.'

The flat tone was gone; there had been warmth in his voice, and more colour in his cheeks. And he looks different too, Janet thought. Away from those two awful men he's probably quite a decent person. How on earth did he manage to get mixed up with them?

'Were you an engineer?' she asked.

'Sort of. My boss ran a garage and filling-station. I was only the dogsbody around the place, but he taught me a lot. Particularly about boats — he was as crazy about them as I was. Only he was an expert, and I was a novice.' His eyes again sought the mountains. 'How far can one go up the loch?'

'All the way. About thirty miles.'

'Ever been that far?'

'Once or twice. There's not much point

to it, though. The scenery doesn't change much. Usually we stick down this end.'

He nodded. 'It's pretty,' he said. 'No, not pretty, but — well, sort of satisfying, if you get me. If I had a place like that I reckon I'd never want to leave it.'

'Wouldn't you?' she wondered aloud. 'There's not much to do, you know. Messing about in the *Stella* — a little shooting and fishing — looking: after the cows and the hens and the garden. Not very exciting, really — particularly in the winter.'

'Depends on what you like doing, I suppose,' he said. 'It'd suit me fine.'

'Would it? You've knocked around a bit, haven't you? Wouldn't you miss the cinemas — the people — the bright lights? I do, sometimes.'

He shook his head. 'Not me,' he said stubbornly. 'I could do without them easy.'

Then why haven't you done without them before? she wanted to ask. Why didn't you look for a job in the Highlands or in the colonies instead of taking up with Bull and Fred and getting involved in robbery and attempted murder? You're young and strong, you could have carved out a decent life for yourself. Why didn't you at least try?

Or had he tried?

She said haltingly, after a fortifying sip at the sherry, 'What — what made you do it, Joe? Team up with Bull and Fred, I mean — go in for all that — that beastliness? They look what they are, but you don't. You're different to them. Why did you do it?'

It was the first time she had addressed him by his name.

He turned his gaze from the mountains to look at her. The blank expression had come back to his eyes. But he did not answer her question.

'We'd better go,' he said, standing up. 'You wait here while I get the booze.'

He drank off the rest of his beer in long, choking gulps, as though he no longer enjoyed it, and then went over to the bar.

I suppose I shouldn't have said that, she thought. And yet — why not? I wasn't preaching at him, I only wanted to know.

Or perhaps he wasn't offended; just ashamed. And so he ought to be. But if he *is* ashamed he certainly isn't repentant, or he wouldn't have watched me so closely this morning, he'd have let me go to the police. No. Despite all that talk about boats and mountains and the simple life, he's a crook like the others. Not so brutal as Bull, perhaps, or as evil as Fred. But he's still a crook.

She wondered why that thought should trouble her.

4

A howling monster; a drunken monster!

The Tempest, Act II, Scene 2

The islanders went early to bed that night. After the evening meal had been cleared away Bull and his companions settled down to play cards. It looked as though they intended to make a night of it, for bottles of beer and whisky were stacked around them — a sight which angered Traynor almost as much as the presence of the men themselves. But he was wise enough to express his anger in looks rather than in words. Bull had been drinking heavily and was in an ugly mood — although, to every one's astonishment except Kay's, he was unusually affable to Donald. Kay guessed the reason for that; it was done to annoy her, to widen further the rift between husband and wife that his coming had provoked. He had sensed that to infer a camaraderie between himself and Donald would infuriate and humiliate her. And the unfortunate Donald, surprised and embarrassed, had accepted the affability in his eagerness to avoid conflict, to ease the tension.

But Kay had on this occasion refused to be provoked; she would not give her enemy that satisfaction, despite her repressed indignation. She was even able to feel surprise that he should be astute enough to seize on such a method of attack. She had regarded him as an animal, possessed, possibly, of an animal cunning. She had not expected subtlety.

What is it, she wondered, that makes us instinctive enemies? I think Uncle Robert feels much the same about him as I do; but not the others. The others hate him because he's here, because of what he's done. There is nothing personal about it, as there is with me and Uncle Robert. And why is it always me he tries to humiliate? He doesn't do it to Uncle Robert; he did at first, but not now. I think he even has a sort of odd respect for Uncle for standing up to him. But why doesn't he respect me? Is it because I'm a woman, and he has no use for women? Or is it simply that hate begets hate?

If she could not fathom the reason for Bull's animosity she could at least try to analyse her own. What was it about the man, she wondered later as she lay in bed, that made her hate him so intensely? She didn't hate Joe; his presence on the island annoyed her, but she didn't hate him. She didn't even hate the loathsome Fred. Fred disgusted her, she longed to be rid of him, but she couldn't care less what might happen to him after she *was* rid of him.

It wasn't like that with Bull. To be rid of him wasn't enough. She would rather have him with her for ever than let him slide out of her life unpunished. She wanted to see him hurt and humiliated, to have him taken away by the police in handcuffs, to know that nothing less than years of imprisonment and degradation awaited him. But why? Why should she feel like that about this particular man, whom she had known for little more than twenty-four hours? He was a criminal — but so were the others. He was dirty and common and unkempt — but so was Fred. He was brutal and uncouth. Well, no one could describe either Fred or Joe as polished — and Fred, despite his physical handicap, could no doubt be equally brutal in a sadistic, more subtle manner. What was it about Bull that singled him out for her hate?

She had not felt that way at first, she reflected. Not in the car. In the car she had been intimidated — even fascinated — by his bulk and his ugliness, had actually experienced a perverted feeling of pleasurable anticipation of the excitement that the men's arrival on the island would cause. It had been on the jetty, when he had deliberately ignored her, had told Fred to 'give the lady a shove,' that the seed of hate had been sown. And he had gone out of his way to nurture it since — by his reference to her as a windbag, by . . .

From his twin bed on the other side of the lamp Donald said irritably, a hand marking the place in his book, 'For Heaven's sake, Kay, what's the matter with you? You're as restless as a flea in a bear-pit.'

Kay sat up. Viciously she pummelled the pillows into place behind her back. Donald had not helped. He had even prompted, however unwittingly, the greatest humiliation of all. 'You ain't got a chance,' Bull had said, jeering at her. 'I'm choosey about dames.'

'How charmingly you express yourself,' she said. 'So like your friend Bull.'

'Cut that out!' He peered round the lamp to look at her. 'You've really got your knife into that brute, haven't you? Why? Because he hasn't fallen for your feminine wiles, I suppose.'

She was shocked into silence.

All her adult life Kay Grant had lived on the admiration of men. By look, by word, by deed they had showered it on her, had paid tribute to her beauty and her charm, both publicly and in private, openly proclaiming their adoration or whispering it in her ear. She had come to see herself through their eyes, to know herself through their mouths, because through them the picture was prettiest.

Their admiration had become as essential to her as the food she ate, as the air she breathed. And they had never failed her.

Until now. Until Bull. For Donald, in his clumsy attempt to provoke her, had voiced what she knew to be the truth — a truth she had subconsciously tried to hide even from herself. She hated Bull, not so much for what he was or for what he had done, but because he was the first man to loom large in her life without enhancing it. He had ignored or spurned her, responded to neither her sex nor her charm, had offered no tribute to her beauty — had, indeed, repudiated it. He had not added to the pretty picture, he had done his best to destroy it. He — a common criminal, an animal on two legs!

'Want to go to sleep yet?' Donald asked. She had been silent and still for so long that he had returned to his book. 'Shall I put the light out?'

'No. Not yet.'

She was glad he had not demanded an answer to his previous question. She would have had to deny him the truth as she had hitherto denied it to herself.

'Good. I'd like to finish this book.'

Finish a book! How like Donald, she thought, to be so unpredictable. They had had a flaming row when he had returned from his walk with Bull, and all afternoon he had been sullen and uncommunicative — not because of the row, she thought, but because of something that had occurred on the walk. And now, after an evening of tension and embarrassment, he was so engrossed in his book that he wanted to finish it before going to sleep. It did not occur to him that she might want to talk, to discuss the calamity that had befallen them. He was not interested, as she imagined other men would be under similar circumstances, in seeking a solution to their problem. He only wanted to finish his book.

Her mother had once remarked that Donald only ran true to form when he was out of form. Kay had thought then that being married to a man who could be relied on to do the unexpected thing might be fun. Now, after eight years of it, she found it more irritating than amusing.

Fred had been wrong on at least one count in his summing-up of Kay; she had never been unfaithful to her husband. There had been occasions when she had hovered on the brink of infidelity, for she was a sensual person and Donald had not proved himself a satisfactory partner physically; he had seldom made her feel completely fulfilled as a woman. But it was neither morality nor love for her husband that had restrained her; rather it was pride. Once there was a beginning there might be no end; once she had slipped it would be so damnably easy to slip again. And she had no wish to be labelled 'easy' or a 'push-over' by her admirers. She needed their respect as well as their admiration.

Not that I deserve either, she thought now, in a sudden welter of self-abasement. And with this new knowledge of herself her hate against Bull flared up afresh, almost stifling in its intensity. Bull had not only destroyed the pretty picture, he had undermined her self-respect. For that there was nothing she would not do to be revenged on him.

Nothing? Could she even stomach the repellent Fred?

'Now you're restless again,' Donald said. 'Still thinking about Bull?'

She was glad to talk, to be done with thinking. 'He's the ring-leader,' she said eagerly. 'Fred's a nasty piece of work, but I don't think he'd amount to much on his own. Neither would Joe. If we could outsmart Bull — '

'But we can't, Kay. He's tough and he's cunning — and he's armed. Nobody here can beat that combination.'

'Nobody tries.' Her voice was bitter. 'Only Uncle Robert, and he's too old, poor dear. If you had half his spirit, Donald, we might get somewhere.'

'We might indeed,' he agreed. 'The mortuary, most likely.' He shut his book with a snap. 'In Heaven's name, Kay, what is it you want me to do? Get myself shot? Will that help?'

'No, of course not,' she said impatiently. 'Don't be so damned stupid. I'm not suggesting you should fight it out man to man, or anything heroic like that. You wouldn't stand an earthly. But if with all your education you can't find a way to outsmart those three toughs — well, either education is overrated or you are too lacking in spirit to try.'

For most of that afternoon Donald had brooded on his refusal to accept Bull's challenge of the morning. He had no doubt that he had taken the right course; his distress of mind lay in the suspicion that it was cowardice, not prudence, which had prompted his decision. To learn now that Kay would have approved of his refusal had she known of it made him more content with himself.

'I'll think of something,' he promised. And meant it. 'Just give me time.'

'You've had too much time already,' she said. 'I can't stand much more of these men, Donald. I really can't.'

He was moved by the note of despair in her voice. How lovely she is, he thought. Her warm skin glowed under the thin nightdress, her blonde hair sparkled in the lamplight. Why did they always have to bicker? Why couldn't they sometimes be on the same side of the fence?

'I don't think they intend to stay much longer,' he said, trying to console her. 'They will probably move off in a day or two, when they think the hunt has died down.'

The prospect did not please her. 'I don't want to wait until they go of their own accord,' she said. 'I want to *make* them go.'

'Why? What's the difference?'

'You wouldn't understand.' She spoke crossly, knowing that to him there *was* no difference. 'It's a question of pride, that's all.'

'What has pride to do with it? I should have thought it was more a question of expediency.'

'I know you would. Oh, get on with your book and leave me alone. I want to think.'

She leaned back against the pillows disconsolately. Through the windows lights twinkled in the darkness to the west; the lights of the village, little more than a mile away across the loch. It was galling to see them, to calculate their nearness, and to know that they might be a hundred miles away for all the help they could bring her.

Donald was no use. He might be, perhaps, if he had her hate to urge him. But he hadn't — and in any case he could never sustain any emotion for long. Anything that was to be done she must do herself. There was Fred, of course; he too had a score to settle with Bull — or so he said. But Fred's price was too high, he . . .

She sat up. 'Donald! There *is* something we can do!'

'Eh?' He put his book down reluctantly. There was a vacant expression in his eyes which showed he was still lost in the plot. But Kay did not see it; she was staring out of the window. 'What's that?'

'Have you got a torch?'

'I think so.' He leaned over to fumble in the small cabinet between the beds. 'Yes, here it is.'

'Good. Then why shouldn't we signal to the village with it? If we can see their lights they must be able to see ours. You know Morse, don't you?'

'After a fashion. I've forgotten most of

it. I doubt if I could send a message.'

'We don't need a message. Only an S O S. You could manage that, couldn't you?'

'Yes,' he said doubtfully. He was anxious to co-operate, but this could be dangerous. 'Aren't you forgetting that Fred will be on the boat? If he sees the signal and reports it to Bull . . . '

It seemed unnecessary to finish the sentence.

'He isn't on the boat. He's in the living-room, drinking and playing cards with the others. It's perfectly safe if we send the signal now.'

He thought this over.

'Yes, that's true. Then why don't we climb out of the window and just take the *Stella*? We could push her off without the engines — let her drift for a bit first. Wouldn't that be better still?'

'No, it wouldn't.' She said it without hesitation. 'For one thing, I'm quite sure they have removed part of the engine to prevent us doing just that. Joe was messing about with it this afternoon; I dare say Fred objects to sleeping aboard. And for another, if one of us goes we must all go; we can't leave the others to face the music. You know what Bull threatened to do to Bobby. And can you see us getting your aunt and uncle out of the bungalow without the men hearing? They're in the next room. We wouldn't have a hope.' She shook her head. 'You can forget that one, Donald.'

He turned the torch over in his hands, directed it idly at a dark corner of the room, and pressed the button switch. Despite the soft radiance of the bedside lamp the beam showed white and strong. 'I don't like it,' he said unhappily, cutting off the beam. 'Suppose one of them decides to take a stroll?'

'Oh, for Heaven's sake!' Her voice was scornful. 'In the middle of a game of cards? Here, give me the damned torch. Tell me what to do, and I'll send the signal myself.'

'No.' He pushed hack the bedclothes and swung his feet to the floor. 'I'll do it. But first I'm going to make quite sure that the men are all in the living-room.'

'How?'

'By going along to the lavatory. I'll

either see them or hear them. It depends on whether their door is closed.'

The door was ajar. He could see Fred at the table, but the other two were out of sight, and he waited until he had heard both their voices before going on to the lavatory. He had just closed the door when footsteps thumped noisily along the passage and some one tried the handle. There was a muttered oath. Then the footsteps retreated, he heard a door shut, and all was quiet.

'I told you it would be all right,' Kay said impatiently, when he got back to the bedroom. 'Now for Heaven's sake get a move on, Donald, or there will be no one awake to see the signal. Some of the lights have gone out already.'

He picked up the torch and went over to the open window. 'Even if they see it they probably won't understand it,' he said. 'But we'll try. Do we turn out the lamp?'

'No. Leave it.'

She saw his back stiffen. There was a click, and a beam of light sprang out of the window. Dot, dot, dot . . . dash, dash,

dash . . . dot, dot, dot . . . She could see the message being spelled out on the foliage of a tree near the window. Then the torch swung to the left and the blobs of light vanished.

Suddenly he stopped and turned to her. 'I've just remembered something,' he said. His face was anxious. 'Whoever came along to the lavatory while I was there closed a door when he went back. I heard it. Yet when I passed the living-room later the door was still ajar.'

'What of it?' she said impatiently.

'Well — which door was it that I heard shut?'

For the first time a spark of his fear touched her, to be instantly suppressed. She would not be panicked into retreat now. 'Oh, what does it matter?' she snapped. 'Don't be such an old woman, Donald. Get on with it.'

He shrugged. 'All right. But don't blame me if there's trouble.'

The clicks went on again. Dot, dot, dot . . . dash, dash, dash . . . dot, dot, dot . . . Kay sat upright in the bed, her hands clutching the blankets. This was her revenge. Bull might think little of her as a woman, but he had also underrated her as an adversary. Now he was about to pay for both those mistakes.

Oh, God, let some one see the signal! she prayed. Let them understand!

So great was her concentration that she jumped when Donald said, without looking round, 'How long do I keep this up?'

'Don't stop! Go on, go on!' she implored him, desperate for success.

'Yes, but for how long? I can't keep it up all night.'

'You've got to give them time,' she said. 'Time to see it and understand. If we're lucky we might even get an acknowledgment.'

'All right. But we don't want to bounce our luck.' He shifted the torch to his left hand; his thumb was beginning to ache. 'I'll give it a few more minutes, and then we'll — '

He broke off as a door banged. Heavy footsteps sounded in the passage. They were coming towards the bedroom. 'The lamp!' Donald cried hoarsely, as he ran to the bed. 'Quick! Turn it out!'

They were both too slow. As Kay reached out her arm the door burst open and Bull lurched into the centre of the room, where he stood surveying them, swaying slightly. Donald was still on his feet at the foot of the bed, the torch in his hand. He had forgotten to switch it off, and it cast a wavering pool of light at the gunman's feet.

For an instant the two men stared at each other. Kay watched Bull, terrified by his murderous expression; she had seen him angry, but never as angry as this. His face was purple under the whiskers, veins pulsed angrily at throat and forehead. His waistcoat and shirt were undone, and she could see his great chest, covered with black hair, heaving as he breathed. There was a white fleck of spittle at his mouth.

Then his lips moved, and the spittle dropped and was caught in the beard beneath. 'You — you — ' So fierce was his wrath that the words would not come. He shook his huge frame and tried again. 'Goddam and blast you!' he said thickly. In three enormous strides, moving so fast that his victim had no time in which to escape, he was towering over the unfortunate Donald. His great fist came up from somewhere near his waist and caught the other man directly between the eyes. With a sigh like air escaping from a pricked balloon, Donald went down. His body twitched and was still.

Bull's rage was not appeased by the blow. 'Bloody swine!' he roared, his fists still clenched. His boot thudded into the unconscious man's ribs. 'Get up, you bastard! I haven't finished with you yet.'

Kay had been petrified with horror, overwhelmed by the speed and brutality with which Bull had acted. The sickening thud of that bone-crushing blow between the eyes had for her drowned all other sounds. She had seen but not heard her husband fall; even Bull's trumpet of a voice had reached her but vaguely, a background noise only. But as his boot was raised again the tension broke, and she screamed — a high-pitched scream, piercing in its intensity. Bull put his foot down and turned on her, stepping over the prostrate Donald.

'Shut up, you bitch!' he bellowed. 'It was you put him up to this. He hadn't the guts or the wits to do it on his own.'

The scream had been involuntary, occasioned by fear and hysteria. But the sight of that hated figure standing over her, the sound of his voice, checked the scream. Something snapped in her brain; she was no longer afraid, she could only hate. Viciously, obscenely, she began to curse him, using words she had heard but never before spoken, spitting them out of her mouth like evil things. Her teeth were bared, there was a hint of madness in her eyes. Her nightdress had slipped down over one shoulder, exposing her breast, but she did not heed it. She was no longer a woman; the veneer of civilization had left her. She was a frenzied, snarling, primitive creature possessed of but one thought — to lash him with her tongue until even his thick hide could feel it and rebel.

Bull's fist caught her on the side of the head. It was not a heavy blow, directed downward, but it made her head sing and knocked her still farther over the edge of the bed. She put a hand on the floor for support, desperately fighting off the wave of nausea that swept over her, determined not to be sick or to lose consciousness. She would not give him that satisfaction.

Slowly her head began to clear. She became aware of Donald's white face close to her hand, a dark swelling on his forehead. His eyes were shut, and she wondered vaguely if he were dead. Pressing hard on the carpet, she levered herself up from the floor. One side of her body was numb; the blood still sang in her head. With a deep sigh she sank back on the pillows and closed her eyes. When she opened them again it was to see Fred bending over her.

'He's gone.' Fred's voice was thick. He sucked at his dry lips and leaned over her, his eyes flickering. His breath reeked of alcohol. 'You're lucky. Bull's a killer when he's drunk.'

She stared at him dully. Thought and vitality had drained from her, leaving only an aching body. With what was left of her mind she willed him to go away. She was too tired to speak.

Fred said, 'Anything I can do to help?' His bold eyes gazed in fascination at her breast.

She rolled her head against the pillow in a gesture of negation. Voices, Bull's among them, came to her from the passage. They brought her sharply back to reality; he might come back, she might have to fight him again. And she was in no condition to fight. She needed rest, time in which to recover her vitality, to think and to plan. If he came back now . . .

She pulled the bedclothes up to her chin in an instinctive gesture of protection, her eyes watching the door.

'No need to get the wind up,' Fred said, annoyed. 'He's off back to the bottle.'

For some reason she believed him. Her body relaxed, began to tremble. She felt suddenly cold. 'Go away,' she said weakly.

He looked down at the still unconscious Donald. 'What about him?'

She had forgotten Donald. From where she lay she could not see him. She sat up quickly, wincing at the pain in her head, the blankets clutched about her body.

'Will he be all right?'

'Well, he's still breathing.' Callously he stirred the limp figure with his foot. 'He won't feel so good when he wakes up.'

The action infuriated her. She had little self-control left, but now she was fully conscious. With disgust she remembered the look in Fred's eyes. At the time she had neither accepted nor rejected it; she had been vaguely aware of it, but as something quite unconnected with herself. Now it had become personal. It sickened her to realize that she had remained passive under his gaze, that he might think . . .

But it was Donald she had to consider now, not herself. He needed care and attention, and she could give him neither while Fred was there. Not even for Donald would she get out of bed with Fred's lecherous eyes on her.

'Get out,' she snapped. And, as he stood irresolute beside her, 'Get out of my room. You're as much to blame for this as Bull is. Get out, damn you!'

'Them's harsh words, lady.' He felt no

resentment, only a gnawing sense of frustration. Her old man was out cold; she was alone, had been almost unconscious, her spirit of resistance temporarily numbed. If only he had been quicker to realize and seize his opportunity! 'I thought you and me was going to be friends.'

She checked the angry retort. It would not do to antagonize him; she must keep a tighter rein on her temper. It would be foolish to close that road of escape until she was sure it would not be needed. 'If you want to help, get my uncle,' she said. 'And keep that brute out of here.'

It was not the way in which he wanted to help. But while he hesitated a stentorian roar came from the passage.

'Fred! Come here, blast you!'

Kay shivered. If Fred did not go . . . if Bull were to return . . .

But Fred did go. The woman would keep, Bull's temper would not. And as he disappeared through the doorway Kay scrambled out of bed to kneel anxiously beside her husband.

* * *

Rose Traynor had been dreaming.

Across the island prowled a beast on four legs, its misshapen head and body covered with thick black fur. Great tusks protruded from its drooling mouth. Apparently sightless, it moved with its broad snout close to the ground, its huge, swollen body swinging and rumbling as it went.

She had no fear for herself. It was going away from her, and the stench of its passing made her cover her mouth and nostrils with her hands. But she still watched it, for she knew it was searching for some one — some one whom it hated, who had been its master and whom it wished to destroy. Some one who . . .

It was then that she saw Robert. He stood directly in the path of the beast, his back to it, looking out over the water. She called out to him, but he did not hear her — for the air was full of popping noises and the sound of water falling from a great height. And now the beast was no longer prowling. It had scented its quarry, it was thundering across the island, and the dust from its hooves rose into the air like a great cloud, blotting out Robert and the water and the trees. She screamed. And as she screamed the beast screamed too, a high, piercing scream that rocked the knoll on which she stood, so that suddenly it tilted and she was falling . . . falling . . .

'Robert!' she cried. 'Robert!'

'All right, my dear.' He was already getting out of bed. 'I'm going.'

She shook herself awake. 'What is it? What happened? Did some one scream?'

'Yes. Kay, I think. That brute's in their room. My God, if only I had a gun I'd — I'd — Janet, wake up. Janet!'

'I'm here, Daddy.' Her voice, soft and tremulous, was close to him in the darkness. If she was afraid she did not panic. 'Shall I light the lamp?'

'Yes.' He was struggling into his dressing-gown; he had abandoned the search for his slippers. 'And stay in here and look after your mother. Move your bed across the door after I've gone, in case one of those devils tries to come in here.'

Rose was fully awake now. 'Be careful, Robert.' It was a vain, useless plea, but it was all she could say. She knew him too well to attempt to stop him. 'Oh, please be careful! That man — '

He had already opened the door. As he stepped into the gloom of the passage Bull emerged from the far bedroom and lurched towards him, stopping with a jerk when he found his way barred.

'Get the hell out of here!' he bellowed.

Traynor stood his ground. His anxiety was for Kay; had he been given time in which to think he would have let the man pass so that he might get to her the more quickly. But his wrath was too great for discretion.

'You damned scoundrel!' he roared, his fists clenched. 'What have you done to my niece?'

'Oh, it's you, is it?' Bull's long arm shot out. His hand caught Traynor's dressing-gown at the throat, closing the gap so tightly that the other was nearly throttled. 'I'll tell you what I done, mister. I've slapped her ruddy face for her, that's what.' He pulled Traynor towards him, his breath a wave of alcohol. 'Aye, and that damned husband of hers; he's out cold. They was trying to be clever, see? Flashing a bleeding torch out of the window.' He pushed the other away, releasing him. Traynor steadied himself against the wall, gasping for breath. 'Think they can get the better of me, do they? Well, you tell 'em from me, mister — one more trick like that and I'll make the bastards wish they'd never been born.' He belched, and turned to look back at the open doorway. 'Fred! Come here, blast you!'

Traynor had got his breath again. He said, rubbing his throat, 'Fred? What's Fred doing in there?'

'Tucking her up and kissing her good-night, I expect — the goddammed fool!' His bulk filled the passage. As Traynor, oppressed by a new dread, tried to force a way past him, Bull put a large hand against the older man's chest and pushed him easily away. 'You leave this to me, mister.' Almost casually he bellowed,

'Come here, Fred, damn you!'

Fred limped out of the bedroom, slamming the door behind him and intensifying the gloom. He was annoyed — with Kay, with himself, with Bull. 'What d'you want?' he demanded, his voice surly.

Bull said, 'I don't want you messing about with that ruddy dame, see? Lay off her.'

The mild tone deceived Fred. 'I ain't messing about with her,' he snapped. 'And what the hell's it got to do with you, anyways? She ain't your property.' With the words came a new suspicion, and he stepped closer, peering up into the big man's face. 'Or maybe you think she is, eh? Maybe you fancy her yourself?' He laughed derisively, encouraged by the other's silence, reading into it a confirmation of his suspicion. His anger at the thought of Bull as a possible rival overcame his natural caution, and he said spitefully, 'You got a hope, mate! Why, she's told me — '

Bull's hand shot out, gripping him by the knot of his gaudy tie, yanking him nearer.

'She's told you she hates my guts, eh?' He thrust his face close to Fred's, glaring at him balefully. 'Getting real matey with her, ain't you?' He jerked the knot, twisting it savagely, so that it tightened on his victim's neck. 'Next thing you know, she'll be promising you a tumble in exchange for a bullet in my back. And you'll do it, too, won't you — if I give you the chance?' Traynor watched in dazed fascination as Fred's eyes protruded still farther, his face slowly purpling. 'You bloody fool! Can't you see what her game is? Rub me out, and you and Joe'll be easy. That's what she's after. Nor you won't get a tickle out of her, mate, promise or no promise. I know her sort.' With a final twist he released the tie. Fred fell back against the wall, gasping for breath. Bull stared at him thoughtfully. Almost sorrowfully he added, 'She's out to cause trouble, mate, and by Christ she's doing it! You lay off her, Fred. No dame's worth three thousand smackers.'

5

I long
To hear the story of your life, which must
Take the ear strangely.

The Tempest, Act V, Scene 1

'Mcfee's day,' as it later came to be known on the island, dawned as warm and bright as the two preceding days. The sun shone brilliantly, the soft breeze barely ruffled the surface of the loch. It seemed that the weather was trying to compensate the islanders for the misfortune which had befallen them. Prior to the coming of the three men cloud had sat sombrely on the mountains for almost a week, and a damp drizzle of mist and rain had fallen monotonously.

It was partly because of the weather, partly to help Kay, and partly to escape from the tension and unhappy atmosphere in the bungalow that Janet suggested at breakfast the next morning that she should take Bobby for a day's fishing in the *Stella*. Kay agreed at once. Bobby was already showing signs of being fractious after a night during which his sleep had been disturbed more than once — the last time being when Bull, drunk and almost out on his feet, had stumbled into the room and clumsily attempted to put himself to bed. Kay did not want to be bothered with Bobby; she had plans to make and a husband to nurse. Donald, with sore ribs and an aching head, but with no bones broken, was in bed. Rose Traynor thought he had slight concussion (he had been sick in the night), and Donald was only too anxious to accept any diagnosis which kept him away from Bull and further conflict.

As she ate her breakfast Rose enlarged on her nephew's suffering, hinting at internal damage in the forlorn hope that it might shame Bull into an apology. But Bull was not addicted either to shame or to apologies; and that morning he was in a vile temper. He had mixed his drinks too freely the previous night; his eyes were bloodshot and heavy, his head throbbed, and his mouth felt like the bottom of a birdcage.

'Anything the fool got he asked for,' he growled, his mouth full of egg. Nothing ever spoilt his appetite. He turned to Janet. 'And you ain't taking the boat out, miss. That stays here. I may want it myself.'

'Not thinking of leaving us, are you?' Kay said. 'Such a short visit! But no doubt you'll come again. Let us know in advance next time, so that we can lay in a good supply of rat-poison.'

Traynor frowned. He was furious that this ruffian should give orders about the *Stella*, but to his way of thinking it was more dignified to ignore him. It shocked him that Kay could bandy words with the brute after what he had done. Nor could he understand her apparent high spirits that morning. The blow Bull had given her had left no mark, she looked fresh and radiantly lovely. Compared to her, he thought, looking round the table, the rest of us are a bunch of crows.

Kay was not bandying words at random, she was following a set purpose.

Hers was no passive hate. If she could not bite she must scratch; if she could not hurt her enemy by her actions she must sting him with her tongue. She could not let him rest, any more than she could rest herself. Above all, she had to show him that he could never cow her spirit with blows, that nothing he could do would defeat her.

And she was not defeated. When Donald had been attended to and put to bed the previous night, and the house was quiet again, she had looked for the torch; there had been few lights still showing on the mainland, but she would not neglect the chance that a signal might be seen and interpreted. A second attempt might have more luck than the first. But the torch had gone — Bull or Fred had taken it, she supposed — and for much of the night she had lain awake, listening to Donald's stertorous breathing and planning her next move. Her enemy must never be allowed to feel safe; he must be goaded and pricked and alarmed. Under such constant pressure his spirit might well break, certainly before hers; his position was less secure. He could not even be sure that Donald's signal had not been seen. At that very moment the police might be preparing to act on it.

It was a heartening possibility — and one that had also occurred to Bull. He was puzzled and uneasy at her obvious high spirits; he had expected to see her sullen and cowed. Had that damned husband of hers received an acknowledgment to his signals before he had interrupted them? Was that why she was so cheerful? It seemed unlikely; why should they have gone on signalling if they knew their message had been understood? But he'd keep the boat handy, just in case he had to leave in a hurry. He would also need some one to steer the damned thing. Not Joe; he didn't want Joe and Fred along. Grant could take him. Grant wouldn't argue; he'd know what to expect if he did.

'Funny, ain't you?' he growled. 'Seems like that clip on the ear done you good. Well, maybe I'll do you a bit more good before you'n me's through.' He pushed his plate away and reached for the toast. 'I got news for you, lady; you'll be on your own to-night. I'm having no more truck with that husband of yours; from now on he sleeps in the shed out back. Locked in. He can have a bed, but no light. Come to that, you won't none of you have lights. I'm taking no more chances.'

There was a chorus of outraged protest. Kay alone was silent; she suspected that Bull's sore head, rather than caution, had prompted the pronouncement. And in any case she would ask no favours of him, not even for Donald. Her heart sank, however, as she glanced across at the ever-watchful Fred. There were no locks on the bedroom doors.

'He can't sleep in the shed,' Rose said indignantly. 'It's dirty and untidy. I keep paraffin in there — the fumes would be bad for him.' In her indignation she had forgotten that this would be news to her husband. 'And there's only one tiny window right at the top.'

'That's why I'm putting him there,' Bull said. 'If he don't like the smell of paraffin he can dump it outside.'

'But why can't we have lamps in the bedrooms?' asked Janet. 'You don't think we're likely to set fire to the place, do you?'

'I wouldn't put it past *her*,' he said, jerking a thumb in Kay's direction. 'I reckon she'd do anything to bring the cops over. But lamps is almost as good as torches, miss. I ain't taking no chances, like I told you.'

Kay wondered why she had not thought to use the lamp the previous night, after Bull and Fred had gone and she couldn't find the torch.

Janet decided she would still go fishing, even without the *Stella*. The prospect of a whole day spent in the company of Bull and Fred (mentally she had already placed Joe apart from them) appalled her. She would walk over to the old jetty; even if she didn't catch any fish it would at least be peaceful there. Bobby would be less enthusiastic when he knew that the *Stella* had been ruled out, but the delights of a picnic might lure him. Bobby adored picnics.

She was putting the gear together in

the shed (the shed in which Bull had ordained that Donald should sleep) when she saw Joe watching her from the doorway. She had not heard him approach; his quietness was one of the things about him that she liked. He walked on his toes, with the lively grace of a panther. She did not think that his mind was as agile as his body, but even when he was interested and the flatness had left his voice he spoke more softly than most men.

She gave him a quick nod of recognition and went on with her preparations. She felt annoyed with him. Most of the previous afternoon they had spent together; they had climbed up through the trees behind the bungalow to the crest of the hill, and from there they had surveyed the island, the loch, the world — and each other. An intimacy had developed between them. Although he had avoided all reference to the topic that interested her most — the crime that had brought him to Garra — he had otherwise talked freely about himself. He had not had an easy life, and his undramatic recital of it touched her. She had come down the hill filled with a sentimental zeal to reform him, to help him find a way out of the mess he seemed to have made of his life. It was not a completely unselfish resolution; playing at God, trying to shape other people's lives, can be a fascinating pastime. To Janet, imbued with many of her father's rigid principles, starved of human contact and yet full of a restless will to impress her personality on some one or some thing, it was irresistible.

But Joe had been quick to disappoint her. Despite their new intimacy and her happy belief that already she had begun to influence him, he had not come to their rescue the previous night, he had made no attempt to restrain the rampaging Bull. His very absence from the scene, thought Janet, indicated a tacit approval of his confederate's behaviour.

'Going fishing?' he asked. And, when she nodded, 'I thought Bull said you wasn't to take the *Stella*.'

'One can fish from the shore,' she said.

He came over to the bench at which

she was working. 'You'll have to take me along, then. Bull won't let you leave the bungalow else. He's scared you might hail a passing boat.'

Janet shrugged. 'I'm still going fishing, even if it means an escort. I can't disappoint Bobby.'

His brow puckered. 'What's wrong?' he asked. 'I thought we were friends.'

She turned on him angrily. 'So did I — until last night. Why didn't you stop that drunken brute from going into my cousins' room? You didn't even try.'

'Why should I?' he demanded, immediately on the defensive. 'They were trying to bring the cops over, weren't they? You think I want that?'

That silenced her. It reminded her that, although she might look on him as a sinner to be saved, he was still very much a sinner in the eyes of the law. If Donald and Kay had succeeded it would have meant imprisonment for him; she could not expect him to acquiesce in that. Not yet. Not until the reformation was in a more advanced stage.

'All right. But he didn't have to behave

the way he did — knocking my cousin senseless, hitting a woman. Don't tell me you approve of *that*!'

'No.' He frowned. 'Though I dare say she asked for it; she's always baiting him. If she tried to take the mickey out of him when he was drunk — well, she ought to have known better.'

'She didn't know he was drunk,' Janet said frigidly. 'We're not used to drunks on Garra.'

'Maybe not. But she's different to you. I bet she's met a few drunks in her time.'

Janet stared at him. 'Aren't you jumping to conclusions on a very short acquaintance? You only met her the day before yesterday.'

'I know her sort,' he said doggedly. 'She's what I'd call a — ' He stopped, his pale cheeks tinged with pink. He began to tug at the sleeves of his jacket, trying to pull them down over his thin, flexible wrists. Janet had seen him do it before when he was embarrassed. 'The boss's wife was like that,' he said. 'The one that used to lend me the boat. That's why I left.'

Janet was not certain that she knew what he meant, and it seemed wiser not to ask. But she could not help saying, 'You don't like her, do you?'

'No.'

She could feel some sympathy with him there. She was not over-fond of Kay herself. But loyalty made her hide her sympathy, and she said, 'Was that why you kept out of the way when you heard her scream? Because you don't like her?'

'Of course not. I just happened to be in the garden, that's all. By the time I got back Bull was in the passage talking to your father. There was nothing I could do then.'

'What were you doing in the garden?' she asked suspiciously.

He gave her a sheepish grin. 'I was in the garden because I couldn't get into the lavatory. And Bull came out with me. That's how he come to see the signals.'

Janet flushed, annoyed that she had not guessed the answer. She said brusquely, 'If we're going fishing we had better get a move on. I haven't cut the sandwiches yet.'

‘I’ve never caught a fish,’ he said, as he followed her across to the kitchen. ‘Never even tried.’

‘You probably won’t catch one to-day,’ she warned him.

By the time they set out she had recovered her good humour. She was not sure that Joe could be completely exonerated of callousness toward her cousins, but at least he was less guilty than she had supposed. And since she had accepted him as a sinner she must not reproach him if occasionally he exhibited a sinner’s traits. She must accept those too.

Bobby’s acceptance of Joe was less whole-hearted; he had not seen as much of Joe as he had of Fred and Bull. In the boy’s eyes Joe was a rather colourless individual whose place in the island community had yet to be determined. He lacked Bull’s swashbuckling arrogance and Fred’s apparent geniality, and had nothing to offer in their place. Most damning of all, he had no gun.

Bobby did not make this last discovery until they were nearing the old jetty. For most of the journey he was roaming ahead, running down to the shore to throw stones into the water, climbing the climbable trees, hiding in the long bracken and jumping out at them as they approached. And it was after one of these ambushes that a large black-and-brown bird, its breast a metallic green, whirred noisily up from a near-by patch of tall grass.

Janet and Joe stopped to watch it. Bobby reached for his gun, banging away with his mouth. As the bird disappeared over the trees he turned to his companions.

'Why didn't you shoot it, Joe?' he demanded. To the boy Joe was Joe and Fred was Fred, but Bull was Mister Bull. Thus did he recognize authority.

'I haven't got a gun,' Joe said.

'You mean you left it at home?'

'No. I haven't got one at all.'

'Mr Bull's got a gun,' the boy said. There was scorn in his voice. 'So's Fred.'

'I know. But I don't happen to like guns. Never did.'

Such a sissy admission was beyond

Bobby's understanding. He turned away in disgust. 'If Mr Bull had been here I bet he'd have shot it. I bet he *never* misses,' he said, stooping to uproot a tall frond.

'Maybe,' Joe said. 'But it isn't all that easy to hit a pheasant with a pistol, you know.'

But either Bobby was already too far away to hear, or this outspoken doubt of his hero's marksmanship was too close to *lèse-majesté* to be permissible comment. He skipped ahead, brandishing the frond.

'I was hoping that after last night he might have lost some of his admiration for that brute,' Janet said, as they walked on. 'I thought children were scared of drunks. But it doesn't seem to have worked with Bobby, unfortunately. By the way, that was a capercaillie, not a pheasant.'

'A what?' And, when she repeated the name, 'Never heard of it.'

'I think it's peculiar to the North,' she said.

They did not catch any fish. Since the water was too deep for wading, they fished from the end of the old jetty, well away from the trees. It was even more rickety and rotten than the one on the mainland; it took their weight, but only under noisy protest. Janet was relieved when Bobby decided that fishing was a dull sport and went back to the island to play more exciting games on his own. She did not want to have to watch Bobby as well as the fly.

They had only the one rod, but Joe was an apt and interested pupil. Jane showed him how to attach the fly — a Silver Grey — and cast it so that it landed gently on the water, letting it float with the stream before whisking it back into the air and making another cast. After he had watched her for a while he said, 'Why don't you just leave the fly on the water? Wouldn't that be simpler?'

She laughed. 'Simpler, yes. But the salmon wouldn't take it. It's a fly, not a lump of dough.'

'They don't seem to be taking it your way either,' he said.

'Not this morning. They're not rising, I'm afraid.'

But her lack of success did not damp

his enthusiasm for the sport. Janet was a good and patient teacher, and soon he was casting almost as expertly as she had done. The girl watched him with pride. 'You're doing well,' she said. 'Keep it up.'

He turned to grin at her. It was a boyish, infectious grin that wiped all the hardness and unhappiness from his face. Janet smiled back.

'What would a rod like this cost?' he asked.

'About ten pounds. You can pay a lot more, of course. Then there is the reel and the line. And the gaff. Altogether I suppose it would come to nearer twenty pounds than ten.'

He began to pull on the line. 'Doesn't look as though it's worth all that,' he said, examining the rod with a critical eye.

'It's not a cheap sport,' she admitted. 'You'd need waders too. And then there's the licence. Here it costs about five pounds for the season, but in most places it's more.'

They had lunch on a grassy knoll high above the surface of the loch. Bobby stayed with them only as long as the meal lasted. Then, munching an apple, he ran off to track imaginary beasts through a bracken jungle.

Janet stretched herself on her back and closed her eyes. The sun was hot, and she felt lazily content. Joe sat a few feet away, arms clasping his bunched knees, his eyes on the distant moors. Neither felt like going down to the jetty to fish.

'What a heavenly day,' she said, plucking idly at the grass. 'You certainly brought the sunshine with you. Before this we had rain every day for at least a week.'

He turned to look at her. She wore jeans (the shorts had been discarded out of deference to her mother's wishes) and a sleeveless blouse, against the whiteness of which her bare arms and legs, tanned by the sun, were a warm brown. Brown hair — a darker brown than her skin — clustered in untidy curls round an oval-shaped face. Though her eyes were closed, he knew that they too were brown.

'I'm glad there was something good we brought,' he said, his voice flat and expressionless. 'The rest was pretty bad, eh?'

She turned towards him, jerking herself up on one arm. Her remark had been casual, made without thought; until his question she had forgotten what he was, why he had come to Garra. But she made no apology. 'It hasn't been so bad for me,' she said quietly. 'For the others, yes — but not for me. They've had Bull and Fred to contend with. I haven't. Or only occasionally.'

'You've had me,' he said.

'Yes, I've had you. We've been together most of the time, haven't we? It was a strain at first — for you too, I expect. But now — ' She paused. His grey eyes were watching her intently, and she felt embarrassed. But she had to make him understand. It was important for both of them. 'You think Garra is wonderful, don't you? So it is, really, provided you have some one to share it with — some one of your own generation, some one who appreciates the same things as yourself. I've never had that. Ever since I left school there has just been Mummy and Daddy. They may be the best parents in the world — I think they are, in some ways — but they're not *fun*. I've never had any friends. I've never been able to let my hair down, let myself go, do wild, foolish things for no other reason than that I felt like doing them. One can't go gay on one's own.' She sighed. 'Sometimes I've been so bored I thought I'd go crazy. I used to pray for something to happen — something exciting, something unusual, something that meant the next day wouldn't be exactly the same as all the other days.' For the first time her eyes looked directly into his. 'And then it *did* happen.'

'Us?' And, when she nodded, 'You mean you were *glad* to see us?'

She smiled at his astonishment.

'Good heavens, no! I was angry and scared and — well, disgusted at times. I still am. But just now, lying here in the sun thinking, I suddenly realized that for the first time in years I was experiencing something new. It wasn't as good as the old, perhaps, but it was new. That was what mattered. Can you understand that?'

She saw from his puzzled expression that he could not. I suppose his life has been too exciting, too varied, for him to know what boredom means, she thought.

'Don't you ever have people to stay here?' he asked.

'Very seldom. We are too far away from the friends I knew around London and at school; I don't even write to them any more. Daddy has one or two cronies in the village, but they are all older than me. I'm on my own.'

'You could go away,' he said.

'Yes. I've thought about it, often. But it isn't so easy. They need me here; there's a lot to do, and neither of them can drive the car. And where would I go? Besides, I don't know that I really *want* to go away. Not for long. I love Garra — it's my home. What I want — ' She shook her head. 'Am I being terribly inconsistent? If so I'm sorry. I suppose I want the best of both worlds. I know I'll never have it — but that doesn't stop me from wanting.'

He was no longer looking at her. Rather inexpertly, he was rolling a cigarette. When he had lit it he puffed at it furiously, concentrating his whole attention on it as though fearful that if he were to neglect it for a moment it might go out. As it probably would, thought Janet. It's a very sickly-looking cigarette.

It occurred to her that it might be Joe who was bored now. Why should he care about her worries? Compared to his own, hers must seem petty. Nor had she meant to unload them on him; she had been leading up to something very different. But she had never got there. His capacity for listening had carried her away.

'I've talked too much about myself,' she said. 'I'm sorry. I just wanted you to understand that if circumstances had been different — if you hadn't been in trouble with the police, if you hadn't brought those two dreadful men with you — I'd have been glad you came.' She paused, then added defiantly, 'Even now I'm glad, in a way. You see, I — I like you, Joe.'

He turned to her quickly, anxious to embrace and hold that admission before it could be retracted.

'I like you too,' he said, his eyes intent on hers. 'I like you better'n I've ever liked anyone. Ever since I first saw you I've been wishing — ' He puffed vigorously at the cigarette. It had gone out, and he threw it impatiently away. 'Oh, what's the use! No good wishing things was different; they're not, and they're not going to be. Me and the others, we'll be away in a few days. It's not likely you'n me'll meet again after that.'

No, she thought, it isn't likely — and wondered why that thought should sadden her. Through his own acts Joe had made himself an outcast from her world; that she hoped to help him find the way back could not erase what he had done, could not turn him into some one who would be welcomed by her parents. And yet . . .

'We might,' she said. 'If we both want to. It depends on us — not on anyone else. We're free people, Joe.'

She saw his eyes narrow; instantly she realized her gaffe, and wished it unsaid. For how long would Joe be free? But he made no direct comment. He said, 'No doubt about me wanting to see *you*. But how would you feel with a gaolbird for a friend? That's what I'll be — a gaolbird. Or a fugitive — on the run.' He shook his head. 'I reckon we finish right here, you and me.'

A steamer was coming down the loch. She passed close to the island, her passengers thronging the rail in curiosity, their faces etched sharply in the strong sunlight. Gulls hovered and chattered overhead, swooping down to the water to grab the titbits thrown overboard. Away to Janet's right Bobby shouted and waved, redoubling his efforts when the passengers waved back.

'It depends on you, Joe.' She spoke quietly but distinctly, her gaze intent on the steamer. This was her chance — she must not bungle it. 'I haven't so many friends that I can afford to discard one lightly. But are you really a friend? That's what I want to be sure of.' She turned to face him, her eyes wide and serious. 'Just how much can I depend on you, Joe?'

The question surprised him. 'All the way,' he said. 'I just told you, didn't I?'

She had hoped that he would understand, that he would answer her unspoken question. The knowledge that she must put it to him direct frightened and unnerved her. He had shown her plainly enough before that he did not wish to discuss it. If he refused her now there was nothing more she could do.

'Friendship means trust and — and confidence, as I understand it.' She wondered if he could hear the loud beat of her heart. 'You haven't given me yours, have you? How do I know if you are really the sort of person I think you are? I don't believe you're like Bull and Fred, you see. I keep telling myself that you never meant to get mixed up with them — that it happened against your will, or because you were unlucky, or just weak. But I haven't had much experience of people, and I may be wrong. The 'you' I see now may not be the real 'you'; you may be putting on an act just to fool me. I don't think you are, or I wouldn't be talking to you like this; but I've got to be absolutely sure before I feel I can treat you as a friend.' She put out a hand — not to touch him, but in a gesture of entreaty. She was filled with a desperate sadness. He was so young and good-looking, so lost, so — so alone. Far more than herself, he needed a friend; yet his expression had not softened, he seemed to be beyond the reach of her pleading. 'Joe, please! Listen to me — don't shut yourself away. Can't you understand that I only want to help you? But you've got to help me first. I must know what made you do it. That's what is important, you see. Not what you did, but why.'

His hand touched hers gently and was then withdrawn, as though scared of the liberty it had taken. Janet scarcely felt the contact. Her whole being was concentrated on willing him to speak.

'I'm sorry,' he said — and from his voice and the look on his face she knew that he meant it, that her plea would be answered. 'You and me look at this differently, I suppose. To me it don't seem to matter so much *why* I did it; it's what I did that counts most. That's what I'll get nicked for. And it's something I just didn't want to talk about. Not with you.

But if you reckon it's all that important — '

'To me it is,' she said quickly. 'Tell me, Joe.'

* * *

Joe left the filling-station under a cloud — a cloud piled up by the boss's young wife when Joe failed to respond to her invitations. Had the boss not liked Joe there might have been a prosecution for theft, and had Joe not liked the boss he might have told him the truth. As it was, he just left.

For some months he worked as a casual labourer in London's East End. Then, in a Bermondsey pub, he met Fred. Fred was affable and inquisitive, listened sympathetically to Joe's account of his dismissal from the filling-station, and promised to try to fix him up as a driver for a firm of haulage contractors with whom he occasionally did business. Two evenings later they met again. The job was his, Fred told him; if he wanted it he was to report the next morning.

It proved to be tiring work, much of it at night. The loads had to be collected from warehouses in and around the dock area, and delivered to towns in the North and Midlands. Joe didn't think much of Hudson, his boss, and some of the men he met on the job were tough-looking customers. But the pay was good, and he stuck it.

On the long night runs there was always another man in the cab with him. Sometimes they'd start off together from the firm's yard; but more often Joe would pick the man up at his house, or at a prearranged meeting-place. Mostly his companion was a man named Abbott, a big, bad-tempered individual with an unquenchable thirst. Joe was glad when Abbott's thirst kept him away from work. Any substitute was preferable.

It was about three weeks after he'd started working for the firm that he stopped at an agreed street-corner one night and Abbott wasn't there. Instead there was Fred.

'Abbott's sick,' he explained, climbing into the cab. 'Or drunk. But sick is what his missus told Hudson. I'm taking his place.'

Joe was puzzled. Fred didn't work for the firm. 'You sure that's okay?' he asked.

'Of course I'm sure. I was with Hudson when Mrs Abbott phoned. It was too late for him to get hold of one of his own chaps, so I volunteered. This ain't the first time, mate.'

Joe supposed it was all right. It was Fred who had got him the job. And on the few occasions since then that they had had a drink together Fred had always spoken of Hudson as though he knew him well.

It was a wet night, and they made poor time. Fred did not talk much; he seemed nervy and on edge, and replied to Joe's few conversational openings in monosyllables, so that they died with him. Joe was not displeased. He preferred to concentrate on his driving.

It was as they were nearing Stamford that Fred said, 'I forgot. You wasn't told that the destination's been changed.'

'We're going to Leeds,' Joe said. 'That's what's on the ticket.'

'It may be on the ticket, but it ain't where we're going. We're taking this lot to Rotherham.' Fred fished in his pocket and produced a piece of paper. 'Hudson typed the address out for me, so's there wouldn't be no mistake. Want to see it?'

Joe pulled the lorry in to the side of the road and cut the engine. 'Let's have a look,' he said.

There was no mistake. 'Sands and Redding, Cross Street, Rotherham.' And it was typed on the firm's notepaper.

'I don't get it,' he said. 'It's the same firm, but a different address. Why didn't Hudson let me know it was changed?'

'Because he got the instructions after you'd left, that's why. Don't you worry, mate; I been to their place in Rotherham before. Maybe that's why Hudson was glad to have me go along. It ain't easy to find.' And, as Joe continued to stare in disbelief at the paper, 'What's the matter? You think I got it wrong?' Fred clicked his tongue. 'Okay. Ring up Hudson and check.'

'At this hour? Are you crazy?' Joe folded the paper and handed it back.

'How far is Rotherham from here?'

'About eighty miles, I reckon. Might be less.'

Joe looked at his watch. 'We could be there by five,' he said. 'That means hanging around before we unload, blast it.'

'Hudson said it'd be okay,' Fred told him. 'There'd be some one to meet us, he said. Come on, mate, let's get cracking. This ain't no night for parking — nor you ain't the sort I usually parks with,' he added with a snigger.

Joe obeyed reluctantly. He was suspicious, but he had no firm reason for disbelieving Fred. Nevertheless he decided to play for safety. If he didn't like the look of things when they got to Rotherham he would hold up the unloading until he'd had a chance to talk with Hudson on the phone.

Fred obviously knew Rotherham well. When they reached the outskirts of the town he guided them unerringly through a maze of side-streets to a walled yard near the railway. He got out of the cab to open the gates, and as Joe drove into the yard two men came out from the shadows and walked over to Fred.

Joe got down from the cab and flexed his limbs. He hoped it was going to be all right. The rain was still pelting down, and he didn't fancy having to go on to Leeds. Fred and the two men had run for the shelter of a projecting roof, and he hurried to join them.

''S'truth, what a night!' one of the men said. He was small and sandy-haired, with an engaging grin. Joe looked at the other, and his spirits rose. They both looked ordinary enough to satisfy his nagging uncertainty. If they were crooks they weren't toughs; he could take on the two of them. But he didn't think they *were* crooks.

He jerked his thumb at the lorry. 'What's the idea of switching that load here?' he asked. 'I was all set to take it to Leeds.'

Because he was nervous his tone had been truculent. The small man grinned at him. 'You can take it to flipping Timbuktu for all I care,' he said. 'Me and Tom here don't want it. We got better things to do than hang around in the flipping rain at this hour of the morning.'

'We don't know about no switch,' Tom said. 'We was just told to get down here at four to receive a load that was coming in early. But we ain't unloading. Young Mr Sands is coming down hisself to supervise that.'

'And when will that be?' asked Fred.

'When the yard opens. Eight o'clock.'

Fred whistled. 'You mean we got to wait three ruddy hours for the bastard? Have a heart, mate.'

The small man's grin was still there. 'You can wait if you want to,' he said. 'But not us. We're clearing off; we've done our job. 'See the stuff in, then lock up and hop it,' was what the manager said.' The grin broadened. 'It's us for bed and a long lay-in, mate.'

'We got a small van what was lent us for the job,' Tom said. 'We could drop you off in the town. There's a café there stays open all night, if you want something to eat.'

Fred rubbed his hands. 'Me for the café,' he said. 'Okay with you, Joe?'

Joe thought it was. For one thing, he was hungry. For another, the fact that the lorry was not to be unloaded until eight would give him time to check first with Hudson. And for another, Fred would be with him. If the set-up was crooked Fred must be at the bottom of it; as long as he could keep an eye on Fred he'd have no cause to worry.

They did not hurry over their meal; it was still raining, and neither was anxious to leave the warm, fetid atmosphere of the café. Joe watched Fred all the time; despite the reassurance he had gained at the yard, he was taking no chances. But Fred seemed relaxed and quite unconscious of his companion's interest. After they had finished eating he produced a dirty pack of cards and, when Joe declined the offer of a game of poker, proceeded to play patience.

At a quarter-past seven Joe pushed his chair back and stood up. 'May as well make a move,' he said. 'Must be quite a tidy stretch back to the yard, and I want to phone Hudson on the way.' And, as Fred made no move, 'Coming?'

'No.' Fred placed a red eight on a black nine and carefully straightened the line of cards.

'Why not? They said young Mr Sands would be there at eight.'

'Why was you going to phone Hudson?' asked Fred.

'Just to make sure it's all right to leave the stuff there. It's me that's responsible, not you.'

'Don't waste your money, mate. It ain't all right.' Fred looked round the now empty café and then up at Joe. He had abandoned the cards. 'Mean to say you don't know what the game is? Green, ain't you?'

'What game?' Joe said slowly.

'I'll tell you.' Fred hooked one foot round the leg of Joe's chair and pulled it from under the table. 'Here, sit down!'

Joe sat down. He needed to. His knees were wobbly and he felt sick. He wished he hadn't eaten such a large meal. He said, 'You mean — that isn't Sands and Redding's place? We should have gone on to Leeds, like I said?' And, as Fred nodded, 'Those two chaps — Tom and the little fellow. Are they in it with you?'

'Yes.' Fred pushed the cards aside and leaned forward. 'You and me have earned ourselves quite a tidy little packet to-night, mate.' His voice was a confidential whisper. 'Want to hear how we done it?'

Joe nodded. He had no idea what he was going to do — not even what he *ought* to do. But the truth might help, whatever his decision.

Fred told his story with smug satisfaction. He had never met Hudson, he said, but he had a pal in the firm's office. It was this pal who had fixed the job for Joe, who had tipped Fred off when Joe was due to carry a valuable and suitable load, who had typed out for him the fictitious address on the firm's notepaper. All Fred had to do then was to seek out Abbott, ply him with drink until he was incapable (a simple task; Abbott never refused a drink when the other fellow was paying), and, having ascertained from him where Joe was to pick him up, take his place.

'But why pick on me?' Joe asked. 'Why not one of the other drivers?'

Fred eyed him in genuine astonishment.

'Why the hell do you think I fixed that job for you? It had to be a driver I knew, see? One who wouldn't act difficult when I turned up in Abbott's place.' He did not add that Joe's ingenuousness and his obvious grudge against society had made him an ideal choice.

'How many of you is there in on this?' Joe asked. He knew that he ought to take action, that to sit there talking was playing into Fred's hands. But what action?

'Four. Five, counting you. Besides us there's my pal at Hudson's and the chaps up at the yard. Them two get rid of the stuff for us — lorry and all.' Fred looked at the clock on the café wall. 'Two hours since they dropped us here. Must be nearly there now.'

'Where?'

'Never you mind where, mate. That's their business. It's just gone, see?'

'Does the yard belong to them?'

'You kidding?' Fred stared at him, unable to credit such greenness. 'Of course it don't. They borrowed it. That's why we had to get there early, before anyone what works there turned up and started asking questions. Tom forgot to ask their permission — it kind of slipped his memory.' Fred grinned. 'Took you in proper, didn't they? 'Young Mr Sands is coming down hisself to supervise the unloading,' ' he mimicked Tom's high-pitched voice. 'They're good talkers, them two. That's how they get away with it.'

Yes, thought Joe, they were good talkers; they had fooled him properly, even though he had been on his guard against just that. But he felt little resentment. Fred and Tom and the sandy-haired man, they were crooks; that was their job, just as his job had been driving a lorry. And it was part of their job to fool mugs like himself. If they succeeded it was his fault, not theirs.

'Suppose I tell the cops?' he asked.

Fred shrugged. 'It wouldn't do you no good, mate. Think they'll believe that you wasn't in it from the start? Taking me on as a mate when you knew I wasn't employed by the firm . . . switching delivery just because I says so (that piece of paper's tore up, so don't reckon on *that* to help you) . . . handing the stuff over to a couple of chaps you don't know nothing about? There weren't even the name of the firm on the gate.' He shook his head cheerfully. 'If you think you can get away with a tale like that you're crackers.'

Joe knew it was true. Yet the knowledge brought relief rather than despair. From childhood he had had it drummed into him by his reprobate father that the police were his enemies, that once he allowed himself to fall into their clutches he would never escape. It made no difference whether he was innocent or guilty; either way he was done for. That had been his mother's creed too; small wonder that it was his, that he did not abandon it now. Yet he had thought of doing so; with a more plausible tale to tell he might have summoned up the nerve to go to the police. The relief came with the knowledge that such an effort would be wasted, that it was pointless to make it. For even the truth did not leave him entirely guiltless. What was the charge he'd seen in the newspapers? Criminal negligence — that was it. They'd get him for that even if they couldn't manage to pin the rest of it on him.

'What am I supposed to do now?' he asked. 'Go back to Hudson and tell him I've lost the blamed lorry? You got that worked out too?'

Fred nodded, winked, and reached for his pocket, to produce a fat roll of one-pound notes. Slowly, impressively, he began to count them. Joe watched him, fascinated. He had never seen so much money.

'Fifty nicker.' Fred pushed them across the table. There was still a thick wad of notes left, and these he returned to his pocket. 'Not bad for one night's work, eh? Who's going to pay you that for driving a perishing lorry?'

Joe looked at the untidy pile of notes in front of him. Fifty quid was more than he had ever earned in a month. But what would happen to him after it was gone? What would happen to him *before* it was gone, if the police caught up with him?

'Put it away,' Fred said urgently. 'That much money don't look right in here.'

Joe glanced round the café. There were no other customers. The man who had served them was behind the counter, he couldn't see the money from there.

'I don't want it,' he said. 'You think you're smart, Fred. Well, maybe you are. Me, I'd rather work for a living. Maybe it don't bring in so much dough, but it's regular. And safe. And that's the way I like it.'

The other sighed.

'You catch on slow, mate. When you don't turn up at Leeds this morning Sands and Redding will be on the blower to Hudson — and he'll call in the busies. But it ain't me or the others as they'll look for; they don't know about us. It's you they want, Joe.' He smacked his lips. 'You got to lay low for a while, mate, not go looking for jobs. Not unless you fancy a nice little stretch. Now pick them notes up and let's get out of here. Time we was moving.'

But Joe did not move. 'Nice pal you've turned out to be,' he said bitterly.

He had no rigid moral objection to crooks, so long as they abstained from violence; it was the thought that he was one himself that scared and angered him now. His father had supplemented his very casual earnings by petty thieving, his mother had been gaoled for shop-lifting. Home to Joe had been a place of poverty and misery, of deceit and an ever-present fear of the law. At an early age he had determined that if those were the rewards of crime he would have nothing to do with it himself. And now, through no fault of his own other than a too sanguine and trusting nature, he had been branded indelibly as a criminal.

Fred grimaced at his companion's ingratitude. 'There's fifty nicker there as says you're wrong,' he said, pointing to the table. 'And more to come if you act sensible.'

Joe picked up the notes and stuffed them in his pocket. 'There'd better be,' he said. Since it seemed he was committed to crime, he'd get the best out of it. Fred and the others might think they had picked a sucker, but he wouldn't be a sucker for long. He'd catch on. 'Fifty quid won't go far; if I can't go back to my digs I'll need new clobber, for a start. And I reckon there ought to be more than fifty quid apiece out of a haul like that.' Abruptly he pushed his chair back and stood up. 'Where do we go from here?'

They went to Liverpool. Fred said it would be handy for a job he was fixing. At first Joe stayed indoors all day, venturing abroad only at night; but gradually he lost some of his fear of instant arrest, and began to go out during the day. Fred had bought him a jacket and trousers (second-hand, and several sizes too small, but preferable to the dungarees he had been wearing), and soon he was spending most of his time at the docks. Ships had always fascinated him. Now, in addition to his love for the craft themselves, he saw in them a possible means of escape from the unenviable position into which Fate, assisted by Fred, had precipitated him.

When he mentioned his idea to Fred the latter shook his head.

'Fixing a passage for a chap like you is tricky. And expensive. You stick around, mate. There's big money to be made in this racket.'

'I don't like rackets,' Joe told him. 'I'm getting out. How expensive?'

But the other was not prepared to be specific. 'A tidy sum,' he said vaguely. 'More than you got right now. Of course, if you was to make number three in the job I got fixed for next week — ' He paused. 'There could be two hundred nicker in it for you.' Noting the startled look on his companion's face, he added hastily, 'A hundred, anyways. More than enough to get you on to one of them boats, and no questions asked.'

He saw no sense in promising a larger sum than was strictly necessary.

Joe was tempted. A hundred pounds was not a large sum to stake against his liberty, but if it would do the trick it was all he wanted. Yet he held back — not through fear of the police (that was with him already, it could not be augmented), but from a new sense of shame that he had experienced for the first time when talking to the men at the docks. Would they have accepted him so readily, he had wondered uncomfortably, have talked to him so freely, if they had known who and what he was? Only then had he appreciated the wide gulf separating the lawless from the law-abiding. Even his parents' activities had not made him aware of it. He had felt no shame for them, only bitterness and mistrust. When he had finally renounced them it was not because they were numbered among the lawless, but for the misery that their way of life had brought him.

He was not given to analysing his thoughts and emotions; he accepted them as natural phenomena conforming to standard patterns and common to all humans. But during the past few days he had come to appreciate that this shame of his was a personal thing — Fred did not feel it, he thought, would not understand it — depending more on his own opinion of himself than on the opinions of others; it was part of him, and he must deal with it in his own way, there were no precedents to guide him. That way, he knew, was to have no more to do with Fred and his kind. His introduction to crime had been involuntary; that knowledge, when he remembered it, helped to lessen the shame. In time it might enable him to lose it entirely. But he would not lose it if he were voluntarily to abandon, as it were, his amateur status as a criminal, and turn professional.

'I'm not interested.' He spoke sharply, angry that this newly discovered weakness in himself should baulk him now. 'You tricked me into this set-up, but you're not getting me in any deeper. You can count me out.'

Fred was annoyed. He had counted on Joe; Joe was a good driver, and he was cheap. No doubt Tom or Sandy would be willing to take his place. But Tom or Sandy would be expensive, they couldn't be fobbed off with a mere hundred or two. And neither of them could handle a car at speed like Joe.

He said, 'The others reckoned you might make trouble. Seems they could have been right.'

'I'm not making trouble,' Joe told him. 'I just want to keep right out of it.'

'Maybe. But the way the boys look at it,

a chap what isn't with us is against us. They won't like it, mate.'

'I don't care what they like. I'm not doing it.'

'There's nothing to it, really.' Fred's tone was persuasive. 'A hundred nicker for driving a car. Could be two hundred. You're a mug to turn that down.'

'Okay, I'm a mug.' That was a description of himself with which he thoroughly agreed. 'But get some one else to drive your ruddy car.'

Fred nodded. 'Sure. Tom'll be glad to. Tom don't turn down easy money so quick.' He limped over to the window and peered out into the fading daylight. 'I'll have one of the boys pick him up. But I'm kind of sorry for you, mate.'

'I can take care of myself,' Joe said curtly.

'Think so? You don't know the way them chaps work. Maybe they'll shop you, or maybe they'll fix you themselves.' Fred paused to consider the alternatives, then shrugged. 'I wouldn't know. You can't do us much harm with the busies if they pick you up; no names, see, no evidence what counts. But then stiffs can't talk, can they? Maybe the boys will reckon that's safer.' He turned slowly, looked with commiseration at the startled Joe, and limped over to the door. 'Well, so long, mate. And good luck. Reckon you're going to need it.'

'You mean they would actually shop me or — or kill me?' asked Joe, horrified.

'That's about it.' Fred's hand was on the doorknob. 'If I was you, mate, I'd make myself scarce damned quick. It ain't no use me telling them you're on the level. They don't take them sort of chances. It ain't healthy.'

Joe was not a logical thinker; his hands were more active than his brain. With his mind in its present turmoil the illogicality of Fred's argument escaped him. He did not even attempt to analyse it, nor doubt the capabilities of his enemies to implement their professed intentions. To Joe the alternatives were startlingly clear-cut. Either he must do whatever it was Fred wanted him to do, or run the risk of a prison sentence or a knife in the back.

'Wait!' Fred had already opened the

door. Now he shut it and turned hopefully. 'If I drive this car for you, is that the lot? You'll help me to get away after?'

'Sure.' His face wreathed in smiles, Fred came over to him and clapped him on the shoulder. 'It'll cost a bit, like I said, but we'll fix it. Okay?'

Joe nodded. He had made his protest and it had proved unavailing. However unwilling, he must commit this further crime and accept the extra burden of shame that went with it. Yet he was not wholly sorry. At least, if all went well, it would mean freedom — from Fred, from the 'boys,' from the police — and the chance to make a new start in a new land.

'Tell me what I have to do,' he said.

Fred told him.

The raid had been carefully planned. Fred took him over the route several times, showing him where to park the car, the short-cuts out of the city, explaining the timing and the need for accuracy. For a few hours he hired a car similar to the one he had earmarked for the raid, so that Joe might become familiar with its controls and performance. But when Joe asked questions about the raid itself, of what would happen inside the building, he shook his head. 'You worry about your side of it, mate,' he said. 'Leave mine to me.'

Joe did worry.

Yet it went smoothly enough at first. They picked up the doctor's car where Fred had said it would be, and then collected Bull and made for the factory. It was Joe's first meeting with Bull, and he did not like what he saw. Fred had assured him that there would be no violence, that no one would get hurt. Joe had believed that; Fred did not look or act like a man of violence. But Bull did. I hope to Christ no one tries to stop him, Joe thought unhappily.

As they neared the factory a new fear occurred to him. He said, 'What if the cops already have the number of the car, and pick me up?'

'They won't,' snapped Fred.

Joe dropped them at the mouth of the alley that bordered the south side of the factory yard and drove on, edging carefully out from the ill-lit lane into the thinning stream of traffic at the T-junction; an accident now, however slight, could wreck their plans. He turned on to the parking lot, cut off engine and lights, and walked across to the shadows of a neighbouring building. Fred had said to stay in the car, but Joe saw no reason to follow his instructions as rigidly as that. Despite Fred's assurance, he could not believe that there was no possibility of the theft of the car having been already reported. If the police picked it up he wasn't going to be in it.

Exactly fifteen minutes later he drove past the factory again. But there was no signal, and he went on round the prearranged circuit, cutting out the parking lot.

It was as he was approaching the factory for the third time that he heard the shots. This was a quiet district, and by now the city was mostly asleep; the two shots, fired in rapid succession, sounded sharp and clear, echoed for a brief moment against the tall buildings, and then were gone.

Hand-brake off, engine running, his hand on the gear-lever, Joe waited anxiously at the mouth of the alley. Perspiration beaded on his forehead. Across the street a light was switched on, he heard the rattle of a window being raised. Tensely he watched it, clutch depressed, his fingers edging the gear-lever into position.

If they don't come now I'm off, he told himself. I'm not staying here to be put in the nick.

They did come, running and stumbling down the alley. The car was already moving as they scrambled into the back. It gathered speed quickly.

'Steady!' warned Fred. He was badly out of breath. 'Take it easy, you fool.'

Joe braked, recovering his nerve. He took the corner smoothly.

'Some one saw us,' he said hoarsely. 'I heard a window open.'

'Okay. We'll switch cars later.' Fred's eyes never left the rear window. 'Keep going.'

The road ahead was clear. Joe glanced quickly into the driving-mirror. Bull's face was reflected in it, grim and menacing, the bloodshot eyes looking directly into his. Joe said, thinking he already knew the answer, 'Who done the shooting? I thought you said — '

'Shut up!' Fred did not look round. In a more conciliatory tone he added, 'The watchman had a gun.'

In the mirror Joe saw the big man's eyes turn to look at his companion. Was that to warn Fred to keep his mouth shut? There had been two shots. Had Bull — or Fred — returned the watchman's fire? And if so . . .

Joe shivered, though his body felt hot and the steering-wheel was wet under his hands. He'd done it now. This wasn't just another robbery he'd got himself into. This could be murder.

* * *

Janet's attention had begun to wander long before Joe had finished his recital. The details of his escape were not important to her, and she was depressed by the discovery that he had committed two crimes, not one. True, the first had begun by accident (his guilt there lay in his reluctant acceptance of what had been done), and he had been badgered and blackmailed into the second. But in the eyes of the law he must be as guilty as his companions.

Lying there in the sun, she wondered again why this man and his future should have become so important to her. His past, except where it might influence the future, did not matter; a strong character could rise above squalid beginnings. But Joe was not a strong character, it seemed. In the flat, monotonous tone that he adopted whenever he found talking difficult Joe had told his story badly but conscientiously, attempting neither to stress nor to minimize his own part in it. Yet to Janet it had clarified his weakness, and it was that which depressed her. A weak character might be the more malleable; but with such a background could Joe ever be transformed into the man she wanted him to be?

She did not look at him when he stopped speaking. He had expected some comment — reproaches, perhaps encouragement — but she made none. The sun still shone brightly, but clouds were banking up from the west; the slight breeze was freshening, stirring the tops of the trees. Over to their right Bobby still played happily among the bracken.

Joe began to roll a cigarette. The action disturbed her thoughts, and she said, '*Did* the watchman have a gun?'

'I don't know. If he did he didn't use it.'

No. It had been Fred who had used the gun. He had boasted of it. Fred, it seemed, had instigated the robbery, had been the leader in its execution. Yet it was Bull who was the leader now. Why? Had she sized those two up as inaccurately as she appeared to have sized up Joe?

Or had she been wrong about Joe? Had she judged him too harshly? With his unhappy upbringing, and in the difficult position into which Fred had forced him, was he really so much to blame in not going to the police? Until threatened with imprisonment or death he had refused to take part in the second crime. With such alternatives, how many men of his kind would have acted differently?

The thought cheered her. She rolled over and smiled at him.

'I'm sorry, Joe. And thank you for telling me. Circumstances were rather too much for you, weren't they?'

He exhaled a mouthful of smoke gratefully. 'You don't blame me, then?' he asked.

'Yes, I do.' Even to spare his feelings, she would not lie to him. To sugar the pill she added, 'But that doesn't mean I don't sympathize with you. I certainly do. You had a rotten deal. That beast Fred — ' She vented her feelings by striking the ground with her fist. It hurt, and she rubbed it ruefully. 'What do we do now, Joe?' she asked.

'I don't know.' He was grateful for the 'we.' But what help could a girl like Janet give him?

'Do you still want to go abroad?'

'Not particularly. I just want to get some place where I'm safe from the cops. If it wasn't for them I'd as soon stay here.'

She wondered if 'here' meant Garra or

Britain generally. But if he was ashamed of what he had done (and she thought he must be, or why had he refused to talk about it before?) it seemed that he was not repentant in the sense that he wanted to expiate his crimes. That he might do so by surrendering to the police and serving his sentence did not come into his consideration. Escape and liberty were what obsessed him.

'Not me,' he said firmly, when she tentatively suggested this course to him. 'My old man may have been a wrong 'un, but he was dead right when he said never to let the cops get their mitts on you. You hadn't a chance, he said. And he ought to know. He saw enough of them.' He shook his head. 'If that's your notion of help, Miss — Miss Janet — you can forget it. I'm not having any.'

It was the first time he had spoken her name. Janet was so taken up with this thought that she allowed the important issue to go unchallenged. Although she had never fully analysed her hopes for him, she knew that by 'help' she had meant 'reform'; and how could he be reformed unless he first atoned for his sins? But Joe had taken her more literally. He had interpreted her expressed desire to help him in the only way it occurred to him — as help in escaping from the consequences of his actions.

It was a fundamental difference in their approach to the problem, and it would have to be faced. But not now.

'Call me Janet,' she said. 'When we're alone, that is. Not in front of the others. They'd accuse me of fraternizing with the enemy.'

'I'm not your enemy,' he said quickly.

'I know. But you can't expect them to understand that.' She laughed. 'They might cut off my hair, as the French did to girls who were too friendly with the Germans. I wouldn't like that.'

'I wouldn't like it either,' he said seriously, his eyes intent on her face. 'It's pretty hair.'

Janet blushed. She did not believe that her hair was pretty, but if he thought so that was all that mattered. No man had ever complimented her on her looks before. It was a new and exciting experience, and her heart warmed to him.

'It's not really,' she said, compelled to honesty. 'But — '

There was a cry from Bobby, followed by a loud splash. Alarmed, Janet scrambled to her feet. But Joe was quicker. Ahead of her he raced through the bracken to the cliff-edge, paused for a moment to slip out of his jacket, and jumped. She saw him disappear, heard the splash as he hit the water. Then she was at the edge herself, peering anxiously down.

It was Bobby who was doing all the splashing. Joe held him firmly above the surface, some eight feet from the shore, and he was beating at the water with his hands and feet, spluttering from fright and the water he had swallowed. But it was Joe who caused her to cry out. Head tilted back, his white face just broke the surface of the loch. For a brief moment she looked into his eyes, saw the agonized appeal in them. Then she was slithering down the bank and into the water.

She was only just in time. Joe was under the water now, and she snatched the boy from him. Bobby kicked and struggled; out of her depth as she was, she found it impossible to hold him and help Joe at the same time. Desperately she made for a point where the cliff was lowest, almost threw the screaming boy on to the bank, and turned to swim back to Joe. His fair hair showed momentarily, his hands beating frantically at the water. Then he was gone again, and only a swirl and a few bubbles in the otherwise smooth surface of the loch showed where he had disappeared.

Janet was almost as much at home in the water as on land. Without hesitation she dived, groping for him with her hands. She bumped into him as she opened her eyes; he had his back to the island, and she caught him under the armpits and tugged, treading water furiously. His body was limp (later she was to remember that and be thankful for it; she could not have handled him so expertly had he struggled), and he came up easily. Releasing his arms, she caught his head between her hands and kicked out for the shore.

His struggles had taken him farther

out, and it seemed hours before she felt the stony bottom under her feet and was able to stand up. Joe's eyes were closed, his body seemed lifeless as it sagged against her. Oh, God, don't let him be dead! she prayed earnestly, as she dragged him half out of the water and propped him against the cliff. Please, dear God, don't let him be dead!

She felt half dead herself, but she could not leave him there. He needed artificial respiration, and in that semi-upright position she could not give it to him. Somehow she had to get him on to the bank. Almost crying with exhaustion and fear, she managed to scramble up the loose, slippery surface of the cliff. Then, lying on her stomach, she reached down and gripped his arms. But she could not move him; his dead weight was too much for her. Each time she tried to lift him she nearly overbalanced.

Tears welled into her eyes. She would never save him now. 'Joe!' she sobbed. 'Joe!' Hardly aware of what she was doing, she let go of one arm and began to fondle his damp hair — gently at first, then more fiercely, until she was almost tugging at it. 'Oh, Joe! Don't leave me now!'

It was Bobby who brought her to her senses again. He had recovered from his fright and, damp and rather forlorn, came wandering over to her. 'I'm cold,' he wailed, sniffing loudly. 'I want to go home.' With only a faint show of interest, he asked, 'What are you doing, Auntie? Where's Joe?'

It *was* cold. The clouds had darkened and shut off the sun, and Janet was suddenly aware that she was shivering. But with Bobby had come fresh hope. Teeth chattering, she said urgently, 'Joe is sick. He's down there and I can't get him up. I want you to help me, Bobby. Catch hold of my ankles, dig your heels into the ground, and lean back and pull. And pull hard.'

He obeyed at once; it was a game, he had no thought for Joe. She felt his fingers round her ankles, and took a firm grip under Joe's armpits.

'Now, Bobby!' she called, bracing herself. 'Pull hard!'

His nails bit through the thin socks into her flesh, but she scarcely noticed the pain. Exerting all her strength, she hunched her body and tugged, feeling the boy take the strain on her legs. Joe's limp body moved a little farther out of the water, and for a few seconds she relaxed, holding him there. Then, 'Again, Bobby,' she cried, and braced herself for yet another effort.

It was not needed. She felt Joe's body move, saw him turn his head slowly from side to side; a wave of thankfulness engulfed her as she became aware of his heart beating under her hand, and she held him the more tightly, fearful that he might yet slip away from her.

'It's all right, Joe,' she said, a break in her voice. 'I've got you.'

He did not answer or look up, but began to cough, retching violently, so that his whole body shook. Then suddenly he leant forward and vomited. The action caught Janet unawares. Bobby had released her ankles, and she was pulled forward past the point of balance. Slithering helplessly down the slope, she cannoned into Joe and landed head-foremost in the water.

When she came up, spluttering with annoyance, it was to see Joe looking at her with a sickly grin. Cautiously he put out a hand to help her up.

'You're a glutton for water, aren't you?' he said. 'I should have thought you'd had enough.'

Janet did not know whether to laugh or cry. Despite his weak attempt at humour he looked ill; his eyes were still glazed, his face was white and drawn, violent spasms contracted his body. She knew that apart from the water he had swallowed he must be suffering from shock. He ought to be kept warm and dry, she thought, recalling the elementary first aid she had learned at school. Yet the water still lapped his feet, and he was shivering from the cold.

They were close together. Impulsively she moved closer and put an arm about him, trying to infuse warmth into him from her own body, forgetful that she too was cold and wet. And at that close contact, so foreign to her, all restraint left her and she began to cry, clinging to him instinctively, her fingers spasmodically kneading the firm flesh under his shirt, her face hidden against his breast. 'Oh, Joe!' she sobbed. 'I thought you were dead.'

For a moment he held her to him, his free hand stroking her wet hair. This was as foreign to him as it was to her. He had never held a girl in his arms before, and it flashed through his mind that this could not be real, that perhaps he really had drowned out there in the loch. But, real or not, he wanted that moment to last. Cold and wet as he was, with death only a few minutes past, he knew that this was the most wonderful and important thing that had happened to him, that nothing could ever sweep it from his memory.

He bent his head to brush her wet hair with his lips.

Janet was unconscious of the caress; but she felt him stir, and the practical side of her nature reasserted itself. Reluctantly she drew away from him.

'We must get you home,' she said. 'You need some dry clothes.' She shivered, hugging her wet body with her arms, and gave an unromantic sniff. 'Are you all right now? Do you think you can climb up the bank if I help you?'

Could he? With her beside him he would have tackled Mount Everest. 'I'm fine,' he assured her. 'You watch me.'

She watched him. His feet kept slipping on the loose surface, his arms were too weak to take the strain when he tried to pull himself up. It took the combined strength of both of them to get him to the top, and when he had reached it they were both glad to rest.

Bobby was waiting. He said petulantly, 'When are we going home?'

'Soon,' Janet told him. 'Take off that wet jersey, darling, and run around until we are ready.' When he had stripped and trotted off she turned to Joe. 'And you get that shirt off. You can rub yourself down with a serviette from the lunch basket. Thank goodness you took off your jacket first. At least that is dry.'

Joe did not argue. He was happy to have her boss him; it implied an intimacy which seemed to bring her closer than any caress could do. He peeled off his shirt and rubbed vigorously to restore the circulation, while Janet sat on the grass and watched him, secretly delighting in the play of his muscles, in the breadth of his shoulders and the firm whiteness of his body.

'That's better,' he said. She brought him his jacket, happy to be waiting on him, and he sat down and took off his shoes, tilting them to let the last drops of water run out. As he was wringing out his socks he said quietly, not looking at her, 'That was a pretty close shave, wasn't it?'

'It certainly was. What on earth possessed you to jump in like that?'

'Sorry.' He grinned. 'I forgot I can't swim.' Then, serious again, he said slowly, 'You saved my life.'

'I suppose so.' To Janet what she had done seemed insignificant beside his own action. 'But you probably saved Bobby's. It was crazy of you, Joe, but — well, it's just about the bravest thing I've ever known.'

He shook his head. 'I didn't save nobody — just gave you more to do. You pulled us both out. It's you that's the brave one, not me. I'm just crazy, like you said.'

Janet felt herself blushing — not at his praise, but at the look in his eyes. She was suddenly aware of the thin texture of her wet blouse, of the way it clung to her body, moulding her tiny breasts so that for once they stood out proudly. Yet his look did not embarrass or disgust her. He did not look at her as Fred had looked at her bare legs that first evening, as Fred always looked at Kay. There was admiration in his eyes, and a deep longing. She had never seen that in any man's eyes before, and it warmed and gladdened her, so that she no longer felt the cold and would have been happy to stay there with him for hours.

But they had to get back. She jumped up briskly and called to Bobby.

They went back over the south side of the hill; it was the more direct route, but hard going in places. Joe insisted on helping her over the worst of these; and Janet, who had done the journey many times before and was far more agile than he, meekly submitted, secretly delighting in the pressure of his hand on her arm. To be weak and feminine and dependent was suddenly a luxury, and one she had never before indulged.

As they came out of the trees above the bungalow Joe's grip on her arm tightened, and he stopped, holding her back. Janet turned to him in surprise.

'What's the matter?'

'A boat. See? Alongside the *Stella*. Looks like we've got visitors.'

She looked to where he pointed. A small dinghy, an outboard motor in its stern, bobbed merrily up and down on the waves that, whipped by the freshening breeze, disturbed the previously smooth surface of the loch.

'It's Angus McFee,' she said slowly.

6

The visitor will not give him o'er so.
The Tempest, Act II, Scene 1

It seemed to Fred that morning that if he was ever to make any definite progress with Kay this must be the day; with her husband in bed and Bobby taken care of it looked, as he thought, dead easy. But Kay spent most of the morning closeted with Donald; she appeared at lunch, snubbed Fred when he hinted at what was in his mind, and once more retired to her room. Bored and irritable, he took a deck-chair on to the lawn, armed with one of the few books on the living-room shelves which promised salacious reading.

But the promise was not fulfilled, and after a while he threw the book down in disgust, closed his eyes, and tried to visualize the moment when Kay should finally succumb. In some ways imagination could be more satisfying than reality;

it demanded no restraint, either from him or from her. In imagination she was no longer frigid and scornful, but lascivious and yielding; he was the master, she the slave. And to anticipate thus, to enjoy in imagination the delights he expected eventually to enjoy in reality, was to extend the ultimate pleasure rather than to blunt it.

But thoughts cannot always be compelled. Sometimes they may be taken so far towards the desired goal, only mutinously to diverge and confuse when the thinker is momentarily distracted or in doubt over some finer point. And Fred was constantly in doubt; he knew what he wanted, but he had no fixed idea of what it would be like or how it could best be achieved. When, for the third time, he found himself back in the preliminary stages, he gave it up and opened his eyes.

It was then that he saw the dinghy.

For a few seconds he watched it idly, focusing his eyes in the strong light. It was only when he realized that it was headed for the island that he scrambled hastily to his feet and made for the bungalow.

Bull was stretched out on his back, breathing stertorously, his mouth wide open. At another time Fred would have hesitated to wake him, knowing his sudden temper. But he dared not hesitate now.

Bull took some waking. As always he reached automatically for his gun. When he saw Fred he belched forth a stream of oaths and obscenities and told him to get the hell out of it. Then he lay down again and closed his eyes. He had no fear of Fred; not with the money securely hidden. It would profit Fred nothing to put a bullet into him now.

Fred was annoyed. And scared. Time was short, and he could not handle this on his own. 'Listen to me, you perishing hulk,' he snapped, his fear of Bull's wrath swamped in the urgency of the situation. 'There's a boat. It'll be here in a few minutes. What the hell do we do now?'

Bull rolled his great body over and sat up, sticking the gun into his hip-pocket. 'A boat? How many aboard?' he demanded, ignoring the insult.

'One.'

The other grunted. 'Probably a friend of the old boy's. We'll make him handle this.'

They found Traynor at his desk in the living-room. Usually he was annoyed at being disturbed; but their news intrigued him, and he went to the front door and looked out at the loch. Visitors, whoever they might be, could cause difficulties for the three men. And difficulties were what he most wanted them to have.

The dinghy was now less than a hundred yards from the jetty. Its occupant waved a greeting when he saw Traynor. 'Who's the guy?' asked Bull. 'Friend of yours?'

'Yes.' Traynor gave a wave of acknowledgment to the man in the dinghy. 'A man named McFee. He's a frequent visitor here.'

Behind them in the hall Rose Traynor exclaimed gleefully, 'Angus McFee! How nice! I'm sure he'll be able to help us, Robert. He's so clever.'

The men ignored her. Bull said, 'Go

down to the jetty, mister, and tell him to clear off. He's not to land, see?'

'Just like that, eh?'

'You can tell him the tale, can't you?' Bull said angrily. 'You're too busy — the old lady's sick — ain't you got no imagination? But keep your trap shut about us if you don't want to get hurt. Fred, you go with him. If he starts talking out of turn let him have it.'

Traynor stared thoughtfully at the approaching boat. 'Very well,' he said, a faint smile on his face. 'I'll do my best.'

His back was towards them, and they could not see the smile; it was his docile submission that was his undoing. Bull was immediately suspicious, without knowing of what to be suspicious.

'You cooking something?' he demanded, laying a heavy and restraining hand on the older man's shoulder. 'This 'gentle Jesus' act ain't natural. Not from you it ain't.' He stared hard at the dinghy, trying to fathom what was in the other's mind. His grip tightened. 'I got it,' he said triumphantly. 'You're reckoning this here guy will know something's wrong when he ain't allowed ashore. That's it, eh?'

'It did occur to me,' Traynor admitted. Since his scheme looked like going awry, the best he could do now was to use it as a further trip-wire for his enemies. And he had not put much faith in it; his estimate of Angus McFee's intelligence was less sanguine than his wife's. 'Illness or no illness, it isn't usual to tell one's friends to clear off when they pay one a visit. Not on Garra. But it's your worry, my friend, not mine.'

Across the water came a hail. 'Ahoy there, Prospero!'

Traynor waved again. 'Well?' he said to Bull. 'What now?'

'Go and meet him,' growled Bull. 'Fred'll go with you. Bring him up here and keep him in the bungalow. You can give him a meal if that's what he's expecting, and then get rid of him. But get this, mister, and get it good; wherever Mister Bloody McFee goes, there goes Fred. And keep a check on that tongue of yours, like I said. Fred ain't as fussy as I am about using a gun.'

Fred grinned. It sounded like a

compliment to him. And compliments from Bull were rare.

'And who, may I ask, is Fred supposed to be?' Traynor asked mildly. For the first time since the men had come to the island he was beginning to enjoy himself. It was a pleasant change to see this domineering brute in a quandary. 'The prodigal son?'

'He's the hired man,' Bull said, without hesitation. 'The one your daughter told the villagers about when she went shopping.'

'It was Joe went with the girl, not me,' Fred objected.

'I know that, damn you! But Joe ain't here, and neither's the girl; we'll have to take a chance that this bastard McFee didn't meet 'em.' Bull raised his hand from Traynor's shoulder and gave him a shove. 'Git going, mister. And watch your step.'

'What about you?' asked Fred.

'I'll stay out of sight in the kitchen.' Traynor was already on the path, and Bull raised his voice to call warningly, 'But not out of hearing, mister. Don't forget that.'

Traynor nodded and went on, trying not to appear too eager. One hope had failed, but another had taken its place. Janet had mentioned to him — but not, apparently, to the men — that she and Joe had met Angus in the village. And not even the short-sighted Angus could accept Fred for Joe.

How could that be used to advantage?

The dinghy was already alongside the jetty when the two men reached it. Traynor apologized for his tardiness.

'I was thinking you didna look too pleased to see me,' McFee admonished him in the broad Scots he delighted to affect, clambering nimbly ashore. 'Come at an awkward time, have I?' And, when Traynor started to protest at this slur on his hospitality, 'Ah, well, it makes no difference. I'm no' going back till I've said what I've come to say.'

He was a short, stocky man of sixty, with close-cropped, grizzled hair and a straggling grey beard. Behind his spectacles his eyes were the colour of the loch — grey-blue shot with green — set in a square face that shone like polished oak.

He wore a dark blue fisherman's jersey with stained and shapeless flannel trousers and a heavy pair of rope-soled canvas shoes. On one stubby finger was a thick band of gold.

'And what might that be?' asked Traynor.

'It'll keep a while.' McFee peered inquisitively at Fred, hovering watchfully a few feet away. 'Who's yon?'

His host hastened to introduce them. 'This is Fred,' he said. 'I've taken him on to give me a hand here.'

'Have ye, now?' The Scotsman took off his spectacles, polished them on a large maroon handkerchief, and replaced them on his nose. 'But he's no' the laddie I met with Janet in the village yesterday. Does that make two of them, then?'

Traynor smiled blandly and turned to Fred. 'Well, now — what do you say to that, Fred? *Are* there two of you?'

Fred scowled, shuffling from one ill-shod foot to the other in nervous indecision. What the hell was he supposed to say to that? Bull had said to take a chance; but it was he, Fred, who had to take it — not Bull, damn him! The bastard should have known that Traynor would create difficulties if he got the chance.

'Of course there are two of us,' he said surlily, playing for what he thought was safety. Joe and the girl might return before the old geezer left. 'You know that. Me and Joe.'

McFee's eyebrows went up — not only at the answer, but at the tone. He looked at his host, expecting an angry reproof. Bob Traynor was not the man to be spoken to like that by an employee.

But no reproof was forthcoming. The bland smile remained. 'Thank you, Fred,' Traynor said courteously. He turned to his visitor. 'You were right, Angus, there *are* two of them. Fred and Joe.'

Angus McFee was not easily shaken, but this was almost too much for him. He swallowed hard.

'Ye wouldna be pulling my leg, would ye?' he demanded suspiciously.

'Of course not. Why should I?'

'You mean you didna know whether you hired one man or two?'

'A temporary lapse of memory,' Traynor assured him. 'But it all comes back to me now. I hired two. Fred and Joe. Now come on up to the house, Angus. Rose will be glad to see you.'

McFee grunted. Had he not known Bob Traynor for a lifelong teetotaller he would have suspected him of being drunk.

'Aye,' he said. 'I've no doubt she will. With her husband gone daft in the head she'll be needing a friend to comfort her, poor thing.' With short, bouncing steps he followed his friend along the jetty, the watchful, anxious Fred in close attendance. 'Lapse of memory, eh?' he muttered. 'I didna know — ' He stopped abruptly, so that Fred nearly bumped into him. 'Good God, man, what for would ye be wanting two men to help you run a postage-stamp of a place like this? You that's done it single-handed for sixteen years! Prrrh! Ye may be daft in the head, but by the looks of ye ye're no' an invalid yet.'

Traynor turned and smiled at him.

'A good question, Angus,' he said. 'We

must try to supply an answer.' He looked over his friend's grizzled head to the man behind. 'Fred, why do I — '

Something in Fred's eyes stopped him, warning him not to overplay his hand. Fred was an unstable character; he might be as great a ruffian as Bull, but he lacked the big man's nerves. Push him too far and he might whip out that gun and use it, as he had used it on the unfortunate watchman.

Well, no doubt there would be other tricks to play. He must bide his time. 'You could put it down to laziness, I suppose,' he told McFee. 'Or old age.'

'I could — but I won't.'

'No? Then we must think up something else.'

McFee made no comment. He felt flustered and confused; the situation was beyond him. Either Bob was mad, or he was putting on an act. But why should he do that? Had he some deep scheme afoot that he wished to conceal from his visitor? If so he was going about it in a most extraordinary way.

Perhaps Rose could make that clear.

But Rose made nothing clear. She greeted him effusively, and this alone told the visitor that something was wrong. It wasn't like Rose. But neither she nor her husband seemed surprised when Fred accompanied them into the living-room and settled himself in one of the easy-chairs.

'What's this about Bob needing two men to help him on the island?' he asked Rose. 'Two of them, he says there are — though he was a wee bit doubtful at first about the number.'

'Two?' Rose looked doubtfully at her husband, and saw him nod. Yet Bull, who had drilled both Kay and herself in what they were to say, had said that there was to be only one. 'Are there two?' This time she looked at Fred, who also nodded. 'Yes, of course there are. The garden, you know, and the animals; they're getting too much for him, Angus. And it's nice for him to have company when he's working.'

Company? McFee stared at the sprawling Fred, taking in the mean face, the long, dank hair and the 'sideboards,' the dirty collar and loud tie, the greasy blue suit. If that's company for Bob, he thought grimly, then Bob's no company for me.

'Know me again, won't you?' Fred said insolently.

There was silence in the room. McFee waited expectantly for his host to rise from his chair in wrath and hurl the offending hireling from the room. But Traynor did not rise. Nor was there any apparent wrath — except McFee's.

'How's Jenny?' Rose asked equably. 'Why didn't she come with you, Angus?'

Slowly, almost reluctantly, McFee shifted his gaze from Fred to her. He shook his head. Maybe it's I that's daft, he told himself sadly.

'Jenny's away out,' he said. This had been a stock question made out of politeness. He never did bring his wife with him. Jenny disliked islands and boats and the people who went with them. It was a constant source of wonder to the Traynors that she had consented to marry Angus, to whom Garra was a second home, the loch his playground.

Kay joined them for tea, and helped to

restore McFee's belief in his own sanity. Though she made no demur to Fred's presence at the table, it was obvious that she bitterly resented it. He noticed that none of them engaged Fred in conversation, speaking to him only when addressed — which was seldom. Gradually McFee came to realize that, although for some reason they were prepared to accept the man's presence among them, they would not accept his person. They were not rude to him, but in so far as they could they ignored him.

He set himself to study Fred. The man ate sparingly, constantly fingering his food, sucking the tea from his cup in noisy gulps. His hands, although not over-clean, were not the hands of a manual worker; he'll be as out of place working on the island, thought McFee, as he is at this table. And Fred, he thought, probably appreciated the incongruity of his position; although there was an air of bravado about him, his restless eyes betrayed his uncertainty. They were still only when concentrated on his plate — or on Kay Grant.

Appreciating the significance of this latter fact, McFee understood why Kay should so resent Fred's presence.

'Isn't your husband here with you?' he asked her, pursuing his train of thought. He had met the Grants on one of their previous visits.

Kay explained that Donald had a headache and was lying down.

'I'm sorry. And the boy?'

'He's gone fishing with Janet.'

McFee was reminded that there was yet another member of the island community not accounted for. 'And Joe?' he asked. 'Doesna he take tea with you?'

'He's out with Janet,' Traynor told him.

Inured by now to surprises, McFee took this in his stride. But Traynor was less complaisant. It had been his plan to confront his visitor with so many incongruities, so many paradoxes, to leave so much unexplained, that McFee would return home with his mind full of the problem, would not let it rest until he had solved it. But it seemed that McFee, having absorbed the initial shock, was rapidly becoming inured. Either the shocks were too infrequent, or they lacked punch.

Maybe he could rectify that. 'You told me down at the jetty that you had something to say to me, Angus,' he said. 'What is it?'

McFee had been about to raise the same topic. His visit had been inspired by his meeting with Janet and Joe the previous morning, and a desire to discover just why Traynor should have found it necessary to employ labour on the island. But his curiosity then was as nothing to his curiosity now, and he suddenly realized that since he had landed on the island Fred had never been out of earshot. Perhaps something was afoot that his friend did not wish to discuss in the man's presence. Traynor's remark seemed to substantiate that possibility; he could be hinting at a private talk.

'Aye,' he said. 'I hadna forgotten. But it's a personal matter, you'll understand. Suppose you and I take a wee bit walk, Bob? It's too grand an afternoon to be spending indoors.'

He did not get the expected response. Traynor said, 'It's not so grand. The wind is freshening — could be treacherous. If you don't mind, Angus, I'd rather not go outside. I don't want to get a chill.'

McFee stared at him in disbelief of his own ears. This from Bob Traynor, the man who had tramped his island and sailed the loch in all weathers — and for pleasure! He said, not attempting to hide his scorn, 'Verra well. But since ye dinna fancy the fresh air maybe we could talk in another room? Or are ye feared there'll be too great a draught in the passage?'

Traynor flushed. His refusal had had the desired effect, but it gave him no pleasure. It was not pleasant to have an old friend look at him as Angus McFee was looking at him now. He was suddenly sick of the whole business; for a brief, desperate moment he was tempted to blurt out the truth, heedless of what Fred might do. But sanity asserted itself. Confronted with such open defiance Fred might panic and start shooting; he dared not risk that. And even if Fred did nothing there was still the unseen but menacing bulk of Bull in the kitchen to contend with.

'Later, Angus,' he said weakly. 'And don't think — '

McFee never learned what he was not to think, for it was then that Bobby pranced into the room. Though some time had elapsed since he had been pulled out of the loch, it was still obvious that he had had a close and thorough contact with water. And his journey home had added dirt to wetness.

'What on earth have you been up to?' demanded his mother.

'I fell into the loch. So did Joe. Auntie Janet had to rescue us. And Joe was sick, and we tried to pull him up — but we couldn't, he was ever so heavy.' His eyes strayed to the table. 'Can I have a bun, Mummy? I'm hungry.'

'Yes, darling. Of course.'

While his mother continued to question him, horrific visions floated through Rose Traynor's mind. From the boy's meagre account it seemed certain that Joe was dead, that his rescue had been effected too late. Sick . . . too heavy to pull up . . . they had had to leave him . . . it all added up to that. Well, the man was a thief and deserved no sympathy; nevertheless it seemed dreadful that he should die like that. And what a terrible experience for poor Janet! Bobby seemed unmoved by the tragedy, and that was something to be thankful for; death could make a shattering impression on the young. But Janet . . .

She was saved from further mental agony by the appearance of Janet herself. And behind Janet came Joe.

Though cleaner than Bobby, they looked more bedraggled. Joe's jacket was dry, but under it his chest was bare; his trousers had shrunk still higher up his legs, losing what little shape they had formerly possessed. Janet's blouse still clung wetly to her; her jeans were wrinkled and darkened by the water, her shoes squelched as she walked. Yet in neither of their faces was reflected the harrowing experience through which they had passed. Both looked apprehensive, but Janet exuded a radiance that startled her mother.

'Scarecrows, aren't we?' she said gaily, relieved that Angus McFee's arrival did not appear to have precipitated a further catastrophe. The family all seemed normal enough — though there was no sign of Bull, and Fred looked strangely ill at ease. 'How are you, Angus? Sorry to greet you like this, but Bobby took us all for a dip.'

'What happened, my dear?' asked her father.

Janet told them, stressing the part Joe had played. When she had finished Kay said simply, 'Thank you, Joe.' But that seemed inadequate, and she added softly, 'I won't forget what you did. If there's any way in which I can repay you I'd be glad to do it.'

Joe flushed. He was not accustomed to having beautiful women look at him as Kay was looking at him. He said clumsily, 'I did nothing; just got in Miss Janet's way, that's all. It was her rescued the kid. Me too.'

'I dare say,' Traynor said. 'But it was a gallant impulse, young man, and does you credit.' He shook Joe warmly by the hand.

'Thank you. As Mrs Grant has said, we won't forget it.'

They turned to Janet then, fussing over her, praising her, pressing for greater detail. Joe breathed a sigh of relief, glad to be out of the limelight. Their praise had embarrassed him. He didn't deserve it, and he didn't want it.

Fred limped quickly across the room and led Joe to the door. With all that pother over the girl it seemed unlikely that anyone would notice that for once he wasn't eavesdropping. He could take a chance, trusting that McFee was temporarily forgotten. Joe had to be briefed.

But he had seen the look that Kay had given Joe, and he had not liked it. 'Quite the little hero, ain't you?' he sneered. 'Thinking of marrying into the family?'

'Shut up!' There was such venom in the words that Fred was startled. 'Quit trying to be funny and tell me what's going on here.'

Fred told him.

Janet came over to them. She said, smiling up at Joe, oblivious of Fred's presence, 'Daddy is going to lend you some clothes until yours are dry. You ought really to have a hot bath, but Mummy says the water's cold. You'll have to make do with a good rub down instead.' Fred left them, reminded of his duties, and she touched Joe's fingers gently with her own. 'Hurry up. You mustn't catch a chill.'

'What about you?' He did not want to move while she was still there beside him.

'Me?' She laughed. 'Oh, I'm tough. But don't worry, I'll change too. I must look an absolute sight.'

'Not to me you don't.'

Once more her fingers sought his, as though secretly conveying a message. Then she was gone.

It was while helping Bobby to change out of his wet clothes that Kay had the idea of writing a note to McFee. They were in her room, and she had looked out of the window — and there was the dinghy, rolling and bobbing on the water. And in a little while McFee would get into it, start the motor, and sail back across the loch to the mainland without the least notion of what was wrong on Garra.

Unless she did something about it.

Donald was awake and feeling better. When she outlined her plan to him he frowned. 'I don't like it, Kay,' he said. 'Using the boy, I mean. Isn't there another way?'

'No, there isn't.' She spoke sharply, annoyed that he should criticize this plan as he had criticized the others, and forgetful that he had good cause to be wary. 'Fred sticks to McFee like a leech. And what chance would you or I have of getting near the boat without one of them chasing after us to see what we were up to? But Bobby — they'd never suspect him.' She glanced across the room at her son, who was examining a scent-spray. 'Leave that alone, darling, and put your shoes and socks on.'

'He might fall in,' Donald said. 'Isn't one ducking a day enough?'

She had thought of that; the dinghy did not sit steadily on the water. 'But it's shallow there,' she said. 'He can't come to any harm. And we can keep an eye on him from the window.' She went over to the dressing-table. 'Shall I write it, or will you?'

'It's your baby. But keep it short.'

She wrote without pause; words were seldom a problem to Kay. When she had finished she said, looking out of the window, 'Where would be the best place to hide it?'

'Goodness knows! If it's too conspicuous one of the men might spot it. Yet McFee's got to see it.' Reluctantly he got out of bed and padded across the carpet to join her. The dinghy was half hidden by the jetty, but he could see the top of the outboard motor. 'Don't they start those things with a piece of rope? He could put it under that. It would be on the floor-boards, I imagine — near the stern.'

Kay turned. Bobby had picked up the scent-spray again and was tentatively squeezing the bulb. She took it from him and knelt to face him.

'Listen, darling,' she said. 'I want you to do something for me. Only it's terribly secret, so you mustn't tell anyone. Understand?'

He nodded. 'Secret Service,' he suggested. 'Like catching spies.'

'Sort of.' She stuffed the note into his pocket. 'I want you to take that piece of paper down to Mr McFee's boat — not the *Stella*, the other one — and hide it on the floor under a piece of rope. If the rope isn't there you'll just have to leave it on the floor. I expect there will be some rag you can put over it. All right?'

'Yes.' His eyes shone gleefully. 'Is Mr McFee a spy?'

'I hope not. But we don't know.' Aware of his admiration for Bull, she did not dare to name the real enemy. 'Now, off you go. Be careful getting in and out of the boat, darling; you don't want to fall in again, do you? And remember, it's terribly secret. No one but you and I and Daddy must know about the note. No one. Understand?'

He nodded, put one finger to his lips, and darted from the room. Anxiously they watched from the window, relieved when they saw that he had reached the jetty without being followed. But their relief was short-lived. As he climbed gingerly down on to the dinghy's gunwale the boat tilted and he disappeared.

'He's fallen in!' Kay exclaimed, turning to run. But Donald stopped her.

'It's all right. He fell into the boat.'

Bobby picked himself up and began to fiddle with the motor. He fiddled for so long that Kay feared he had forgotten his mission. But presently he bent down out of sight, and for a few tense moments they waited anxiously.

'I hope there *is* a rope,' Donald said.

Bobby's face reappeared above the level of the jetty, and he looked up at the bungalow and waved vigorously. 'He's done it,' Kay exulted, waving back. 'Oh, I do hope he'll be careful getting out of the boat. If he fell in now it would draw attention to the dinghy.'

'Spoken like a doting mother,' Donald said.

But Bobby had no intention of getting out of the boat. Not yet. His mission accomplished, he felt at liberty to enjoy himself, and the dinghy offered endless possibilities. The rocking motion particularly delighted him; it would be more delightful still if it were aggravated. Gripping a gunwale with both hands, he started to move his body backward and forward, thrilling to the sound of the boat slapping the water and the feel and sight of the spray.

'Be careful, Bobby!' breathed Kay. She dared not call to him.

'He'll be all right,' Donald said. 'It would take more than Bobby to overturn a boat like that.'

Kay drew in her breath sharply and clutched at his arm. A blue-suited figure had emerged from the bungalow and was limping purposefully down the path to the jetty. The look on his face was not pleasant.

'Fred!' she exclaimed. 'Oh, Donald! He must have been watching!'

Amid the confusion which had arisen after the return of Joe and Janet Fred could not be sure that some one had not managed to whisper a few words of the truth into McFee's ear. But the uncertainty did not worry him greatly; his mind was grappling with another and more personal problem. Having previously convinced himself that Kay Grant was a nymphomaniac, he had suddenly become obsessed with the belief that she was setting her cap at Joe. That look she had given him . . . the soft voice in which she had thanked him . . . she was not the sort of woman to melt so completely just because Joe had tried to rescue her ruddy brat from drowning. There was more to it than that. What had she said? She wouldn't forget him, she would gladly repay him. And to Fred's way of thinking repayment by a beautiful woman could take only one form.

He swore savagely, trying to shut out from his tortured brain the image of Kay, warmly naked, clasped in the strong arms of Joe. If Joe tries to make her before me, he told himself, I'll do him. By Christ, I'll do him! I'll plug him so full of lead . . .

He steadied himself, wiping away with his sleeve the sweat that had suddenly beaded his forehead. Getting rid of Joe might satisfy his lust for vengeance, but it wouldn't help him with the woman. If she were hot for Joe she would not fall into the arms of his murderer, it would take time to make her after that. And time was something he hadn't much of. Not where Kay was concerned.

Joe. How did Joe stand in this? He had spent most of his time on the island with the girl, Janet; but that couldn't be because he preferred her, it could only be because he reckoned he didn't stand a chance with the blonde. Joe was the quiet, shy type; he wouldn't have the nerve to go after a haughty dame like Kay, he'd want something easier, something that purred, not scratched. Only Kay wasn't scratching now. Not for Joe. She was purring so loud even Joe must have heard her. So — what would Joe do?

Fred ran a damp finger round the inside of his collar as he thought of what he would do if he were Joe. A black rage seized him, and he glared across the room at his presumed rival, looking self-conscious in borrowed shirt and trousers. For Joe would do it too, he decided; Joe wouldn't be mug enough to pass up an opening like that. Not unless he'd got himself so deeply involved with the girl that he couldn't cut loose.

This latter possibility brought with it a gleam of hope, and Fred seized on it gratefully. Joe had been out with the girl for most of the day, and to Fred's way of thinking that could mean only one thing. Fishing wasn't the only sport they'd had, he reckoned. Joe wouldn't find it so easy to ditch the girl after that, however much he might fancy the blonde. It was even possible, incredible as it seemed, that Joe didn't *want* to ditch the girl, that he was content with what he'd got. When the two of them had walked into the room that afternoon there had been a look on both their faces that Fred had seen on the faces of young lovers; a soft, smug, satisfied look that he had found vaguely irritating at the time, but which he now recalled with satisfaction and relief. If that was how matters stood he had no need to worry. Kay would get the brush-off from Joe without any prompting from him. He might even catch her himself on the rebound.

It was an encouraging fancy, but it was still only a fancy. Before he could start to build on it he had to find out for sure about Joe and the girl. And that wouldn't be easy. If they'd been up to their tricks that afternoon they wouldn't talk about it, and there was no one else he could pump for information. They had been alone except for the kid.

The kid! He had been with them. But a kid that age wouldn't know what it was all about, would he? Still, he might have seen or heard something that would give a clue if only it could be prised out of him.

Fred reckoned he knew how to do the prising.

He had seen Bobby go down to the jetty; through the open doorway he could see him now, playing in the dinghy. He went over to Joe.

'I'm going out,' he said, hoping he sounded more friendly than he felt. He didn't want to quarrel with Joe if there was nothing to quarrel about. If Joe didn't want the blonde, if it was true about him and the girl, then Joe could be useful. 'Keep an eye on this lot until I get back. And stick close to McFee, so's none of them can talk to him private like. Okay?'

Joe nodded. He was content to stay

there and wait for Janet.

Fred reached the jetty just ahead of Kay. For once annoyed at her presence (how could he question the kid with her there?), he stood scowling down at the dinghy, wondering how to get rid of her. But Kay mistook the cause of his anger. Guiltily aware that she had allowed her hatred of Bull temporarily to deaden her maternal instinct, she had convinced herself that Fred's anger was directed against Bobby. And since Fred could not possibly know of the note, it must be because Bobby was playing in the dinghy.

'Come out of that at once, Bobby.' Her nervousness made her speak more sharply than she had intended. The boy looked up at her in surprise, but she did not see the look. Her attention had been caught by the note; its whiteness showed up clearly beneath the loosely coiled rope, and she knew that if Fred were to look down he could not fail to see it. 'You mustn't play in the boat without permission. It's Mr McFee's — he might not like it.'

'But you told me — ' He stopped,

puzzled by her reproof but remembering in time that his mission had been secret. 'If he's a spy it doesn't matter, does it, Mummy? And you said he was.'

'I said he might be, dear.' She turned to Fred, forcing a smile. Fred must not be given time in which to ponder the significance of the boy's words. 'It's just a game we were playing,' she said, hoping to stifle his curiosity. 'I told him — that — Mr — McFee — '

The words died away. Fred was not listening to her. He had moved closer to the edge of the jetty and was staring fixedly into the boat. Fists clenched in an agony of suspense, Kay waited. There was nothing she could do.

Fred said slowly, 'That piece of paper under the rope. You put it there, son?'

The boy eyed him uncertainly. There was an edge to the man's voice that he mistrusted. But his mother had said . . .

'Pick it up. Give it to me.'

There was no mistaking the rasping fierceness in the order. Bobby shifted his feet in the tossing boat and looked appealingly at his mother.

'Do as he says, darling,' Kay said quietly. 'It isn't a secret any more.'

She was suddenly calm. Her fear had been based on Bull, not on Fred. When she had sent Bobby with the note it had been Bull she was plotting against, it was of Bull's reaction she instinctively thought when she believed the plot discovered. But Bull need never know; it was Fred who had found the note — and Fred she could manage. She had nothing to fear from Fred. For once she was able to find satisfaction in the desire she had aroused in that repulsive ruffian. If necessary she would even exploit it; though not to the full, and only as a last resource.

She watched him as he read the short note, curious as to his reaction; her references in it to himself and his companions had not been flattering. He read slowly, mouthing the words as if unaccustomed to reading. But his expression told her nothing.

'Well?' she challenged.

'Get rid of the kid,' he said.

It was what she herself wanted. Yet perversely, because it irked her to obey an order — and particularly an order from him — Kay hesitated. But not for long. The order, even more than the new hoarseness to his voice, told her the way his mind was working. He wanted to bargain — if blackmail could be considered bargaining. And she could handle him better without Bobby there to listen. Bobby might not understand the bargaining, but he was apt to repeat what he overheard.

She bent to give the boy a hand up from the boat. 'Run up to the bungalow, darling,' she said. Then, remembering that Donald was watching from the window, that he might question Bobby, she changed her mind. 'No, wait for me. I want to talk to Fred, but I shan't be long. Go and play on the beach until I'm ready.'

Fred said slowly, refolding the note, 'Asking for trouble, ain't you?'

He was highly jubilant. That little piece of paper was an unexpected treasure, a trump-card he could never have anticipated holding. Whether she was after Joe or not was no longer important. She would have to dance to *his* tune now, no matter which way her fancy went.

'Don't tell me you're surprised,' Kay said, determined to put up a fight before admitting the need to bargain. 'You knew very well we would take any chance that offered to get rid of you. Why else have you stuck so close to Mr McFee since he arrived?'

'Me, I'm easy-going,' he said, turning the note over in his fingers as though to keep it constantly before her, and ignoring the question. 'I don't hold no hard feelings. But Bull — well, he's different. He ain't as easy as me.'

Though she had known this was coming, she could not repress a shudder as imagination pictured the kind of action Bull might take were Fred to implement the implied threat. No feminine lures would help her with Bull. But the shudder was only momentary. Fred, she knew, had no intention of telling Bull about the note. Not unless she refused to submit to his blackmail.

'No, he isn't easy,' she agreed, turning to face him squarely. 'And he wouldn't be easy on you either, would he, if he discovered that you hadn't watched us as strictly as he ordered? He wouldn't be too pleased to learn that we nearly fooled you.'

The suggestion that he was subservient to Bull, that he was afraid of him, touched him on the raw. Now more than ever he wished to impress her with his manhood, his virility.

'He ain't my boss,' he said sharply, glad that she had not been a witness to Bull's handling of him the previous evening. 'I don't take no orders from Bull unless I want to. Nor I ain't feared of him, either.' He patted the bulge under his breast-pocket meaningly. 'I can talk as big as him.'

'All right,' she said. 'So what?'

The freshening wind pressed her thin skirt and blouse hard against her, moulding her legs and body into sharp outlines and contours. Fred's irritation slipped away from him, melted by desire. He licked his lips.

'I seen Bull handle a kid once,' he said slowly, impressively. 'It weren't pretty.'

Kay caught her breath; her heart missed a beat. This was something she had not foreseen. She had been prepared to gamble on her conviction that, even though she were to promise nothing, Fred would still hold his tongue; that he would not deliberately destroy the goose that might yet be persuaded to lay him a golden egg. But she could not gamble with Bobby's safety and well-being. That was too high a stake.

'I don't believe it,' she said fiercely. 'He wouldn't dare. Bobby's only a baby. I told him to put the note in the boat, and he did. He thought it was a game.'

Fred shrugged. 'It was the same with this other kid. He hadn't done nothing, and Bull knew it. But beating the kid up was the best way to punish the parents, see?' As an afterthought he added, 'They put the woman in a looney bin after.'

Kay's face went white. She did not believe him, but she could not call his bluff. Recalling what Bull had said that first evening, when he had announced his intention of sharing Bobby's room — 'start something, and I take it out on the kid' — she knew she was beaten.

'What do you want?' she asked dully, abandoning the first round without further fight.

'You know what I want.' He stepped a pace nearer, his eyes glittering with triumph. 'I been wanting it ever since I seen you back there on the road.' His voice thickened. He put out a hand to touch her, but she moved away, blindly aware of Donald at the window. Desperately though she wanted Donald to interfere now, she must not let him. In helping her he would be sacrificing Bobby.

Fred was amused, not angered, by her withdrawal, by the look of disgust on her face. It appealed to the sadist in him. A tussle rather than a willing surrender would add spice to the final triumph. No sad and listless whore could give a man that.

'Okay,' he said. 'It'll keep till to-night. I'll come to your room, eh?' He grinned at her horrified expression, at the startled 'No!' 'Worried about your old man? Bull's taken care of him. He's sleeping in the shed — remember? You'll be on your own to-night, blondie.'

Kay shuddered at the new and horrible familiarity. The look on his face made her feel sick, and she turned away, unable to meet it. Her whole being revolted at the prospect his words and his look envisaged, and she knew that if she had ever contemplated surrendering her body to him — and in the heat of angry hatred against Bull she *had* contemplated it — it was because until that moment she had never fully realized just how loathsome that surrender would be, what it would cost her mentally and physically. But she realized it now — knew that not even for Bobby could she go through with it. Her revolt had little to do with moral values; it was not concerned with chastity, or the sanctity of marriage, or her love for Donald. It had something of pride in it, but mainly it was a physical revulsion against the person of Fred himself. Through necessity she might have accepted infidelity, but she could not accept Fred.

There had to be another way. There *had* to be.

A wave of relief swept over her. She had bowed to her body's revolt, she no longer had to fight against it. Now she had only Fred to fight. But he must not know that; until she had found a plan he must believe he had won, that the battle was over. He must be made to grant her the time she needed.

'I hadn't forgotten,' she said slowly. 'I wasn't thinking of my husband, but of my cousin. She's sharing my room to-night.'

He muttered an oath, spat into the water, and rubbed his hand over his mouth. But he was not greatly put out. 'I ain't all that fussy about a bed,' he said. 'It's fancy, but it ain't necessary.' His voice hardened. 'Ain't thinking of pulling a fast one, are you? You be down here by midnight or I'll wake Bull up and show him this here note.' He laughed shortly. 'He'll be drunk — but not too drunk. And he don't like being woke up, neither. What he'll do to you and the kid won't help neither of you to win no beauty contest. So you be here, see?'

She nodded. 'You needn't worry,' she said, amazed at her own calmness. She had no illusions about Fred. Pity was not in his make-up. 'You keep your side of the bargain, and I'll keep mine.'

His eyes narrowed. 'Bargain? I ain't made no bargain.'

'Oh, yes, you have. I want that note back, and I want your help against Bull.'

'How?'

'I don't know how. Not yet. But I'll find a way.' Momentarily she had forgotten that the bargain would never be struck, and added vindictively, 'I'm going to make that brute suffer, if it's the last thing I ever do.'

He grinned. 'Friendly, ain't you? What about me and Joe?'

'I don't care about you. It's Bull I'm after.'

'You are, eh?' Fred looked thoughtful. It would give him great pleasure to jettison Bull if it could be done with no danger to himself, and provided he could first make sure of the money. But Bull was a tough and ugly customer, and not easy to outsmart. 'Well, maybe I'm with you and maybe I ain't. I'm making no promises. But you can have the note. Not now,' as she put out her hand expectantly. 'To-night. If you're there.'

'I'll be there,' she said, without a tremor.

Fred watched her as she walked off the jetty, calling to Bobby as she went. Suspicion clouded his brain. He didn't trust her — she was suddenly too calm, too assured. She meant to trick him, damn her! She wouldn't come — she'd find some other way out . . .

Kay was looking at a pebble that Bobby held in his hand. A gust of wind sent her skirt whirling and dancing about her; Fred had a sudden glimpse of white lace, and dug his elbows into his sides in an effort to control the fit of shivering that seized him.

The wind caught him and he staggered. Slowly he began to limp along the jetty, his eyes never leaving the woman ahead, his fists clenching and unclenching spasmodically. A fleck of foam showed whitely at his lips.

If she don't come, he told himself fiercely, I'll go get her. By God, I will! She ain't going to cheat me now.

McFee and the Traynors were talking

together, with Joe keeping an uneasy watch. Janet stood close to him, listening to the conversation but taking no part in it; occasionally she gave a fleeting glance at Joe's tense face, ready to smile at him if he should look her way. She had changed into her gayest summer frock; Kay noticed it as soon as she and Bobby entered the room, and wondered idly why Janet should have bothered to 'dress up' for McFee. It seemed a most un-Janet-like gesture.

'How are ye, laddie?' McFee stood up and held out a hand to the boy. 'None the worse for your ducking?'

Bobby scowled at him, ignoring the hand. His eyes searched the room. 'Where's Mr Bull?' he asked.

Joe cursed under his breath. Traynor smiled grimly; Bull, he knew, would be listening, and it pleased him that the ruffian's scheme looked like being punctured — and by Bobby, of all people.

Kay said hurriedly, 'Darling, say 'hello' to Mr McFee.'

Bobby shook his head. 'You said he was a spy.'

His mother flushed, and looked apologetically at the Scotsman. 'It's my fault,' she said. 'I'm sorry. We were playing a game, but he seems to have taken me literally.'

McFee chuckled. 'And whom or what am I supposed to be spying on?'

'We never got that settled,' she said, with a faint smile. And to Bobby, 'He isn't a spy, Bobby. I was wrong. He's a friend of Uncle Robert's. Now shake hands properly, there's a good boy.'

Bobby did so. But by shedding the sinister rôle of spy McFee ceased to be of interest. 'Where's Mr Bull?' he demanded.

'And who,' asked McFee, his eyes gleaming behind his spectacles, 'is Mr Bull? Joe I've met, and Fred.' He turned to his host. 'Ye wouldna have miscounted again, Bob? There wouldna be *three* men working for ye now, I suppose?'

Traynor hesitated. He looked up to see Fred watching him from the doorway.

'I don't think so,' he said slowly. 'There aren't three of you, are there, Fred?'

The kitchen door was thrown violently open and Bull came stamping out, his whiskers bristling, his belly quivering with wrath. There was no further point in concealment. Brushing Joe aside, he strode across the floor to stand threateningly over the startled Scotsman.

'You're damned right!' he roared. 'There are three of us, mister. Want to make something of it?'

For a brief moment McFee stared at him incredulously. Then his astonishment gave way to a throaty chuckle.

'Caliban!' he exclaimed, and slapped his thigh. 'By Sycorax! So Prospero has his Caliban, after all!'

7

I would not wish
Any companion in the world but you.
The Tempest, Act III, Scene 1

Since McFee could not be allowed to return to the mainland to spread his news, he had to be kept a prisoner on the island. McFee himself accepted this dictum with cheerful grace. So did Traynor, though less cheerfully. Both knew that it was inevitable; they also knew that it must cause their captors considerable embarrassment. Not only was McFee another man to be watched, but his failure to return home would have to be accounted for to his wife. Her immediate anxiety could be contained by sending Joe with a message. But whereas she might consider it reasonable for her husband to decide on the spur of the moment to spend a night on the island, she was unlikely to remain indifferent if he stayed for two or three.

In case his captors might not have appreciated this aspect of his detention, McFee enlarged on it with a cheerful volubility that irritated the enraged Bull to the point of danger. But the Scot either ignored or did not recognize the danger. 'And it's no' herself will be coming to look for me,' he concluded with evident relish. 'She wouldna trust herself to a boat in this breeze for all the whisky in Scotland. It's the men from the club she'll be sending. And ye willna find them so easy to handle, I'm thinking.'

It was too much for Bull. An enormous fist caught McFee on the chest and sent him sprawling on to a chair. 'Shut up, you old fool!' he roared, and kicked him savagely on the ankle.

Involuntarily Traynor stepped forward, possessed by the instinctive desire to protect his friend from further savagery. Bull saw in the movement an attack upon himself. He seized Traynor by the throat, shook him furiously, and hurled him backward on to the sprawling McFee. But he did not kick him. He stood over the two prostrate men, panting as much from anger as from exertion, his fists clenched menacingly.

'That's how I'll handle them,' he growled.

At the first blow Rose had screamed. So had Janet; she had clutched with both hands at Joe's arm, instinctively seeking his protection. But her scream died abruptly as Joe tried to free himself, and she clutched the harder; she did not want him hurt, nor was she so sure of him that she could tell his purpose. And Joe, perhaps aware of her uncertainty, did not persist in his struggle. Poised and tense, he waited expectantly.

Kay did not scream. She was perhaps less startled than any of them by Bull's sudden violence. She knew that it was not McFee's mild taunt that had provoked him, but the realization that the tide was turning against him, that he could not for much longer control his and their destinies so autocratically. McFee could not be kept a prisoner indefinitely. Even if Bull could handle the men from the boat club there would be others — and others after them.

With wide eyes she watched him, clutching the terrified Bobby tightly to her. It was Bobby who had betrayed the big man's presence to McFee, who had been the innocent cause of Bull's present outburst of savagery. If Bull in his mad rage were to recognize that . . . were to turn on the child . . .

She shivered, her body weak with fear. Yet deep inside her she knew a savage satisfaction at the desperation and presage of defeat that goaded her enemy now. Hate is like love, she thought. You cannot fully experience either unless you can understand.

From the doorway Fred watched the scene with grim satisfaction. Violence, provided it was not directed against himself or his interests, always satisfied him. And this particular outburst had been singularly opportune. She'll think twice now, he told himself, eyeing the white-faced Kay, before letting Bull get to work on that brat of hers.

Slowly McFee and Traynor sorted

themselves out. The latter was winded but not hurt; ignoring the brutal face so close to his own as he stood up, he went over to the frightened Rose and tried to comfort her. But McFee was in worse shape. Traynor was a big man and a heavy one, and his falling body had caught the Scot with his back against the chair-edge, jarring his spine. When he gingerly put his foot to the floor he winced in agony.

But it took more than a beating to curb McFee's indomitable spirit. Heaving himself back into the chair, he glared up at Bull.

'Ye hulking great animal!' he gasped. 'I'll get even with ye for this. Ye havena finished with me yet.'

Bull ignored him. He went over to the desk and rummaged in it, eventually producing notepaper and envelope. He came back with these and thrust them at McFee.

'Write a note to your wife,' he ordered. 'Tell her you're spending the night here. Joe can take it.'

Joe started at the sound of his name. Janet still held his arm, and she glanced up at him quickly. He looked dazed and haggard, and she wondered what agony of indecision racked him. Sooner or later he would have to declare himself. On which side would he stand then?

'Write it yourself,' growled McFee, bending down to examine his injured ankle.

Bull caught hold of his close-cropped hair and jerked his head up. 'Write it, damn you!' he bellowed. He released McFee's hair and caught him a stinging blow on the cheek.

'Do as he says, Angus,' Traynor said quietly. And added, hoping that the blow had not dazed his friend's wits, 'It can do no harm. It might even help.'

The Scotsman's head sang; he shook it violently to clear it. But Traynor's meaning was plain. Without further argument he adjusted his spectacles and snatched the paper from Bull's hand.

They were silent while he wrote. He took his time over it, pausing frequently for reflection. When Bull told him impatiently to get a move on he replied curtly that it was a difficult letter to write.

If it was to be of use it had to be convincing.

Bull read it when he had finished, the puzzled frown on his face growing gradually deeper.

DEAR SPRITE,

I have been persuaded to stay the night on the island. Prospero has some project in hand (as per the book) which, as he puts it, 'gathers to a head.' He insists that I promised my help — and I believe I did say so when first he raised the matter. Anyway, I'm staying.

The King and his followers are just as you left them, and send their love. So do I — and hope you will understand.

Yours ever,

ANGUS

'What's all this bloody nonsense?' Bull demanded angrily. 'Why can't you write plain English?'

'For the same reason as you canna speak it,' McFee retorted equably. 'It isna my habit. Did you never read Shakespeare?'

'No.'

'Ah! Then you wouldna understand,' McFee said, as though that put an end to the matter.

Bull threw the paper at him. It zigzagged to the floor. 'Then write it so as I can, damn you!'

The other shrugged. 'That's how my wife would expect me to write it. If ye want it in your own words ye'd best dictate it.'

Bull hesitated, caught between two doubts. Was McFee speaking the truth, or was there some code here that was gibberish to him but might make sense to the woman? He bent and picked up the note. 'What's this about a king?' he demanded.

'My wife always refers to Mr Traynor and his family in that fashion. I call him Prospero — as ye may have heard. Prospero, ye see, was a character from Shakespeare who ruled over a small island.' He stared thoughtfully up at his enemy. 'It wouldna be a bad idea if ye were to read the play,' he suggested. 'Your education has been sore neglected. I've no doubt Mr Traynor here would lend ye a copy.'

'I got no time for reading.'

For a few minutes Bull continued to study the note. Apart from the odd wording it seemed innocent enough: there was no appeal for help, it gave no hint of foul play. And McFee had certainly addressed Traynor as Prospero; there at least he was speaking the truth.

He made up his mind and turned to Joe. 'Find out where he lives and see his missus gets this. And don't answer no questions if she asks them. Just hand her the note and git.' His eyes narrowed as he saw the girl. 'And keep away from that damned skirt. Skirts mean trouble. We got enough of that.'

Janet flushed, loosing Joe's arm. She dared not look at him, but as he put out his hand to take the note she saw that it trembled.

She had no opportunity to speak to him alone before he left, but she was waiting for him on the jetty when he returned. The wind was blowing hard now, whipping the tops off the waves into a damp mist that swirled low over the water before being swept away. She watched the *Stella* anxiously as it came up the loch into the teeth of the wind. Joe handled the boat well, keeping her head-on, not letting her fall away as she skidded down into the troughs; but the *Stella* was a small boat, with a tendency to wallow, and not easy to handle in rough water. Each time she was lost from view in a cloud of spray or behind a large wave Janet waited anxiously for her reappearance.

Joe was drenched. Water trickled down his face, and he looked cold as well as wet. But he seemed cheerfully unperturbed, and grinned at her as he climbed on to the jetty.

'Quite a tub, isn't she?' He shook himself like a terrier, and looked ruefully down at his legs. 'Now I've soaked your dad's trousers as well as mine.'

Janet said, 'I thought you might not come back.'

The grin faded, and he nodded.

‘I thought about it,’ he said, pressing his hair back firmly, until the water dropped from it on to his collar and he had to hunch his shoulders to prevent it from running down his neck. ‘When I was in the car I thought how easy it would be. No one would stop me, you see; they wouldn’t know I’d stolen the car. When I didn’t come back you’d all guess what had happened, but you couldn’t do anything about it. Bull wouldn’t let your dad go to the police.’

‘What stopped you, then?’

‘There was two things, really,’ he said slowly. He moved closer to her. ‘One of them was you.’

‘Me? How me?’ she asked innocently.

‘Because — well, because I hadn’t said good-bye to you, that’s why.’ But she knew that that was not what he had started to say, and smiled to herself. ‘And I reckoned Bull might cut up rough when he found I’d skipped it. I didn’t want to cause you more trouble.’

A sudden gust of wind caught them. Janet had her back to it, and stumbled forward, clutching at Joe. His hand was cold to her touch. 'You must go in and change,' she said, feeling his wet jacket. 'I ought not to have kept you here talking.' As they started to walk along the jetty she asked, 'What was the other reason that brought you back?'

'The money. I want my share of that.' He frowned. 'I told you, I didn't want no part in the job at first. It was Fred talked me into it, blast him!' He kicked angrily at a pebble which had somehow found its way on to the jetty. 'I must have been crazy to listen to him. But I'm not crazy now, and at least I'll make sure that I get something out of it. There's over three thousand quid in that satchel, wherever Bull's hidden it, and a thousand of that's mine. I'm not leaving it behind for him and Fred, damn them! When I go it goes with me.'

She could not accept his attitude, but neither would she at present outwardly condemn it. The money, she guessed, was to be the rock on which most of her hopes might founder; yet to tackle it now might be to put a gulf between herself and Joe which she might not have time later to bridge. She must choose a more propitious moment.

Yet she could not entirely ignore what he had said. She told him sadly, 'You'd do better without it, Joe.'

'Would I? You can't get far if you're broke. With a thousand quid and a lot of luck I might get out of the country.' Sensing her disapproval, he added more gently, 'If I stay in this country I'll never be rid of them two. They'll always be catching up with me. Them or the cops.'

Janet was tempted to try him. 'Would you go now — to-night — if you had the money?' she asked. And waited anxiously for his reply.

It was some time in coming. They were almost at the bungalow when he said slowly, 'I don't know. I guess not. Not until — well, there's something I got to settle first.'

She did not need to ask him what that something was. His answer encouraged her to press her luck, and she said quietly, 'I think I know where Bull has hidden the money. It's in the fuel-store.'

That stopped him. He caught her arm,

swinging her round to face him. 'How do you know that?' he demanded. 'Have you seen it?'

'No. But while you were out in the *Stella* I found we needed some more paraffin, and I asked Daddy for the key. He said Bull had it. And when I asked Bull he wouldn't give it to me; he said he'd fetch the paraffin himself. He did, too.' She smiled faintly. 'Bull wouldn't put himself to that trouble, would he, unless he had something to hide? He's never been helpful before.'

At first her news excited him. An hour before he had been contemplating escape, believing that only a lack of funds lay between him and freedom; and the impact of that thought was still with him. But as he looked into her troubled eyes, so plainly asking a question she could not bring herself to voice, the excitement died in him. The desire for freedom was still strong in his mind, but it was no longer paramount. It could not be separated from other desires.

He asked mechanically, 'Could one break into the store?'

‘No. Daddy had an extra-strong lock fitted; people used to land after dark and steal our petrol. I expect that’s why Bull chose it as a hiding-place.’

He accepted her judgment without question, glad to be rid of the need to make a decision. ‘That’s that, then,’ he said, and turned to mount the bungalow steps.

‘No, it isn’t,’ Janet said. ‘What Bull doesn’t know — and I think Daddy must have forgotten — is that there’s a duplicate key to the lock. And I’ve got it.’

⋆ ⋆ ⋆

To Bull’s mind Donald Grant was only dangerous when exposed to his wife’s influence; by himself he was no more so than Janet or her mother. He hadn’t the wits or the guts, thought Bull, to act on his own. It was for that reason — and also to annoy Kay — that he was being banished to the shed to sleep. But he was not to have it to himself. Since there was nowhere else to put him, McFee also was to sleep there — an arrangement which the Scot regarded with greater equanimity than did its proposer. Bull trusted McFee no more than he trusted Kay or her uncle.

It was Janet who, at Kay's insistence, obtained Bull's permission to move into her cousins' room in place of Donald. Kay would not ask him herself. And Bull, much to their surprise, raised no objection. He saw in Janet a possible brake on Kay's genius for causing trouble. Fred would be certain to take advantage of the fact that she was alone; and he had not banished Donald for Fred to supplant him. Bull did not rate Kay's morals highly; she might not fancy Fred, but he had no doubt that she would accept him if by so doing she could encompass his, Bull's, downfall. And Kay and Fred were a more dangerous combination than Kay and her husband.

It was while they were remaking Janet's bed that Kay told her of what had happened that afternoon down at the jetty. Janet was appalled. 'You mean you're going to do what he wants? You're going to meet him and . . . and — '

'No,' Kay said sharply. 'I'm going to meet him, but there'll be no 'and' to follow.' She shivered. 'At least, I hope not.'

Janet shivered also. She had less cause than Kay to mistrust Fred, but mistrust him she did. Fred was evil. That Kay should consent, even under pressure, to meet him alone at night — that, knowing what he wanted of her, she should actually intend to keep the appointment — shocked her utterly.

'Don't do it, Kay,' she implored. 'It's — it's horrible even to think of it.'

'Don't think of it, then,' Kay snapped. She did not want criticism or advice, she wanted help. 'And don't look at me like that, damn you! Do you think I'm looking forward to it?' She gave a nervous tug at the blanket between them, and it slipped out of Janet's fingers to fall in a rumpled line across the bed. 'I loathe the creature — you know that. The thought of even letting him touch me makes me squirm. But I'm not taking any risks with Bobby. You haven't seen Bull in a drunken rage, but I have. This afternoon's effort was a picnic in comparison.'

She did not add that it was not only concern for her son's safety that prompted her to keep the appointment. Fred represented a challenge — and she had never yet failed to meet a challenge. Fred was a means to an end. If she could enlist his aid against Bull without making too many concessions to his lechery . . .

'There must be another way,' Janet said. She picked up the blanket and began to straighten it. 'We could tell Donald. Or Daddy. One of them would think of something.'

'You're not to tell anyone,' Kay said fiercely. In a calmer voice she went on, 'I know what I'm doing, Janet. I wasn't born yesterday. Fred isn't the first amorous male to make a pass at me.'

Janet did not doubt that. She was under no illusions about her cousin's wife. 'But Fred's different,' she pleaded. 'Sometimes I think he's even worse than Bull. That look of his — it's — it's horrible. You can't ever have met a man like him before, Kay, no matter how much experience you've had. Fred just isn't civilized.'

'All men are alike where their appetites are concerned,' Kay told her. 'Fred's less subtle in his approach than most, that's all. I can handle him. But I'll need your help.'

'Mine? How can *I* help?'

Kay gave the coverlet a final straightening tug. 'You get on pretty well with Joe, don't you?' she said.

Janet flushed crimson. Guiltily she read an accusation into the other's words, as though there were a similarity between her own friendship with Joe and the disgusting and unholy lust that Fred felt for Kay. 'It isn't like that at all,' she defended herself hotly. 'I'm just sorry for him. He's not wicked like Bull and Fred, he only took part in the robbery because they tricked him into it. He told me all about it this morning. And you should be the last one to accuse him,' she added reproachfully, unmindful that Kay had done no such thing, 'after what he tried to do for Bobby.'

'I haven't accused him, and there's no need for you to defend him,' Kay said briskly. 'I'm sure he's a very estimable young man at heart.' Was that sarcasm? wondered Janet. 'All that interests me now is how much influence you have over him. Could you persuade him to go for a stroll with you to-night at about the time I'm due to meet Fred?'

The fading blush returned to Janet's cheeks. 'You mean you — you want me to invite him?'

'Yes.'

'But, Kay, I couldn't. He'd think I was — well, you know.'

'If he's the nice young man we're agreed he is, then he won't think anything of the sort. And if he isn't — well, you will have been warned in time, won't you? So you've nothing to lose. But I must have some one handy in case I need help. I *think* I can manage Fred, but these weedy specimens sometimes develop unexpected strength in their lustful clutches. I know — I've had some. And they don't come any more lustful than Fred.' To the inexperienced Janet it sounded almost like boasting, and she looked at the other in disgust. How could she talk like that? Was she actually proud of the desire she had awakened in Fred's dirty little mind? 'If he proves too strong for me physically, that's where you and Joe step in and prise us apart.'

Kay had not been boasting. She had spoken lightly because it was not pleasant to dwell too deeply on what lay ahead of her. Fred and his desire must be treated as a joke. If she allowed herself to visualize too clearly what that desire might lead to she might panic, she might not be able to nerve herself to meet him. And meet him she must. So much might depend on that.

Janet was bewildered, and said so. She had little doubt that Joe would accompany her if she asked him; but if Kay had no intention of yielding to Fred why meet him at all? Whatever the outcome, it would be a degrading and disgusting experience — and to no purpose. Fred, expecting so much, would be furious at finding he was to get nothing. He wouldn't stand for that; there were no niceties about Fred. If he couldn't get what he wanted by force — or if Joe and she were to interfere — he'd be so mad at

Kay he'd be certain to carry out his threat of telling Bull about the note.

Kay shook her head. 'He'll be mad, all right. But he won't go to Bull. He daren't.'

'Why not?'

'For several reasons. He won't have the note, for a start. I'll get that from him when we meet. I'll have made my gesture by turning up; he must make his by handing over the note.'

'Suppose he refuses?'

'Then I won't go a step farther. But he won't refuse. Not if I make that plain. Fred knows what he wants, and he wants it bad. He won't throw it away when he thinks he's almost home.'

Janet's virginal mind, steeped in her father's puritanism, revolted at the, to her, coarse and boastful words. But at least they were expressive. She said, 'Bull would believe him without the note.'

'Oh, yes, he'd believe him. And he'd take it out on me and Bobby. But what would he do to Fred when he learns that Fred had had the note for over six hours without showing it to him? Particularly if

I tell him *why* Fred kept his mouth shut. You saw how he reacted when he caught you and Joe holding hands. He — '

'We weren't holding hands,' Janet said hotly.

'All right. But the inference is the same, whatever you were doing. Bull's dead against skirts, as he so politely refers to us.' Why is it, wondered Janet, that she can never speak of Bull without that note of venom creeping into her voice? Why does she hate him so much more than Fred? 'I'll remind Fred of that, just in case he has forgotten. Besides, he knows how I loathe him; he expects me to put up a struggle. I think the little horror would actually be disappointed if I didn't. If he doesn't get what he wants he'll be mad all right, but he won't go squealing to Bull. He'd know he'd never have another chance with me if he did that.' She pushed the bed straight with her knees and walked across to the dressing-table. 'Not that he'll ever get another chance, of course. Angus reckons the fun is likely to start about this time to-morrow.'

'Fun? What fun?'

'Well, maybe it won't be fun,' Kay conceded, selecting a lipstick. 'It might even be rather grim, I suppose. But I can put up with a little grimness if I can see that hulking brute in the hands of the police.'

'Police!' Janet's hand flew to her throat. 'Why should the police come?'

'Because of that note Angus wrote to his wife.' Kay pursed her lips, applying the lipstick skilfully. 'Apparently it was full of quotations and misquotations from the last scene in *The Tempest*, alluding to people in captivity. Angus says his wife is sure to recognize the allusion, but he doesn't think she'll take it seriously at first. Not until he fails to return to-morrow. Then, he says, she'll go to the police.'

⋆ ⋆ ⋆

Joe was surprised by Janet's request, but very willing to accede to it. He did not ask why she should want to go walking in the middle of the night (it was enough that she did, and in his company) and Janet did not tell him. Kay had been insistent that she should not. 'I'm not so proud of this assignation that I want it broadcast,' Kay had said. 'If I can handle Fred on my own Joe won't need to know about it. But keep within earshot of the wood this side of the kitchen-garden. That's where we'll be.'

She had refrained from adding that she did not share Janet's trust in Joe. Joe had shown himself more human than the other two, but that was all. Until he proved himself an ally she preferred to consider him an enemy.

They went down to the jetty, and walked along the pebbly beach to the edge of the wood. Joe held her arm; the wind had temporarily abated, but heavy clouds obscured the young moon, and often they stumbled. When she asked rather nervously about Bull Joe said he had gone to bed; not drunk, but not entirely sober. He didn't know where Fred was, he said.

Trees loomed up to their left. To Janet, who knew that somewhere in the midst of them were Kay and Fred, they had become a symbol of evil. She wondered how Donald would react if he knew what his wife was doing.

'Let's sit down,' she said. They must not go too far.

'I thought it was a walk you wanted,' Joe said, surprised.

'I wanted fresh air. I said a walk because I thought it would be too windy to sit. But it isn't, is it? And it's not easy walking on such a dark night.' She wondered whether they would be able to find their way through the trees if Kay called. Would they be too late? 'I wish the moon would come out.'

They sat close together in silence. Joe was content to be with her, to know that she wanted him there. It was a new experience for him, and he was a little nervous, not knowing what was expected of him. He would have liked to put an arm about her, to draw her still closer. But would that displease her? Rather than spoil the harmony that existed between them he decided to do nothing. Something — a word or a movement from her, perhaps — would tell him when she wanted him to do more.

Janet was not aware of his indecision. She was frightened — not only for Kay, but for Joe. And for herself. Ever since Kay had told her of Angus McFee's message to his wife she had been worried about what she ought to do. She was torn between two loyalties: the old loyalty to her parents, the new loyalty to Joe. How could she serve the two?

What would Joe do if she were to tell him what Kay had told her? Would he warn the others, help them either to escape together before the police came or to prepare against a possible landing? They were armed. In addition to Bull's and Fred's pistols they had her father's shotgun and rifle; they could wound and kill before they were taken prisoner. Or would he, if she asked him, keep the information to himself? What use would he make of it? What use *could* he make of it? Unless Bull sent him on some errand in the *Stella* he could not escape. Bull had the sparking-plugs of both the *Stella* and the dinghy in his keeping.

What did she *want* him to do?

And if she did not tell him? What then? The police would come (in the night, perhaps), the men would be taken unawares. But there would still be shooting; some one might still get hurt or killed. And Joe need not know that she had betrayed him.

But *she* would know. And she would have to live with that knowledge. Was it selfishness, then, that prompted her to tell him?

'Joe,' she said. He turned to her instantly. 'What would you do if you knew the police were coming — to-morrow, say, or the day after?'

He was disappointed. He had hoped that she was about to make a more intimate remark, that she had wanted to talk about themselves. But he tried not to show his disappointment.

'Do you mean me? Or the three of us?'

'Just you. If you knew, and Fred and Bull didn't.'

He was silent for a while. Then he said, 'I suppose I'd try to get away in the dinghy. Bull doesn't know it, but there was a spare plug in the forward locker. I'm hanging on to that.'

'Oh!' Why had he not told her that before? Well, at least he had told her now. 'Where would you go?'

Did she want him to go? To be a fugitive, without food or money or friends, to be hunted down and finally cornered? Would it not be better to give himself up to the police when they came, and accept without protest whatever punishment the law decreed?

And yet — could she bear to see them take him away?

'I don't know,' he said.

There was a long silence. Guiltily Janet remembered Kay; in her concern for Joe she had temporarily forgotten her reason for being there with him. Surely if Kay were to need help she would need it soon? How long had she been in the wood with Fred? Kay had left the bungalow before them, she had . . .

'Janet.' The sound of her name (was it only the second time he had used it?), the sudden touch of his hand on her arm, made her jump. She turned to look at him. 'You said you had a second key to the fuel-store. If the money's there . . . if I was to take some of it . . . only some of it, only what's mine . . . would you — '

He hesitated. Now that he had reached the crux of his question he did not dare to speak it. And while he hesitated Janet said quietly, 'None of it's yours, Joe. It belongs to the people you stole it from. So — '

His eyes were accustomed to the darkness now, and he could see her more clearly. She was staring over his shoulder, her mouth still pursed to the sound of that last vowel, her hands tightly clasped. Turning to follow her gaze, he saw that a light had gone on in the bungalow. A moment later the front door was flung open, and the unmistakable figure of Bull was silhouetted against the light.

Something of Janet's fear was transmitted to Joe, and he put an arm round her, drawing her close. She did not draw away.

'It's all right,' he whispered. 'He's not looking for us. Bull hasn't no use for lavatories. He prefers the open.'

It was then that Kay screamed.

Although Janet had been expecting it,

waiting for it, she had been so startled by Bull's appearance that for a moment the scream had no particular significance for her. It was just a scream. Then she remembered, and scrambled to her feet.

'It's Kay.' She spoke breathlessly, panic gone in the need for action. Both hands on the bank, she tried to pull herself up. 'She's in trouble. Help me up, Joe, please. Quickly.'

Two strong hands caught her by the waist and lifted her bodily on to the lawn. At another time Janet would have found it an exhilarating experience. Now she could think only of Kay. Without further explanation she began to run.

They were only a few yards from the trees. As they reached them Joe caught her arm, so that she was jerked backward against him. His action was so unexpected, so untypical, that for a shocked instant she wondered if she had been mistaken in him, if he were another Fred.

'Let me go!' She struggled unavailingly. 'You — you — '

'Ssssh!' He held her tightly. 'Look!'

Janet looked. Moving across the lawn like a black and menacing shadow, only just discernible against the dark background of the tree-studded hill, went the ungainly figure of Bull. For such a big man he moved fast. Although he had had several times their distance to cover he was almost level with them now.

As he disappeared into the trees above them Joe released her arm.

'She's in real trouble now,' he said grimly. 'Come on.'

Kay had screamed only once; they had only the echo of that scream to guide them. It had seemed to come from the top of the wood, and they stumbled towards it as quickly as the trees and the all-embracing darkness would permit. Joe went first, with Janet's hand in his.

'He'll find them,' he panted. 'He's got cat's eyes. That's why he's so good at his job.'

She did not have to ask what that job was. Nor was it until much later that she recalled — and wondered at — his use of the word 'them.' She did not know that he had seen both Kay and Fred leave the bungalow, and had drawn his own conclusions.

They reached the track that led to the kitchen-garden and paused, listening. Janet could hear only the thumping of her heart, but Joe's ears were sharper. 'This way,' he said, and started to run down the track.

They did not have to go far. Almost at once, it seemed to the startled Janet, a light showed suddenly to their left. She cannoned into Joe and clung to him.

'Bull.' His mouth was close to her ear. 'He's got a torch. I wonder why he didn't use it before? Wanted to catch them red-handed, perhaps.'

Cautiously he began to tiptoe towards the light, Janet's hand clasped tightly in his. The numbing, physical fear that Bull always inspired in her had seized her once more, and had she been alone she could not have gone forward; she would have run blindly, desperately, back to the bungalow, heedless of the buffeting of the trees. But Joe was between her and her fear, and she drew courage from him.

They stopped a few yards from the

light. Bull stood with his back to them, the torch directed at the couple on the ground. Fred lay sprawled on his back, glowering through narrowed eyes at the figure towering over him; the knot of his gaudy tie had slipped down, his lank hair hung wispily over face and ears, there was an angry weal on one cheek where pointed finger-nails had clawed their way down it. A few feet away Kay half sat, half crouched. She looked dazed. Her blonde hair was tousled; the lipstick on her mouth was smeared, so that her lips had lost their outline and looked bloated and swollen. Above the waist her tight woollen jumper had rucked up, exposing a thin band of flesh that gleamed whitely in the torchlight. One of her shoes was missing, and there were scratches on her bare legs.

'You bloody fool!' Bull kicked out savagely at the recumbent Fred, his foot thudding into the man's side. Janet winced at the sound and clung tighter to Joe. She saw Kay's hand go to her cheek, and for the first time noticed the red flush that scarred it. Had Bull done that? 'Didn't I tell you to lay off that damned bitch? Can't you see what her game is? Like hell you can! One wiggle of her fat little tail and off you go, randy as a bloody tyke!'

He spat in disgust. They were all so still that even at that distance Janet heard the faint *plop* as the spittle hit the ground.

Kay stood up slowly, pulling at her jumper, mechanically straightening her twisted skirt. The movement drew Bull's attention. He turned and took a pace towards her, the pool of light moving with him so that now she was in the centre of it. Kay blinked, and put up a hand to shield her eyes.

Janet thought he was going to hit her. So did Joe; she felt him stiffen and strain forward, and she clung to him frantically, holding him back. She was so saturated with fear that not even to save Kay could she let him leave her.

But Bull did not hit Kay. He hunched his shoulders, so that to the pair behind him his fat neck appeared to bulge sideways, and spat again. The spittle fell at Kay's feet, and she looked down at it in dazed fascination.

'Get back in there, you.' Kay's head shot up as he barked the words at her. He jerked a thumb in the direction of the bungalow. 'I didn't lock your old man up so's you could take a tumble with Fred, damn you! You lay off that little rat, see? Let me catch you with him again, and I'll tan your dirty little tail so hard it won't ever wiggle at a man no more.' Another step forward. 'Go on — git!'

For the first time Kay seemed fully aware of him. Both cheeks were flushed now, and there was an angry gleam in her eyes; the scorn in his voice had roused her quicker than any blow. Dirty and dishevelled as she was, balanced on one foot, her head still buzzing from the blow he had given her, her pride and anger and hatred enabled her to match his scorn.

'Why, you — you — ' Fists clenching and unclenching, she swallowed frantically, seeking for words bitter and venomous enough to hurt him. So fierce was her rage that she had no fear of what he might do. 'You filthy, misbegotten ape, you! How dare you — '

Bull sprang — not at her, but at the still

prostrate Fred. Janet saw the gleam of metal in Fred's hand as Bull's boot crashed into it, sending the gun flying. Above Fred's shrill scream of agony she heard the crack as the gun went off, heard the bullet thud into a near-by tree. Then the trees and the figures swayed and merged mistily before her frightened eyes, and she fainted.

When she recovered consciousness it was to find herself alone with Joe. She was lying on the ground, her head pillowed in the crook of his arm. The darkness was all about them, but his face was bent close to hers, and she could see the anxiety in his eyes.

For a little while she was content to lie there looking at him. She even managed a faint smile. Then memory returned and she sat up, her eyes searching the darkness.

'Where are they? What happened?'

'They've gone.' He touched her forehead with his fingers. 'Feeling better?'

'All of them?'

'Yes.' His arm tightened, and she felt herself lifted gently. 'You didn't half give me a fright when you flopped out like that. I thought you'd stopped that damned bullet.'

'I'm all right.' She was on her feet now, leaning against him. 'Was anyone hurt?'

'No more than what you saw. They left under their own steam, but Fred only just made it. I reckon his wrist's broke. Ribs too, I shouldn't wonder. Bull's boot ain't no powder-puff.'

Janet sighed. A feeling of contentment and lassitude stole over her. After the noise and the terror and the reflected agony and shame of the scene she had just witnessed it was wonderful to stand there in the warm darkness with Joe's arms about her.

Impulsively she lifted her face. 'Dear Joe,' she murmured softly.

There was no passion in their kiss. His lips touched hers gently, and stayed there while her arms crept round his neck and her hand cupped the back of his head.

She felt his lips move, and leaned away from him, her eyes searching his face.

'I love you.' He sounded surprised that he had at last managed to utter those new and exciting words.

'I'm glad. I love you too, Joe.'

After a while he said, 'What are we going to do?'

'I don't know. You mustn't worry about that now, darling. Something will happen to make it all right. It must.' Snugly engulfed in her new-found love, she had no thought for the morrow, had forgotten what Kay had told her. 'Do you know that you are the first man ever to kiss me like that? The first man ever to kiss me at all, apart from Daddy. And I think I like it. Could we try again?'

'Suits me,' Joe said. He laughed. 'But it makes you dizzy, don't it?'

* * *

When Janet got back to her room Kay was lying face-down on the bed. She looked up at Janet's entrance, glared at her, and flopped down again. Janet saw that she had been crying. Wrapped in her new happiness, she forgot the shame and disgust she had felt for Kay, and was filled with pity.

'Kay, dear, I'm so dreadfully sorry.' She sat down on the bed and placed a hand gently on the other's shoulder. 'Was it — did you — '

Kay's head lifted slightly. 'No, it wasn't. And I didn't,' she snapped. She looked up. 'And a fat lot of help you turned out to be!'

'I'm sorry. We came as soon as you called. But Bull — '

'Bull!' Her tear-streaked face twisted into a mask of hatred. 'I'll kill him! By God, I'll kill him, the beast! He — '

She stopped, staring wide-eyed at the door. Janet turned. Donald stood there, with Bull behind him. Save for two red patches high on his cheeks, Donald's face was chalk-white. His lips were set in a thin line.

'Surprised to see me?' He walked a few paces into the room. 'Bull has just told me what you get up to when I'm out of the way. Nice of him, wasn't it? He thought I might have a few words to say to you.'

'Words!' Bull spat in disgust. ''Tain't words you want, mister, it's action. If she were my woman — which thank the Lord she ain't — I'd wallop the damned hide off her, the dirty little slut.'

Donald turned and slapped him across the face.

'Get out!' His voice throbbed with suppressed fury. 'Get out and stay out. I'll deal with this.'

Bull's astonishment was ludicrous. Slowly his hand went up to his cheek. His mouth opened, showing the blackened teeth and the dark cavern within. Then the red lips lengthened into a broad grin.

'Well, I'll be damned!' Almost playfully, he punched Donald in the chest. 'I'll be ruddy well damned!'

8

Wilt thou go with me?
The Tempest, Act II, Scene 2

Neither Donald nor Kay ever revealed what passed between them in their room that night. When they appeared at breakfast the next morning there were dark circles under their eyes, while their faces — and Donald's in particular — looked drawn and haggard. Kay had taken more than usual pains over her toilet that morning, hoping to hide the ravages which the events of the night and lack of sleep had imposed. Her fierce pride rebelled against the possible solicitude of Donald's family; it sought to deny her enemies the satisfaction which any sign from her of shame or defeat might give them. Neither she nor Donald entered into the spasmodic and uneasy conversation. When she had come into the room Bull had been waiting for her, his great bulk filling the doorway; he had placed himself there on purpose, maliciously eager to note her reaction. Kay's lips pressed a little more tightly together when she saw him, and her eyes narrowed. But those were the only signs of recognition she accorded his presence.

'Sleep well?' he inquired, scratching a whiskered cheek. Since she could not look past him, she looked through him, waiting for him to move. A malicious grin stretched his full lips. 'Maybe you'd rather eat your grub standing up, eh?' He scratched the other cheek reflectively, remembering the slap Donald had given him. 'Or ain't your old man as handy on the fanny as he is on the face?'

Kay gritted her teeth, refusing to be baited into a retort. She was through with words now. Her eyes were fixed steadily on a tuft of coarse hair that sprouted untidily above the open V of his khaki shirt. She stood like that until he let her pass.

After that she did not look at him. Fred she ignored completely.

Fred was in a sorry shape that

morning. He carried his right arm in a sling, his ribs ached abominably, the scratch Kay had given him showed a dull red almost the entire length of his cheek. The sling had been improvised by Rose; the wrist was broken, she thought, and she had fashioned a splint and bandaged it as best she could. It ought to be X-rayed and possibly reset, she had told Fred. Bull, who was in the room at the time, had said roughly that Fred would have to lump it as it was; a bit of pain might learn him not to disobey orders. And Fred had glared at him, saying nothing but looking plenty. Bull had taken his gun, and with it had gone most of his courage. Fred felt lost and naked without his gun.

He continued to glare at Bull all through breakfast. Occasionally he cast a thoughtful eye at Kay; Donald he ignored. He knew nothing of the scene in the bedroom the previous night — he knew little of anything except pain after Bull had surprised him with Kay in the wood — and, like Bull, he despised Donald. But always his eyes returned to

Bull. He found difficulty in using his left hand, and ate little. No one offered to help him. Even Rose, who delighted in doling out medicine and medical advice and in tending the sick and injured, left him to manage as best he could.

Rose's main concern was for Kay. Something — either Kay's scream or the shot — had woken her, and she had sent Robert to investigate. When he found the far bedroom empty they had got up and dressed, to be ready for any emergency. They were in the passage when Kay had returned, running past them to her room and slamming the door behind her. They had followed, alarmed by her distraught and dishevelled appearance; but Kay had screamed at them hysterically to go away and, after some hesitation, they had gone. Then Fred had come in, bent with pain and holding his injured wrist, and Rose had done what she could for him. She had felt some sympathy for him at first, when she heard who was responsible for his injuries. In her indignation she had even plucked up courage to berate Bull for his brutality. Bull had told her roughly to mind her own business.

Even when Janet returned she did not get the full facts. Janet gave her only a garbled version of the truth, saying that she had awoken to find Kay's bed empty, and had dressed and gone out to look for her. She had heard Kay scream, and Joe had come out of the bungalow, and together they had gone to investigate. Janet told her mother that she thought Fred had made a pass at Kay, that Bull had knocked him down and kicked him, and that Fred had drawn his gun and tried to shoot Bull. Bull had promptly kicked the gun out of his hand, breaking his wrist.

With that Rose's sympathy for Fred had vanished. But she was a shrewd if a dull woman, and she guessed that there was more to the incident than Janet had cared to tell her. Despite her admiration for Kay, she knew that her nephew's wife was worldly and sophisticated and not unused to masculine attention; Kay would not have been so distraught had Fred merely made a pass at her. Nor was she altogether satisfied that she had been told the truth about her daughter's part in the matter. Janet's detached manner in the telling of it, her obvious preoccupation with her own apparently pleasant thoughts, intrigued Rose. So did the girl's appearance. She looks like a holiday poster, thought Rose, and wondered what her daughter had been up to.

McFee was the most cheerful member of the community. He hobbled into the living-room declaring that he had slept like a top and was as hungry as a Highlander. Janet suspected that, bruised ankle notwithstanding, he was enjoying himself hugely; the adventure fed his love of the dramatic. And, like her father, he was obviously — far more obviously — filled with a secret excitement, an anticipation of the denouement he confidently expected to occur that day. He kept casting sly glances round the table, peering between the heads of those opposite him and through the open doorway to the loch beyond, and occasionally bursting into an irrepressible chuckle. Robert Traynor was less demonstrative. Although he too hoped for rescue, he knew that if it came it would not come peaceably and without danger.

Bobby too was subdued. Bull's outburst the previous afternoon, his quick and savage violence, had frightened him. It was what in his childish imaginings he had vaguely recognized to be in keeping with his hero's character, yet to see it put into practice so forcefully had robbed violence of its glamour, leaving only the pain and the terror. He sat next to Janet, eating little. His eyes kept straying across the table to where Bull was shovelling food down into his enormous stomach in his usual bestial manner. Every time the big man snorted or belched — and he did both frequently — Bobby started apprehensively, as though he feared the noise was a prelude to yet another outburst of brutality.

Janet tried to distract his attention from Bull by talking to him. But she was in no mood for light conversation, and her efforts met with little success; after a while she abandoned them and devoted herself to her own thoughts and problems. These were many and varied; but the happenings of the previous night had established at least one fact securely in her mind. Where before there had been two conflicting loyalties, now one was paramount. Joe must come first. Somehow, and soon, she must tell him what Angus and her father believed, that the police might come that afternoon or evening. She must not let him be taken unawares; he must be given the chance to make his decision, to shape his own destiny.

Joe sat on the other side of her. She was glad to have him there; if he had been opposite her she could never have stopped looking at him, she would have betrayed — to her mother, if to no one else — the secret of her new happiness. And her mother must not know it yet. No one must know it. Not until she and Joe had decided what they should do.

Like Kay, but for a very different reason, Janet had taken considerable pains over her appearance that morning. Normally she would have put on shorts or jeans, and a woollen jersey; she seldom used cosmetics on her face, and her hair was only cursorily combed and brushed. That morning she had brushed her hair until it shone, she had devoted what little artistry she possessed to the making up of her face, she had put on a gay cotton frock. I can't make myself beautiful, she had thought, but at least I can make the best of what I am.

She had awaited her meeting with Joe with trepidation. Instinct, not experience, told her that the night was a time for romance, the morning for doubts and, possibly, regrets. Would Joe regret that morning what he had said to her the previous night? But all her doubts vanished when she saw him. The way his eyes lit up, the look he gave her — of admiration and humble adoration and devotion — told her without any words what she wanted to know. Joe was hers as surely as she was his. All that remained to know now was how to achieve their love.

Again like Kay — and again for a very different reason — Janet had slept little that night. For one thing, she had not wanted to sleep, to sink into unconsciousness when consciousness was Heaven itself. She had lain awake for hours, enjoying in memory over and over again those delicious moments when Joe had kissed her and told her he loved her. She was back in her parents' room, since Donald had been permitted to stay with Kay; but not even her mother's snores (Rose Traynor suffered badly from catarrh) or her father's heavy breathing could distract her.

The doubts and fears came later. What would her parents say when she told them that she loved Joe, that she was going to marry him? They were fond of her, but neither was particularly indulgent or understanding. All they knew of Joe was that he was a criminal, an associate of men like Bull and Fred. He did not speak their language, or understand the things they understood and respected; his school had been hard experience, he had no money (or none that was rightly his) and no job. Above all, he was wanted by the police, he was likely to spend the next few years of his life in prison. Could she blame them if they used every means in their power to prevent the marriage?

Yet her parents did not constitute the only hindrance to that marriage. There was Joe himself. Although he had told her that he loved her, he had not mentioned marriage. She suspected that about that he thought as did her parents — that he was not good enough for her; that their love was a dream, an idyll snatched out of reality; that when the time came he would go away and never come back, never seek to see her again.

Janet's heart missed a beat at the prospect. She had not waited all those years for her man only to lose him almost as soon as she had found him. I don't care what he is or what he's done, she told herself; I love him and I'm going to marry him. I'll fight them all — Joe as well, if I have to — but I'm going to marry him.

For the first time since they had sat down to breakfast she allowed herself to look at Joe. It was only a brief look, and he did not see it; but somehow it satisfied Janet. He was beside her now — big, solid, and (despite the cheap, ill-fitting clothes) handsome — and he would be beside her in the future. They might have to wait, they might even have to fight for their happiness. But they would find it eventually, and together.

After breakfast Rose Traynor went out to feed the chickens and collect the eggs. She put on a mackintosh, for it was a dull, grey morning, with a fine rain driving across the island. Janet always suspected that her mother had taken this rural ritual upon herself to escape the washing-up. Rose loved cooking, but the menial chores that accompanied it had tended more and more to devolve upon Janet. What else was a daughter for?

Bull peered suspiciously out at the rain, decided that it was not for him, and went back to bed to plan, locking the door behind him. Janet was amazed at his complete confidence in himself. The whole island was against him now, yet he seemed to have no fear. Angus McFee said it was because Bull was, probably unconsciously, a fatalist. Like the boatswain in *The Tempest*, his complexion was perfect gallows. 'Stand fast, good Fate, to his hanging!' Angus quoted, with another of his chuckles. 'I canna think of a more fitting end for the brute.'

Kay too retired to her room; not to sleep, but to plot and plan. Nothing mattered now except Bull. Completely obsessed by her hatred of him, she was prepared to do anything, take any risks, to humble and destroy him. She could not wait for the police; she was not even sure that she wanted them to come. For her revenge to be complete she had to be the cause, if not the actual means, of his humiliation and destruction.

Donald did not go with her. He put on his raincoat and went out — to tramp the island, Janet suspected, and wrestle with his jealousy. Angus McFee donned an oilskin, borrowed rod and tackle from his host, and limped down to the jetty to fish, taking Bobby with him. McFee was too knowledgable a fisherman to anticipate much success in such rough water. But he was a man inured to all weathers, to whom to be out of doors was to be happy, and his injured ankle prevented a more energetic pastime. And from the jetty he would be the first to see the rescuers that he was confident would come.

Janet cleared the breakfast table and went into the kitchen to wash up. Joe went with her. Closing the door behind him, he looked at her in a turmoil of indecision. The same doubts and uncertainties which had assailed Janet earlier were his now. Did she still love him? Had last night been merely an episode, born of the darkness and proximity and her release from fear, to be forgotten when another day dawned?

She did not leave him undecided for long. She ran across the room and into his arms. Their kiss signified both a release and a promise; a release from doubt, a promise that doubt would never recur. It set a seal on their love, made it real and permanent.

Janet was the first to draw away. 'We must be careful, darling. Daddy may come in.' She smiled at him, gave him a quick kiss, and firmly detached his arms from her waist. 'That's enough for the present. I want to talk to you.' Recalling what she had to tell him, the smile vanished. 'Remember what I told you last night, Joe? Well, it's true. I wasn't just supposing.'

'What's true? That you love me?'

'That always. But I meant the police.' She gripped the lapels of his jacket. 'Angus is sure they'll come, Joe. This afternoon, perhaps, or this evening. But he's sure they'll come, because of the message you took to his wife.' She had thought about it for so long that now she was as sure as Angus. 'Oh, Joe! What are we going to do?'

In the living-room Traynor was at his desk. He always worked for a couple of hours after breakfast; it had become a habit that even the advent of Bull and his companions could not break. But that morning the thoughts would not come, and after a while he gave it up and sat staring out of the window. It may have been the restless presence of Fred which distracted him. Fred twisted and turned in an armchair, unable to find a position in which he could rest his aching ribs. Like Kay, his mind was centred on Bull, pondering the means of revenge. I'll get that bastard if it's the last thing I do, he promised himself savagely.

'There's not much we can do,' Joe said quietly. He did not ask her to explain about the note.

His calmness surprised her. 'You could get away in the dinghy,' she said. Last night that was what he had said he would do; she was glad he did not suggest it now, that he had left it to her to do so. Yet she was still not sure that she wanted him to adopt the suggestion; she could only make it, and leave it to him to decide. 'But if you're going you must go now, before it's too late. Bull's in his room; there's no one to stop you. Fred's not dangerous any more. He hasn't got a gun.'

'There's McFee. He's down on the jetty.'

Yes, there was Angus. Angus would try to stop him; and there must be no violence, no altercation. If Bull were to hear them . . .

'I'll come with you,' she said slowly. 'I'll ask Angus if you may take me for a trip in the dinghy. He won't mind that. We can go round the island, and you can put me ashore by the old jetty. Would that be all right?'

'No.' He drew her to him. 'Not unless — '

'Unless what?'

'Unless I don't put you ashore. Unless you come with me. All the way.' Janet was so startled by the suggestion that she could think of nothing to say except 'Oh!' Not giving her a chance to protest, he went on quickly, 'I tried to ask you last night when we were on the beach, but I couldn't quite make it.' Unconsciously his arms tightened about her. 'If the money's in the fuel-store, like you think . . . ' He felt her strain against him, and released her. 'What's the matter?'

'It's me or the money, Joe. You can't have both.'

'Does that mean you'll come with me if I leave the money?' he said eagerly. 'Honest?'

She shook her head. 'It's not as positive as that, darling. If you take the money I certainly won't come. That's definite. But otherwise — oh, I don't know. We wouldn't just be going off on a picnic.

There are so many things to consider.'

His face fell. 'No, it wouldn't be a picnic,' he agreed. 'I just thought that if you loved me enough . . . '

'Of course I love you enough. I'd go with you anywhere . . . anyhow . . . any time.' She put up a hand to stroke his cheek, and he caught the hand and kissed it. 'But where would we go? We've no money. I'd be just a drag on you, Joe. Without me you might get away; if I came with you you wouldn't have a chance. You must see that, darling.'

He nodded, recognizing the truth of what she had said. He knew, too, that he had been selfish in his plea; being hunted by the police was no game for a girl. And without money in their pockets they would have to live rough, go hungry, do most of their journeying on foot. He could not ask that of her.

'I'm sorry,' he said. 'I wasn't thinking straight. I just didn't want to leave you, you see. I got to thinking that maybe I'd never see you again. I couldn't bear that.'

'I couldn't bear it either,' she assured him, giving him a hug. 'But it won't happen, Joe, will it? We won't let it happen.'

'We'll try not to,' he said, his optimism unequal to hers. She would be free to go where she pleased, to decide her own actions. But not him. When he left the island his every thought and movement must be directed towards keeping one jump ahead of the police. Everything else must be subservient to that — there would be no real freedom for him. And if they caught him what would he get? Two — three — five years? Maybe more — he didn't know. He didn't even know if that watchman had died. Bull wouldn't have the radio on.

'And you'll take the dinghy?' She was still uncertain of what she wanted him to do, of what would be best for him. It was not easy to think clearly, to assess the pros and cons, when one was in love. Joe wasn't just any man, he was her man. 'Alone? And without the money?'

'I suppose so,' he said slowly. He hesitated. 'You know, I've been thinking about what they said on the radio. That woman they mentioned — she didn't see me, she only *thought* there was another man in the car. The cops have got Bull's description, and Fred's; but they haven't got mine. They're not really looking for me — not for that job. If they don't find me here when they come — if there's just Bull and Fred — maybe that'll satisfy them, eh? They'll think the woman was wrong — that there was only them two in it.'

'But wouldn't Bull or Fred give you away?'

'Why? It won't make it any easier for them if I'm nicked as well, will it? I'm not taking the money, I'm not doing the dirty on them; they've got no reason to be sore at me. Come to that, it was them did the dirty on me, wasn't it?'

She did not argue further; there would be no point to it. She knew that his old fear of the police was once more crowding him, that because of it he was trying to invent a justification for leaving her. His argument did not convince her (even if Bull and Fred kept silent her family were unlikely to do so), and she doubted if it convinced him either; but so long as she did not seek to destroy it it would serve, it would save his face. And that was all that mattered.

'I hope you're right, darling.' She smiled at him, though she felt nearer to tears. He was going — not soon, not to-morrow or the next day, but now. And after he had gone when would she see him again? 'I'll put on a woolly — it has stopped raining, thank goodness, but it will be chilly out on the loch in this wind — and then we'll go down to the jetty and see if we can fool Angus. The sooner you're off the better. We mustn't waste time.'

'We haven't washed up,' he said.

'Oh, that! That can wait.' She gave him a last desperate kiss, clinging to him for a brief moment before pushing him away. 'See you outside, darling.'

Fred and her father were still in the living-room. Fred had given up trying to be comfortable in a chair and was standing by the door, looking out at the tumbled loch with a jaundiced eye. I hope he doesn't stay there long, thought Janet. If he sees us leaving in the dinghy he may warn Bull.

But Fred was still there when she came out of her room, and she wondered anxiously what they should do. They might fool Angus, but could they fool Fred?

Her mother was talking to Joe on the path. 'Two of the girls are sick, I think,' Rose said, as Janet joined them. Rose always referred to the hens as the 'girls.' 'I was asking Joe if he knew about them, but he says he doesn't. I'll have to get your father. Where is he, dear?'

'In the living-room. With Fred.'

'Good. I think we'll have one of them for supper.'

Janet did not smile at this seemingly cannibalistic intention. 'We'll have to wait, Joe,' she said, as Rose disappeared indoors. She told him about Fred. 'Why on earth does he have to choose this morning to admire the view?' A new and alarming thought occurred to her. 'Or — perhaps it isn't the view! Perhaps it's *us* he's watching. Oh, Joe! Could he have heard us?'

'Shouldn't think so.'

To fill in time they walked slowly across

the lawn to the wood. Joe was nervy and on edge, and Janet suspected he was worried at the enforced wait. She was worried too — not because she was convinced that it was best for him to go, but because she knew that that was what he wanted. And if he wanted it she wanted it too.

Fred was still there when they turned to come back; they could see him through the open doorway. We may have to take a chance on him, Janet thought; after all, he hasn't a gun, he isn't dangerous in himself. And we dare not wait much longer. Bull won't stay in his room all morning, and once he's about again we may not have another chance.

And the weather was getting worse.

'Maybe you were right,' Joe said curtly. 'Maybe it's us he's watching.'

He's angry now, she thought unhappily. And they had so little time; it should not be wasted in anger. She said, 'Darling, what's the matter? You're not upset at leaving the money behind, are you?'

'No.'

'Then what is it?'

'Nothing.' He kicked petulantly at a stray pebble. 'At least — well, I just don't like running away, that's all. It don't seem right, somehow. Sort of cowardly.'

It isn't right, she wanted to say. But she knew his thoughts were running on different lines to hers, that it was a physical, not a moral, cowardice he had referred to. 'You mean you don't like leaving Bull and Fred to face the music alone?' she suggested, purposely misinterpreting him.

'Oh, them! I told you, I don't owe them nothing.'

'Hey, Joe!'

There was no mistaking that bellow. They turned together. Bull stood on the steps, his arms folded across his chest. 'Didn't I tell you to lay off that skirt?' he shouted. 'You seen Fred this morning? He tried to make the blonde last night; don't look so good now, does he? You watch your step, mate, or you won't look so good either.' He paused for breath. 'Come on up here. I got a job for you.'

He did not wait to see if his command would be obeyed, but turned and went back into the bungalow. Janet looked at Joe. His fists were clenched, his body tense. The expression on his face frightened her.

'Don't do it, Joe!' she implored him, guessing what was in his mind. 'Don't do it. You'll ruin everything.'

'I'll ruin him.' He spat the words out.

'Joe, please!' Heedless of who might be watching, she put a hand on his arm, keeping it there until she felt him slowly relax. 'You won't have to put up with him for much longer.'

'All right.' He took a deep breath, filling his lungs with the damp air. For the first time since he had left the kitchen he smiled at her. 'You win. He'd probably have busted me, anyways.'

'Thank you, darling.' She squeezed his arm. 'Now go in and see what he wants; you can't leave the island with him around. And for goodness' sake don't pick a quarrel with him.' She looked anxiously across at the mainland, her eyes searching the far shore. 'Angus said the police wouldn't come until afternoon or evening. I hope he's right.'

It wasn't for a job that Joe was wanted, but as an instructor. 'Show me how to work that damned boat,' Bull said. He made no further reference to Janet. 'The *Stella*. Ain't difficult, is it?'

'Why?' Joe asked. Was Bull also intending to skip?

'Never you mind why, mate. You show me, that's all.' And then, to allay any possible suspicion, 'It ain't safe having only one of us knowing. Suppose you was to get hurt, or something?'

He spoke without rancour. His handling of Fred the previous night had put him in a good humour. Victory over the islanders had been a hollow triumph; a couple of old men, women, a sissy — not much satisfaction to be got from browbeating or manhandling *them*. But to stand up to a man with a gun and beat him — that was different, that was good. It did something to a man. And he'd put the blonde in her place, too. She wasn't so free with that sharp tongue of hers this morning.

He had it all worked out now. McFee had been right. He'd lost his temper when the old fool had started bleating about the men who would be coming to look for him, but it made sense. Right from the start he'd known that the island could provide only a temporary shelter from the law. Now was the time to get out, and get out quick.

He'd fixed Fred. Fred couldn't cause trouble now, not without his gun. Fred could be left behind. He could fix Joe too; why split the lolly when it was all his for the taking? It was that damned boat that was the snag. He'd have to take Joe along to handle the boat.

Unless Joe could be persuaded to teach him.

He would have preferred Grant as an instructor. Joe was green, he shouldn't be difficult to kid; but there was the odd chance that he might get suspicious and gum the works. Joe knew about boats and engines. So did Grant. Only Grant, unlike Joe, would be glad to see him go, he wouldn't try to stop him.

But Joe was there and Grant wasn't. He'd have to take a chance on Joe.

'Okay,' Joe said. 'What about the plugs?'

'I got them,' Bull said.

He had not noticed Fred in the passage. He did not notice him when they left the bungalow. Furious, Fred watched them go. He had no doubt what was in Bull's mind, and his fury was increased by the knowledge that he was powerless to prevent it. He'd be left on the island — without money, without a gun, his wrist broken. He wouldn't stand a dog's chance.

That Joe would also be left behind did not enter his head. To Fred Joe was a tool, not a confederate. Joe didn't count.

As he watched Joe fitting the plugs into the engine it occurred to him that he was now alone in the bungalow. McFee, the girl, and the kid were down on the jetty, the Traynors had gone to look at the hens. Grant was out, and . . .

No. He wasn't alone; the blonde was in her room. There was just him and her — and her door wasn't locked. Bull's was — but not hers. Fred grinned evilly. This could be his opportunity.

She didn't answer to his knock, and he opened the door and went in. Kay was lying on the bed, her hands behind her head, staring fixedly at the ceiling. She was fully dressed, even to her shoes. When she saw Fred she sat up quickly, angry but not afraid. With that broken wrist he presented no menace. 'How dare you come in here?' she stormed, venting on him a little of the frustrated rage that was bottled up inside her. 'Get out at once, damn you!'

He made no move to go. He said, 'Bull's clearing out. I thought you'd like to know.'

She gazed at him, uncertain if this were a trick. But she was not left in doubt for long. The *Stella's* engine broke the silence, firing evenly. Kay leapt off the bed and ran to the window.

'He ain't off yet,' Fred told her. 'Joe's learning him how to handle the boat. He'll be back; he won't go without the money. And he don't want Joe with him either. Bull ain't one for sharing when he don't have to.'

Kay turned slowly from the window. 'Why are you telling me this?'

Fred leered at her. 'I thought as how

you and me might have a little talk,' he said.

* * *

Doubt and misgiving in her heart, Janet stood beside Angus and watched Joe screw the plugs into the engine-head. She wanted to know where he was going, why Bull was going with him; but she dared not ask. McFee, however, had no such qualms. He had long since abandoned his fishing-rod, and welcomed the interruption to Bobby's persistent chatter.

'If ye're away for good then bad riddance to ye,' he said cheerfully. He was a man without malice or grudge. 'If ye hadna damaged my ankle I'd have given ye a parting kick to set ye off.'

Bull grinned at him from the cockpit. He was in high spirits. 'We'll be back, mister, don't you worry. We ain't leaving you. This is just a pleasure trip.'

McFee sighed lugubriously.

'That's what I was fearing. Well, it's rough out yon; maybe ye'll be seasick. Ye wouldna care to let me have my own sparkplug back before ye go, eh? Just in case? The *Stella's* no' that safe in bad water.'

'I wouldna,' Bull mimicked. 'If it's no' safe for the *Stella* it's no' safe for that orange-box of yours.'

They'll be falling into each other's arms next, thought Janet. But Angus had been right; it *was* rough. The *Stella* should be all right; Joe knew how to handle her. But in the dinghy . . .

With sudden dread she remembered that Joe could not swim.

Anxiously she watched the *Stella* move out into open water to meet the full force of the wind. Joe was slow in turning, and a big wave caught them beam-on, so that the *Stella* listed alarmingly, her lee gunwale practically under water. She righted herself slowly, water pouring from the scuppers. Then Joe had brought her round, and they were heading north into the wind, the spray sweeping over them as they hit the crests. Joe's taking her too fast, Janet thought. He'll tear the engine out of her if he's not careful.

It was as she walked slowly off the jetty,

with Bobby chattering beside her, that she realized the importance (to her) of the fact that the *Stella* had gone up, not down, the loch — that, for a little while at least, Bull would be off the island and out of sight.

And so would Joe.

She hurried into the bungalow for a torch; it would be dark in the cave. As she left her room she could hear Kay's voice in the end bedroom, and wondered if Donald were back. Bobby was waiting for her, but she told him to go down to the jetty and watch for the *Stella*'s return, and was relieved when he did so. She wanted no companion on her present errand.

She made for the wood, forcing herself to walk sedately across the lawn; she must not appear to be in a hurry, as though she were setting out on a definite mission. It was a relief to reach the shelter of the trees, and for a moment she paused there, looking back. Fred was her main concern; she could not understand what had become of him. He had been looking out of one of the passage windows when Bull had appeared on the steps and shouted for Joe, and she had not seen him come out; yet there had been no sign of him in the bungalow when she had gone to her room later.

But at least he had not followed her. Relieved, she ran on down the path to the vegetable garden.

At the far end of the garden she paused again; there was no sign or sound of pursuit, and she went through the gap in the wire and began to climb the slope to the outcrop of rock that marked her objective, anxious to reach the shelter of the tall bracken and the few bushes that partially screened the fuel-store from the loch. She could hear the *Stella*'s engine; was it her fancy, or was it nearer now?

The key turned easily in the lock. The heavy door swung open, and she slipped quickly into the cave, closing the door behind her; to leave it open would be to attract inquisitive eyes. The pungent fumes of petrol and paraffin assailed her, and she switched on the torch, thankful that she had thought to bring it. The cave was ventilated, but only a faint light penetrated the interior.

She saw at once that she had been right about the haversack. With her father's shotgun it was propped against the rock wall, and she swooped on it eagerly, her fingers trembling as they wrestled with straps and buckles.

The money was there; bundles and bundles of notes. She gazed at them awestruck. Three thousand pounds had not sounded a vast sum when she had heard it mentioned on the radio; not a sum for which men would risk years of imprisonment, for which they had even been willing to kill. Yet now it looked almost staggeringly vast.

She picked up one bundle, riffled the notes in fascination, and put them back quickly. She must not waste time. But what was to be done with the money now that she had found it? Even if she got it back to the bungalow without being spotted by Fred or the others there was no safe hiding-place for it there. Nor would she leave it in the cave. Because of her Joe was willing to forgo what he believed to be his share. At least he should have the satisfaction of knowing, before he left, that Bull and Fred would not benefit by his sacrifice.

She pushed the door open cautiously and peered out. No one was in sight. She could still hear the *Stella*, but it sounded no nearer. Closing the door behind her, she began to climb the steep side of the hill.

The going was tough. After a few yards rocks gave way to trees; but the undergrowth here had not been cleared, and brambles and bushes impeded her progress and tore at her frock. And the haversack was surprisingly heavy; it was a relief when at last she found a suitable hiding-place and was able to slip it from her shoulders. Then, having satisfied herself that she could find it again, she hurried back down the hill. She must lock up the store and get back to the bungalow before Bull and Joe returned.

As she opened the door — 'Come in, Janet,' Kay said. 'And leave the door ajar. It's dark in here.'

Janet went in. Fred was there too. He had the shotgun in his left hand and was leaning on it, grinning at her uneasily. Apart from having found the gun, Janet couldn't see what he had to grin about. And what use was the gun to him with a broken wrist?

'I suppose you followed me,' Janet said slowly. 'Why?'

'Just a hunch,' Fred told her. 'You looked like you was going some place, and blondie here said it could be the fuel-store.' At this familiar reference to her cousin Janet looked sharply at Kay. Kay gazed back at her stolidly, apparently indifferent. 'So we come after you, thinking you might have a key we didn't know about.' His tone changed. 'Did you find the money?'

So they had guessed. Well, guessing wasn't knowing; she had hidden the haversack, she could still fool them. But what on earth had made Kay team up with Fred? He couldn't have forced her to accompany him, she must have come of her own accord. Why?

'What money?' she asked.

'The money what was in the haversack.' Fred's eyes roamed the walls of the cave, peered into the dark corners, and came back to Janet. 'Bull must have hid it here. What have you done with it?'

'Nothing.'

'But that was what you were after, wasn't it?'

'Yes. But I couldn't find it.'

Her voice told him plainly that she was not afraid of him. The knowledge angered him, and he snapped at her, 'You found it all right.' Forgetful of what he held in his left hand, he lifted the shotgun and slammed it down again. The clang as the butt hit the granite floor of the cave startled him, and he jumped. 'What was you doing outside just now? Hiding it?'

He leaned forward, staring at her, his eyes blinking nervously. Janet stared back, fascinated by the change in him. He was no longer the bold-eyed, cocksure little man who had first come to the island. He looked defeated, uncertain of himself. There were still traces of the old familiarity, as when he had referred to Kay as 'blondie.' He could still produce flashes of anger; but it was the anger of frustration, unsupported by weapon or physical strength. Like a mangy cur, he could bark. But he could not bite. His teeth had been drawn.

'I thought Bull might have hidden it somewhere outside.' She turned to her cousin. 'What are you doing here, Kay? It's obvious what Fred is after, but what made you come with him? You're not interested in the money, are you?'

'Yes, in a way.' Her voice sounded flat, almost indifferent, but Janet was not deceived. She knew Kay was boiling up for something, that she was holding herself in — and with difficulty.

'But, Kay — '

'Did you know he was planning to leave?' Kay's voice had lost a little of its control. 'Alone?'

For a moment Janet was frightened. How could they know about Joe? Then she gave a deep sigh and relaxed. Kay would only refer to one man as 'he.' To Joe she would have given a name.

'Bull?' she asked. Her voice was not quite steady. She might so easily have betrayed Joe inadvertently.

'Who else? Isn't that just what the

swine would do?'

Now the venom showed clearly. The veneer of indifference was gone. 'How do you know?' Janet asked.

'Joe has taken him out in the *Stella* to show him how to work it. Fred heard them talking. Doesn't that show what's in his mind? He wouldn't choose a day like this for a lesson unless it were urgent.'

Janet had forgotten the *Stella*. Now she listened for it. Faintly, as from a long way off, she heard the throb of an engine. So they were not back yet. And when they did return, what then? How soon would Bull come for the money? When he couldn't find it, would he go without it? How would that affect Joe?

'It doesn't explain what you're doing here,' she said.

'Doesn't it?' Fred was impatient of this chatter. 'I wanted the money, she wanted one of your dad's guns. We reckoned Bull would have hid 'em together. That made sense, didn't it?' He banged the shotgun on the floor, less heavily this time. 'So when he comes for the money we'll be waiting for him, see? With a gun. And that suits both of us.'

Janet nodded. She was not greatly surprised. It was an unholy alliance cemented by their common hatred of Bull. 'Who's going to use it?' she asked, her eyes on the sling that supported his right arm.

'I am,' Kay said calmly.

'You mean — you'd actually shoot him?'

'With the greatest of pleasure.' Her eyes glittered in anticipation. 'I can hardly wait.'

Janet did not doubt the truth of that. 'Suppose he doesn't come?' she said. 'The money isn't here. Only the gun. He could have hidden the money wherever he's hidden the rifle.'

Kay frowned. So did Fred. He peered anxiously round the cave again and then at Kay. The absence of the rifle had raised doubts in their minds; apparently it did not occur to them that Janet might have hidden both money and rifle. Janet herself was surprised that the rifle was not there, although she had not given it thought until now. She supposed that Bull must have hidden it nearer the bungalow, in case of sudden need.

Into the silence came the throb of an engine. It sounded nearer than before. ‘Shut the door,’ Kay said urgently. ‘If he sees it open he’ll know something is wrong.’

Janet did not move. She stood listening. Then she shook her head. ‘That’s not the *Stella*,’ she said.

Cautiously she opened the door farther and peered out. Across the loch, still some distance away, a big launch was buffeting and bucketing its way towards the island.

9

Why speaks my father so ungently? This
Is the third man that e'er I saw; the first
That e'er I sigh'd for: pity move my father
To be inclin'd my way!

The Tempest, Act I, Scene 2

Janet did not wait to see what Fred and Kay would do; all her thoughts were for Joe. As she ran through the bracken and down the sloping pasture she heard Kay call after her; but the words were swept away by the wind, and all that reached her ears was a thin, faint cry that still seemed to retain some of its original urgency. She did not heed it. Kay's troubles were not hers.

As she reached the gap in the wire she had to catch at a post to stop herself, and swung round, jarring her body against the far post. Her heart thumping, she gave a quick look over her shoulder at the launch. Already it seemed to be much nearer. Then she was off again, across the vegetable garden and along the path through the wood. From the fuel-store the trees obscured the bungalow and the lawn and the jetty, stretching up from the shore in a wide band to near the crown of the hill. Was the *Stella* back? she wondered as she ran. Or had Bull seen the launch and decided not to return to the island but to make for the eastern and more desolate side of the loch, taking Joe with him?

It was that last thought which agitated her. If she wanted Joe to escape — and she was no more certain of that now than she had been at the beginning — she did not want him to escape with Bull. Bull would do him more harm than prison, both physically and morally.

She came out from the trees on to the lawn and looked anxiously at the jetty. The *Stella* was there, and so was the dinghy. But jetty and beach and garden were deserted. It must be about lunch-time, she thought. If they are all indoors maybe they haven't seen the launch.

She stepped on to the granite-flanked path and turned to look back at the loch. The launch was little more than a hundred yards from the jetty now, and making straight for it. But the waves and the spray obscured it, and she could distinguish nothing of the people on board.

Janet hesitated. I'm always having to make decisions, she thought. What do I do if they haven't seen the launch? Do I tell them? It's too late now for Joe . . .

A rifle cracked sharply from somewhere above her, and instinctively she flung herself to the ground, imagining herself the target. The coarse gravel bit into her through the cotton dress, she could feel it against her hands and cheek; but she lay there motionless, waiting for the next shot. When it came her body jerked involuntarily, but she pressed it down and wriggled towards the edge of the path, seeking the protection of the granite boulders. It was only when she realized that she had not been hit, that there had been no sound of a bullet striking the ground beside her, that she raised her head cautiously. Then came the crunch of shoes on the wet gravel, and Joe was beside her, gathering her into his arms, murmuring endearments.

'Oh, Joe!' she said weakly, as he lifted her up. And burst into tears.

They were all in the bungalow except for Bull and Fred and Kay. As Joe deposited her gently in an armchair they crowded round solicitously, asking impatient questions. Joe moved away to the fringe of the circle, but as she dabbed at her eyes with the handkerchief her mother handed to her she could see him watching her with a dog-like devotion that made her want to get up and go to him, heedless of what they all might think.

But when she tried to rise her mother stopped her.

'You've cut your leg, dear, and there's a nasty graze on your cheek. You stay there and get your breath back while I clean you up.'

Rose went off to the kitchen for hot water. Janet looked idly down at her legs, watching the little rivulet of blood that trickled slowly from just below her left knee, and then veered abruptly off course and ran round her calf and disappeared. She put a hand up to her cheek, and it came away sticky and redly damp. Her once gay frock was dirty and creased and wet.

'You still haven't told us where you've been, Janet,' her father said. His voice and his face were stern. He seemed unable to relax, even with her.

'I went for a walk, that's all.'

'Where?'

'Over towards the fuel-store and the far pasture.' She looked at Joe, but his expression had not changed. Either he did not understand the significance of what she had said, or the money was no longer of importance to him. 'Then I saw the launch, and I ran back.' She was still looking at Joe. Once she allowed herself to look at him it was difficult to look anywhere else. Reluctantly she turned to her father. 'Was he shooting at me?'

He shook his head. 'At the launch, I think. Not necessarily to sink them. To warn them off, more likely.'

'He's no better than a murderer,' Rose said indignantly. She had come back with hot water and towels and bandages and cotton-wool, and was busily wiping the blood from her daughter's leg. 'Even if he wasn't aiming at Janet he could easily have hit her.'

McFee chuckled involuntarily; it was a typical Rose comment. No one else smiled. Joe had gone to the window and was watching the launch. It was beam-on to the jetty now, and level with it; but it was no nearer. It was moving very slowly up the loch with the engine throttled back. He had thought that in that wind the men in the launch might not hear the shots, that the bullets might fall unnoticed into that rough water. But it was obvious that they had changed their minds about coming in to land, if that had been their original intention. They were standing off. Would they go back for the police, he wondered, or would they stay and await developments?

'Where is he?' asked Janet. Joe had rejoined the circle, and she smiled a welcome at him.

'Bull? He's up at the top of the hill,' Joe said. 'We saw the launch as we were bringing the *Stella* in. He told me to keep every one in here, and then off he went. I think he had one of your dad's guns hidden up there.'

'It's a good vantage-point,' Traynor said. 'He can see all round the island. Plenty of cover, too, if he doesn't stick too close to the crest. It won't be easy to shift him if he decides to stay there.'

It was strange — or wasn't it? — how they seemed to be accepting Joe as one of themselves. They talked freely in front of him; there was little restraint. Was that because, in comparison with Bull and Fred, he *seemed* more like themselves? Janet wondered. If there were only Joe would they still accept him?

Donald said quietly, 'Did you see Kay, Janet?'

He had not spoken before. He looked strained and ill, and she felt sorry for him.

'Yes. She was over that way too. I ran on ahead; I wanted to see if the *Stella* was back. I expect she heard the shots when she was in the wood, and decided it might be safer to stay there.'

'I'll go and meet her,' Donald said.

She had not thought of that. She looked appealingly at Joe. Surely he must have guessed?

It seemed that he had. 'I shouldn't do that if I was you, Mr Grant,' he said awkwardly. 'Bull said you was all to stay in here. Your wife won't be in no danger in the wood, but if Bull sees you walking across the lawn you'll probably get a bullet in you. Bull ain't playing games, you know. He's in dead earnest.'

'You're telling me!' said McFee. 'If you'll pardon a Scot borrowing an Americanism.'

Donald hesitated. 'Was Fred with her?' he asked Janet.

'No,' she lied. 'No, I didn't see Fred. I don't know where he is.'

Traynor was staring at his nephew in astonishment. 'Why on earth should she be with Fred?'

'No reason,' Donald said hastily. 'I just thought, as Fred isn't here — well, where is he?'

'Up with that other devil, most likely.

But he won't be much use as a marksman. Not with a broken wrist.' Traynor walked over to the window. 'Hello! They're going back.'

They crowded round him. There was no doubt about it. The launch was nearly half-way across the loch, going fast, heading for the mainland.

As they turned away from the window Janet said fervently, 'Thank God!'

She was thinking of Joe, looking at Joe. As long as the launch was there Joe could not leave. Now it was gone. There was still Bull, but Bull had been there before. Bull, somehow, they could cope with.

It was some time before she realized that they were all staring at her in astonishment — all except Bobby, who had lost interest in the conversation and was fiddling with the forbidden radio. Squeaks and howls issued from it, and occasional snatches of speech and music. No one paid it any attention. All their interest, Joe's included, was concentrated on Janet. Joe thanked her with his eyes. He knew that she had spoken only for him.

'Now there's a traitor for ye, if ever there was one.' McFee grinned at her cheerfully, taking the sting out of his words. 'But they'll be back, lassie. We haven't seen the last of them.'

Janet was all confusion. She had not realized that she had spoken her thoughts aloud. 'I was thinking of the shooting,' she apologized. 'If they had tried to land some of them might have been killed. I didn't mean — '

'Are you in love with this young man, Janet?' said Rose. She was standing beside Joe, looking from him to the girl. As the tell-tale flush crept up Janet's neck and flamed in her cheeks she nodded. 'I see you are. Well, I can't say I'm surprised. I've seen it coming on.' She spoke as though her daughter had contracted an infectious disease.

If Rose was not surprised the others were. They looked like a shoal of fish, Janet thought, with their mouths open and their eyes popping. She looked at Joe. He was frowning, tugging at the sleeves of his jacket, trying to pull them down over his wrists as she had seen him do before, and she knew he was far more embarrassed than she. And suddenly she was not embarrassed at all. She went over to him and took his hand in both of hers, squeezing it, smiling up at him proudly. Then she turned and faced them.

'Yes, I am.' There was no defiance in her voice. She did not have to apologize for her love. 'And Joe loves me, and we're going to be married.'

Into the shocked silence that followed boomed the voice of the B.B.C. announcer. Bobby had the volume full on.

' . . . is still critically ill, but the police hope that he may be well enough to answer questions about the robbery in the course of the next few days.'

'Since this bulletin started news has been received that two men who the police think may be able to help them in their inquiries have been seen on the Isle of Garra, a small island in — '

The voice was cut off abruptly as Bobby idly turned the knob. Oblivious of the others, Joe looked down at the girl, his eyes bright with hope.

'You heard that, Janet? They don't

know about me.'

She pressed his hand. Her eyes were on her family.

'Four days,' Robert Traynor said. 'Four days you've known him. And I don't have to remind you of what he is, Janet, of what he's done. That's common knowledge. Aren't you being rather hasty — a little too free with your affection?' He turned to Joe, cool contempt writ plainly on his face. 'You seem pleased that the radio made mention of only two men in connexion with the crime — though it would have been more becoming to have shown pleasure at the news that the man you and your companions tried to murder is still alive. But let me tell you this, young man. I know — we all know — that you were there, and I shall make it my duty to see that the police know it too. So I suggest it would be most unwise to plan an early wedding. As far as I am aware Her Majesty's prisons make no provision for the accommodation of the wives of their inmates.'

Joe's face went white, but he said nothing. He stared back at the cold eyes, his own unflinching. Janet felt the fingers of his hand contract, so that her own were almost numb with the pain.

'Daddy, how can you!' she cried, angry and hurt. 'Joe didn't try to kill the watchman, he wasn't there. He was outside in the car. He had absolutely nothing to do with the shooting.'

'So he says, my dear. But even if that is true it doesn't absolve him from responsibility.' Her father's voice was stern. 'The shooting would never have occurred if he and his friends had not planned and staged the robbery.'

'They're not his friends, and he didn't plan it. Fred forced him into it against his will. He didn't even know they had guns.' Her eyes flashed. 'You've no right to accuse him when you don't know the facts.'

'Janet!' Rose Traynor was shocked at this *lèse-majesté*. 'You mustn't speak like that to your father.'

Traynor shrugged. 'I'm not accusing him. Others will do that later. And if you prefer to think of him as just a common thief — well, I won't argue with you. I still refuse to accept him as a son-in-law.'

'I see.' Janet turned to Rose. 'How about you, Mummy? Are you on Daddy's side or mine?'

'There must be no question of sides,' Rose said unhappily, with a nervous look at her husband. She had never disputed his opinion on a major issue, and she could not start now. 'But when all's said and done, dear, you must admit that Joe is hardly a suitable husband for you.'

'Isn't he? I should have thought that the most suitable husband for me is the man I love.' She was thoroughly incensed now — there was no question of give and take. She had known that they would be against the marriage, had acknowledged to herself their right to be so. Now reason was swept aside, along with their objections. 'Well, I love Joe. What's more, I'm going to marry him. And none of you can stop me.'

McFee coughed. This was no concern of his, but he loved an argument. 'It seems to me that Janet's suitor is not very eloquent in his own defence. How about it, young man? Do ye consider yourself a suitable husband for the girl?'

'No,' Joe said curtly. 'I know I'm not.' Having broken his self-imposed silence, he went on, with more warmth in his voice and looking directly at Traynor, 'I never asked Janet to marry me — I didn't even mean to tell her I love her. I — well, it just happened. But I *do* love her. I know I'm not good enough for her, Mr Traynor, but I'm not all that bad. And when I've got all this straightened out I'll — well, if she still wants me I'll marry her.'

'Thank you, darling.' Janet looked at her father, her chin tilted, as though to say, There! You see? But if Traynor saw anything to make him change his mind he did not admit it. He shrugged and turned away. As far as he was concerned the argument was ended.

It was Rose who broke the tension.

'Goodness me! The one o'clock news!' She bustled into the centre of the room to look at the clock. 'Yes, it was. And I've done nothing about the lunch.'

* * *

Janet wanted no lunch. She was not hungry, and she would not sit down at table with all their accusing looks directed at her and Joe. Besides, she had to talk to him.

But first she must change. And it was while she was changing that she knew, for the first time with any certainty, just what she and Joe had to do.

He was waiting for her on the steps. The bungalow hid him from Bull's eyrie on the hill-top, and even more than Janet he was reluctant to face her family. He looked up with relief as she came out to join him, but relief turned to astonishment when he saw her.

'What have you put them on for? Going hiking?'

Janet looked down at the brief shorts which had aroused her mother's disapproval. 'I'm going swimming,' she said.

'In this weather? They don't look right for that neither.'

'They're not. But I have to think ahead.'

She told him what she had done that morning. He grinned approval when she explained how she had hidden the money. 'I'd like to see Bull's face when he goes to get it,' he said.

'So would I,' Janet agreed, and told him about Fred and Kay.

Joe looked perturbed. 'Bull isn't easy to kill. You saw what he done when Fred pulled a gun on him. I hope your cousin can shoot straight.' A further thought occurred to him. 'If she kills him she'll be had up for murder. We ought to stop her.'

'How? By warning Bull? It's no use talking to Kay. She just wouldn't listen.'

'You could tell her husband.'

Yes, she could tell Donald. Until Joe had said it she had not thought of Kay as a potential murderess, she had been too wrapped up in her plans for him. But Joe was right; if there was a way to stop Kay they had to try it. Donald was Kay's husband; if he could not dissuade her — and Janet did not think he could — then no one could.

'All right,' she said. 'I'll tell him. He can come with us. It's not safe to go across the lawn.'

'With us? Are we going somewhere?'

'We're going to get the money,' she told him. 'You're taking it with you. What's more, I'm coming too.'

That startled him. 'But you said — '

'I know I did. I've changed my mind. We'll take the money and hand it over to the police. And if that doesn't get you off with a light sentence,' she said, proud of her new-found and unexpected genius for planning, 'nothing will. They might even let you off altogether.'

It did not meet with the response for which she had hoped.

'You hand me and the money over together, eh? That's nice.'

'*You* will, Joe, not me.' She saw the dread in his eyes, and understood. 'Darling, you're all wrong about the police. They're not like that. You think they're vindictive and cruel, but they're not. I know they're not.'

'How? You had anything to do with them?' He shook his head. 'Give me a start and I'll fool them easy. They won't catch me.'

'But they will. And anyway, that isn't the point.' She seized his arm. 'You said you loved me, that you wanted to marry me. Did you mean that?'

'You know I did. But I'm not going to — '

'Listen to me, Joe.' Despair lent urgency to her voice. She had to make him understand. 'I won't marry a coward. I'm not going to tie myself to a man who intends to spend the rest of his life running away from the police. I couldn't stand it. I'll always love you — but if you run away from this I'll never see you again. I mean that, Joe.'

He knew that she did mean it, and his heart sank. But he made one last effort.

'You said before — '

'Don't keep telling me what I said before.' She stamped her foot angrily. 'Yes, I know I said it, but I was wrong. I'm right now — I know I am.' She saw the hurt, lost look in his eyes, and her anger went as suddenly as it had come. 'Darling, I love you. Don't let me down now. Please, Joe!'

He took her into his arms and kissed her. Her parents were probably watching from the bungalow, but it did not matter.

Nothing mattered now except that he must not lose her. Not even his liberty could be more precious to him than Janet.

'It's all right,' he said. 'I'll do it. I won't let you down.'

There were tears in her eyes as she smiled up at him.

'Oh, I knew you wouldn't. But you're terribly stubborn, darling.' She rubbed her eyes and was instantly practical. 'And we're wasting precious time. I'll fetch Donald. We can sneak round the back and get across through the woods. I'll show you.'

He caught her arm.

'Wait a minute. What's all this about swimming? I can't swim.'

'I know. But I can.' She wanted to sound bright and matter-of-fact, knowing he would object to what she was about to propose. 'After we've collected the money you will take it down to the south side of the island — I'll point the spot out to you — and I'll meet you there in the dinghy. Then — '

'Oh, no, you won't! *I'll* get the dinghy.

I'm not having Bull taking pot-shots at you.'

'Darling, please be sensible. You wouldn't have a chance if Bull saw you trying to start the dinghy. You know that. The only way is to swim out to it from behind the bungalow, undo the mooring-ropes, and let it drift down. You can't do that, because you can't swim. It will be easy for me. The way the wind's blowing, I should end up right in your lap. And it's quite safe. I'll keep down below the bank until I reach the jetty, and then swim out under it to the dinghy. Even if Bull sees the dinghy drifting away there's nothing he can do. He won't see me. I'll be on the far side of it, in the water.'

He recognized the wisdom of her proposal, but he would not accept it. He could not let her take such risks, he said, and for him. The water was too rough; the wind might change, she might drift down the loch with no means of controlling the dinghy; now that the launch had gone Bull would most likely come down from the hill and be in a better position to see her and fire at her. 'If you won't let me do it, why can't we just stay on the island and hand the money over to the cops when they come?' he concluded. 'What's the difference?'

'There's all the difference,' she said firmly. 'You'd be handing the money over because you were cornered — or that's what they'd think. You've got to take it to them when you're free, when you have a choice. And the water isn't all that rough; not for me. The wind won't change, either; it will probably blow like this for at least another twenty-four hours. As for Bull — well, I don't believe he'd try to shoot me even if he saw me. You, yes — but not me. Why should he? He only stopped us leaving the island before because he didn't want us to tell the police you were here. It doesn't matter now. They know.'

It was this last argument which persuaded him. Bull might be a killer, but he would not kill wantonly. He had not tried to shoot the watchman; Fred had done that. He had not gone on firing at the launch; only the two shots, near enough to scare them. He had not even killed Fred when Fred had tried to kill him. It was in the use of his strength that Bull exulted. Only when his strength failed him and his liberty or safety was at stake would Bull use a gun.

'Okay,' he said. 'We'll do it your way.'

She gripped his hand and then released it. 'I'll get Donald,' she said.

⋆ ⋆ ⋆

'What was that?' Kay asked.

'A shot.' It was a more familiar sound to Fred than to her. He pushed open the cave-door and peered out. The rifle cracked again; the sound came from the hill-top, and he looked up in time to see a tiny puff of smoke snatched away by the wind. 'Bull's firing at some one,' he told her, as he scurried back into the cave. He jerked his thumb skyward. 'He's up there. And he's using the rifle, damn him!'

'What about the launch?'

'Couldn't see. Must be behind them trees.' The knowledge that Bull had the rifle both scared and angered him. 'We'd best get out; we ain't doing no good here.

I reckon the girl was right. Bull must've hid the money with the rifle, up top.'

Kay was gripped in an agony of indecision. She did not care about the money, it was merely a bait to trap Bull. She did not care about Fred, with his lusts and his fears and his greed. Because Bull had hurt his skinny, misshapen body and his tin-pot vanity he had come to her that morning with his offer of an alliance, and she had accepted it because she had thought she could use him. She would have accepted an alliance with the Devil himself if he had offered her Bull as a prize. But now that she had the shotgun (literally, Fred had it; he had kept it because he was well aware of her loathing for him, he did not trust her. But he would hand it to her when the time came; she could even wrest it from him by force if necessary) she saw no further use for Fred. Yet she could not let him go. She trusted him no more than he trusted her. Despite his avowed hatred of Bull, she knew that his fear was stronger than his hate, and his greed probably stronger than both. He could be bought or bullied into betraying her.

She glanced round the cave as Fred had done, seeking some sign that the money had been there. That was what mattered — that it had been there, wherever it was now, that Bull would expect to find it there, and that he would come for it.

But there was no sign. 'We'll wait,' she said flatly. She had to trust her judgment.

They waited. Fred fidgeted nervously, but Kay was too tense to fidget. Presently she said, 'Give me the gun and show me how to use it. If he's coming he'll come soon.'

Reluctantly he obeyed. His fear of Bull was greater than his fear of her.

Key felt better with the gun actually in her hands, knowing that it was loaded, that she had only to point it and pull the trigger and her enemy would die. The feel of it made that precious moment seem nearer, and she hugged the stock to her breasts, delighting in its hardness, unconsciously stroking the smooth barrel with her hand.

'You be careful with that,' Fred warned,

stepping back. 'Keep the muzzle down. I don't want no accident with me at the wrong end.'

From behind he eyed her covetously as she stood silhouetted against the light from the partly open door. She was a fine piece of goods all right. Damn Bull! If that ruddy bastard hadn't interfered last night he'd have made her. He could make her now if it wasn't for his perishing wrist. With the door closed she could scream her head off and he wouldn't have to worry.

'There's the launch,' Kay said. 'It sounds nearer.'

Fred went to the door and looked out. He could see the launch, it was below the trees now. And it was heading away from the island. When he told Kay she gave a sigh of contentment. 'He'll come now,' she said. 'That's what he was waiting for. Close the door.'

They waited together in the darkness. Kay gripped the gun tightly with both hands. Occasionally her finger sought and found the trigger, touching it lightly, reassuring her that she would not be caught off guard. Beside her Fred breathed nasally; he smelt strongly of stale sweat. Once he touched her side with his free hand, and she jumped nervously at the unexpected contact.

'Do that again and I'll press the trigger,' she snapped. 'I nearly did that time.'

She heard him move away.

But Bull did not come. Presently Kay walked to the door and pushed it open. It was a relief to be out in the air, away from the smell of petrol and paraffin and sweat.

Fred joined her. 'Well?' he asked. 'Who's right now, eh?'

She could not hear the *Stella*, and there was no sign of Bull. He might be anywhere. She turned and looked up at the hill. From where they stood the crest was hidden by the trees.

'We'll go up there,' she said.

'Up top?' Fred was scared. 'Not me. He'll see us coming.'

Kay looked at him in disgust. 'Not the top, you fool. Just high enough to be able to see over the trees to the jetty, to make sure that the *Stella*'s still there, that he hasn't gone.'

He insisted on climbing behind her. Kay did not know if this was because he expected her to protect him from Bull, or because he disliked the thought of her and the gun behind him. She went steadily up, holding on to the trees where the going was particularly steep, pushing her way through the bramble-threaded undergrowth regardless of scratches and tears. Fred climbed more slowly, hampered by his leg and the injury to his wrist. Occasionally he failed to make good a foothold and slipped back, swearing obscenely.

She had stopped for some minutes before he joined her. From where they stood they could see over the belt of trees to the *Stella* tossing at her moorings, McFee's dinghy bobbing and ducking behind it. Kay breathed her satisfaction. He was still on the island, he had not escaped her yet.

'There he is!' Fred exclaimed. 'See?'

Bull came out from the trees on to the lawn; even at that distance he looked big. For a moment or two he stood there, gazing across the loch, the rifle tucked under his arm. Then he turned and went into the bungalow. At the sight of him Kay had instinctively raised the gun, to be checked by Fred. And she knew he was right. The range was too great, and she and the gun were strangers.

'He didn't have the haversack,' Fred said thoughtfully. 'Either he's left it up top, or he thinks it's in the store.' He stared at her, his eyes bright with greed. 'Suppose I was to go up there and look, maybe I could find the money, eh?' Fear came to him at the thought of the risk he might be running, but he shook it off. 'You could watch the bungalow from here, eh? You could let me know when he comes out?'

'Yes,' Kay said indifferently. It was unwise to let him go, but she could not be bothered with him any longer. He had served his purpose.

'You'll wait here until I come back?' he said anxiously.

'I'll wait,' she told him. Fred or no Fred, she had no intention of moving until she saw Bull leave the bungalow. Fred hesitated, fearing to trust her, and yet urged by his greed to do so.

'You be careful with that gun,' he warned her. 'If it goes off accidental Bull will hear it.' He took another look at the bungalow. 'Well, I'm off.'

She did not watch him go. She could hear him cursing and swearing as he fought his way up; but gradually the noise of his progress ceased, and there was only the sound of the wind to disturb the silence. It was blowing a gale now. It fought its way through the trees, snatching at her in spiteful gusts and then whistling off across the loch. Over to the west black clouds were piling up, and there was the sharp patter of raindrops on the leaves above her. Kay did not heed them. She stood erect, her gaze never straying from the green-painted door, the gun in her hands. She felt neither fatigue nor hunger nor thirst. Hate sustained her, uplifted her. She was content to wait.

She was still waiting when Joe and Janet arrived. Donald had already left them, he had gone down to the fuel-store to reason with Kay. They had not expected to find her here, only a few yards from where the haversack was hidden, and for a moment they paused in indecision. But they had to go on. To wait longer was to court disaster.

Kay was not greatly surprised to see them. 'You've come for the money, I suppose,' she said.

'Yes.' Janet hesitated. Should she tell her about Donald? It might be wiser not to. If Kay knew that Donald was looking for her in the store she would not go back there; Donald would not be given his chance to dissuade her. 'Kay, please don't go on with this. He isn't worth it.'

'I don't intend to kill him, if that's what's worrying you.' Kay spoke quietly, her eyes still watching the bungalow. Then her mood changed. 'But I'll hurt him! By God, I'll hurt him!'

It was not a response to Janet's plea; that could not touch her. The decision had come to her gradually as she waited. Death would be too sudden. It could give her one supreme moment of exultation as she saw him fall, and then — nothing. Victory without its aftermath would be flat. But to wound him . . . to have him helpless and in pain at her feet . . . to hand him over to the police herself . . . to go, perhaps, to his trial, to see him in the dock, to hear him sentenced, watch him taken away . . . that would be a multitude of victories. There would even be the years when she could think of him in prison, and gloat over the knowledge that she had put him there, that he would know it was her doing. And to Bull, with his intolerance and his contempt for others, his hatred of restraint and his belief in his own invincibility, prison would be a far greater punishment than death.

'What will you do with the money?' she asked.

Janet told her briefly; she did not say how, and she did not mention that she and Joe were in love. But Kay did not ask for detail; she was not interested. 'You'd better get a move on,' she said. 'Bull will be here soon.'

'Will you wait for him in the cave?' Janet asked, thinking of Donald.

'I expect so.'

She did not watch them as they

unearthed the haversack. The cache was behind her, and she would not interrupt her vigil.

'Has she gone crackers?' Joe whispered. 'Is it all right to leave her?'

He had thought at the beginning that he understood Kay, and had despised her for what he believed her to be. Now he did not know whether to despise or admire. If she were promiscuous in love, at least she could concentrate on hate.

'We must,' Janet said. 'It's up to Donald now. We've done all we can.'

She pointed out to him where he was to wait for her. He kissed her fervently. 'Be careful,' he pleaded. 'I can't lose you now.'

'You won't,' she promised. 'I'll be all right.'

He watched her until she had disappeared among the trees on her way back, then slung the haversack over his shoulder and started down to the shore to wait for her.

It was not until they had gone that Kay remembered she had not asked them what Bull was doing in the bungalow.

* * *

Bull came down the hill humming tunelessly; he was not great on music. Things were going reasonably well, he decided. The launch had gone, it would be at least an hour before it could be back — with reinforcements, presumably. Well, an hour would be plenty. A bite of grub, the money, and then he'd be off — and to hell with the lot of them! It was lucky he'd had Joe show him how to work that damned boat. He wasn't so hot on it yet, he knew that; the launch had appeared before he had properly got the hang of it. But he could start it and he could stop it. If he couldn't get that bucket across to the mainland in one piece, storm or no storm, he'd bloody well shoot himself.

He stumped up the bungalow steps into the living-room and stood surveying them, stroking the raindrops from his beard, secretly pleased at the gaping faces that greeted him.

'Where's Joe?' he demanded.

'Out,' McFee said succinctly.

Bull looked at the empty places round

the table. 'With his skirt, eh? Looks like he don't keep his appetite in his stomach. Fred got his bit out too? Where's her old man? Holding Fred's coat?'

He guffawed hugely, seated himself on the nearest chair, and began immediately to stuff food into his mouth. He had no time to waste. None of his audience (they need not watch, but they were forced to listen) had had much of an appetite before his arrival. Now they had none.

Time passed to the sound of Bull's champing jaws and the suck . . . suck . . . suck . . . as he completed each mouthful. When he had finished he stood up, kicking his chair away, and belched in satisfaction.

'I'm clearing out.' He hitched the rifle to a more comfortable position on his shoulder, and patted the stock significantly. 'And don't none of you get no fancy notions, either. You stay here, see? I ain't toting this around for fun.'

They did not move from the table until he had gone down the path and was half-way across the lawn; then they crowded to the window to watch him.

'Clearing out, eh?' McFee said. 'Where's he off to now, then? He isna making for the *Stella*.'

'Probably collecting the other two,' Traynor said. He looked sadly at the *Stella*, at the heaving loch and the black, threatening sky, and then back at the *Stella*. Am I saying good-bye to her? he wondered.

Bull hurried through the wood and across the kitchen-garden, picking his teeth with a sliver of wood and belching as he went. The rifle was still slung over his shoulder. He had spent less than ten minutes in the bungalow, and it would take him about the same time to collect the money and get back to the jetty. And the *Stella* would be warm after the run with Joe, she'd start easy. Only a plug to fit, and he'd be away.

It was as he began to squeeze his bulk through the narrow gap in the wire that he saw Kay. She was running towards him, with Donald after her. Startled but amused, Bull watched her come, thinking that her husband had surprised her with Fred. You got to hand it to Fred, he thought. Even a broken wrist don't cool him.

It was not until he saw the gun in her hands that he realized his danger, and then it was too late. He reached for the rifle, but in his struggle to get through the gap it had become wedged behind the two posts, and he could move neither it nor himself. Bellowing like his namesake, he looked round at Kay. The gun was at her shoulder, he could see her eyes glinting venomously along the barrel. He gave a final heave, exerting all his prodigious strength; with a sharp *crack* a post snapped, and he stumbled forward, to fall heavily to the ground.

It was at that moment that Kay fired.

She was only a few yards away; it was his fall, and Donald's despairing grab at her shoulder, that saved him. Pain stabbed him in the left arm, and he scrambled to his feet and rushed madly at Kay, knocking the gun from her hands and flattening her with a blow to the head. A red mist danced before his bloodshot eyes, but he saw Donald come at him, and hit out wildly, sinking his fist in the other's stomach. Donald grunted and folded up, to writhe in agony on the ground. Almost automatically Bull let fly with his foot, kicking him in the back.

He stood there breathing furiously, getting his wind and his senses. Then he remembered the money. Panting like a mad dog, he lumbered heavily up through the bracken to the fuel-store.

Kay sat up slowly, holding her head. Every part of her body seemed to ache. A few feet away Donald still writhed on the ground, his hands to his stomach; the air whistled through his lungs as he struggled for breath. She began to crawl towards him. But as she reached him she heard Bull come out of the cave, and she tried to stand up, knowing that he had not found the money, that she must run, that if he caught her he would kill her. But she was too weak to run. She took a few tottering steps, and then he was on her, one hand gripping her arm, the other at her throat.

'Where is it, damn you?' he roared. 'Where's the money?'

She shook her head feebly. She did not

know where the money was; she knew it had gone, but she could not remember where or how. He began to shake her furiously, shouting obscenities at her, jerking her head backwards and forwards until she thought that her neck must snap. Once he let go to slap her on either cheek — one — two — the slaps sounding like pistol-shots. She would have fallen had he not caught her and shaken her again.

And then he stopped. She stood swaying in his vice-like grip, waiting for him to start again. But he did not start. He had begun to think, and thinking led him to one conclusion only.

'Fred!' he bellowed. 'Fred took it, didn't he? Where is he?'

She pointed vaguely up the hill. She did not think Fred had taken it, but she could not remember. But Fred had meant to take it — and he too was her enemy, she did not care what happened to Fred. Anything to stop the jerk — jerk — jerk of her lolling neck.

Bull threw her savagely down, aimed a kick at her which missed, and went.

* * *

Fred was still searching for the haversack when he heard the shot. He knew it was the shotgun — it had a fuller sound than the rifle — and it startled and puzzled him. He had not expected it, and he could not explain it. Kay had said she would warn him when Bull left the bungalow, but he had received no warning. Had she been so wrapped in her hate that the sight of Bull had made her forget everything else? Most important of all, was Bull dead?

He went to the edge of the crest and looked down, but the cave and the pasture below it were obscured by the trees. Should he go down to investigate, or should he remain where he was? If Bull had gone to the cave that meant he had hidden the money there, that the girl had lied when she said she had not taken it. Even if Bull was still alive — and Fred hoped fervently that he was not — he was unlikely to come back up the hill.

He decided to wait.

He was still waiting when Bull came

out of the trees and started to climb the last few granite-strewn yards to the top. Fred did not see him. Bull came from the side, and Fred was watching the jetty; not until a boot rasped on the rock behind him did he turn. It was too late then. Bull picked him up and shook him and threw him down on to a jutting spur of granite. Fred landed on his broken wrist, and screamed in agony.

Bull stood over him, kicking him methodically. Each time the boot thudded home Fred jerked his thin body and screamed. Not until he thought he had softened him up sufficiently did Bull stop. He gave him an extra kick for good measure, and stood back.

'Where's the money, you rat? What have you done with it?'

Sobbing, knowing that the kicking would start again if he did not speak, Fred wrestled with his tongue. But the words would not come; they were there in his throat, but he could not utter them. Piteously he looked up at his tormentor. His eyes rounded in terror as he saw the foot drawn back, and he made a last despairing effort.

'The — the girl,' he croaked. 'She — *aaaaaah!*'

Bull had let the boot thud home. It seemed a pity to waste a good kick. 'Which girl?' he demanded. 'The blonde?'

It took some time for Fred to recover from the numbing pain of that final kick. Bull let him be. Fred would talk now.

'The other one, Janet.' Fred spat blood and teeth from his twisted and swollen mouth; Bull's foot was catholic in its aim. 'She — I think she got the money for Joe.'

Joe! With a shock Bull remembered that Joe as well as Fred had been missing from the lunch-table. *And* the girl.

'Christ Almighty!'

The oath came slowly from between his full red lips. He had been staring down at the *Stella*, giving himself some small comfort from the sight of her, when he noticed the dinghy. Bucking violently in the rough water, it was moving slowly across the bay. Behind it he caught a glimpse of brown legs threshing the water.

'Christ Almighty!' he said again, frozen into immobility.

Slowly, painfully, Fred had dragged himself to his feet. He caught at Bull's arm, hanging on to him desperately, blood streaming from his face. 'Don't leave me here, Bull! Let me come with you,' he sobbed. Bull might kick him until he was senseless, but he would not kill him. 'I don't care about the money, I just want to get away.' He clutched at the tattered waistcoat. 'I've *got* to get away, Bull! If the busies come they'll hang me, you know they will. That watchman — '

Bull's knee came up, catching him in the groin. As Fred doubled up a fist caught him on the side of the head, and he fell, clawing wildly at the air. Bull did not heed him; cursing and swearing, he stumbled down the hill towards the jetty, bouncing off the trees as he went.

Fred too went down the hill, but more silently. He too bounced from tree to tree. But he did not go in the same direction, or of his own volition. And when his limp body finally came to rest he was dead, his neck broken.

10

I have bedimm'd
The noontide sun, call'd forth the mutinous winds,
And 'twixt the green sea and the azur'd vault
Set roaring war.

The Tempest, Act V, Scene I

Janet slipped quietly into the water. Normally it was fairly shallow here behind the bungalow, but now the waves reached to her chest, and she paused for a moment to get her breath back. She had not expected it to be so cold; or did it merely feel colder because she was wearing shorts and jumper instead of a bathing-suit? The rain came at her from over the loch, and she looked at the black sky and the frothing waves in dismay. It was rougher than she had thought, and she wondered uneasily how the dinghy would behave when they got out into open water.

From some distance away came the sound of a shot, and she ducked below the level of the bank, holding her breath as the waves swept over her. The movement had been instinctive; she had no real fear that she was the target, and presently she began to make her way towards the jetty, now about seventy yards distant. The water grew more shallow as she went, always keeping close to the bank, not daring to lift her head. Her family, as surely as Bull, would try to stop her if they saw her.

By the time she had reached the jetty she was clawing her way forward on her stomach. Her knees and her hands were sore from contact with the shifting gravel bed, her body ached from its constant buffeting against the bank. It was a relief to move out under the jetty, to find herself in deeper water, to be able to swim.

She reached the dinghy and clung for a moment to the gunwale, lifting herself cautiously to peer over it; but the dinghy was rocking too violently at its moorings, and the *Stella*, rolling and heaving ahead of her, obscured her vision. She dropped back into the water and began to hack at the stern-rope with the knife Joe had given her.

It took her some time. In order to keep the dinghy between her and the island she had to hold on with her right hand and work with her left. The rope kept jerking as the dinghy pulled at it, and once she nearly lost the knife. But eventually it parted — so suddenly that Janet went sprawling back into the water — and the dinghy swung round, stern first, to tug like an obstinate donkey at the painter.

Janet came up spluttering. She knew then that she should have cut the painter first, so that the dinghy would drift away bows-on; but it was too late to worry about that now, and for a moment or two she clung to knife and gunwale with her right hand, flexing the fingers of her left to restore the circulation.

She did not see the knife go. One moment it was there in her hand, the next it was not.

She gazed dully at her empty hand. Already she was cold and numb and tired, her head ached from the constant pounding of the waves, her body was sore from its contact with bank and dinghy; yet she had not started on her journey, and now it looked as though she never would. When she thought of Joe waiting for her, depending on her, she wanted to cry; but she fought back the tears, knowing that to cry would be to admit defeat. Taking a deep breath, she let go of the dinghy and, arching her body like a young seal, dived down towards the loch-bed.

It was a long way down. By the time she had reached it the blood was singing in her ears. She scrabbled frantically at the murky bottom, unable to see, and then fought her way back to the surface to fill her aching lungs with air. She had swallowed a lot of water, and it made her feel sick. Hanging thankfully on to the dinghy once more, she knew it was useless to dive again. The knife was gone — she would never recover it.

She began to examine the rope. It was spliced neatly into a brass ring at the dinghy's bows. The other end was hitched round a wooden bollard on the jetty; she could not reach it from the water, she doubted whether she could reach it even from inside the dinghy. To unhitch it would mean climbing on to the jetty, where she would be in full view of any pair of eyes that chanced to look that way. If she were quick it might be possible to get back into the water before anyone from the bungalow could arrive to stop her. But Bull had a gun — and despite her confident assurance to Joe that he would not use it, she was not so confident now. If Bull had discovered that the money was missing from the cave he would be in an ugly mood. He would not let anyone leave the island until he had recovered it.

Or had Kay carried out her threat? There had been just that one distant report as she had entered the water, and since then she had heard nothing but the wind and the *slap, slap* of the waves against the sides of the boats. Surely if Bull were dead or wounded Kay or Donald would have returned to the bungalow by now with the news?

Bull isn't easy to kill, Joe had said. Janet believed that. It was far more likely that harm had come to Donald or Kay, she thought unhappily, than to Bull. But it was the jetty or nothing, she decided. She must take a chance on Bull.

Knowing that her courage would fade with every minute she hesitated, she left the shelter of the dinghy for that of the *Stella*, hoping to haul herself up by means of one of the *Stella*'s fenders; from the surface of the water she could not reach the jetty unaided. But it proved more difficult than she had expected; her arms were too tired, her fingers too numb. Even when she had managed to grasp the gunwale, for a while she could do no more than hang on to it; the effort required to drag her body from the water seemed beyond her. Time and again she tried, only to sink back into the loch; and after each attempt it was an agony to force her aching limbs to try again. When at last, exerting every ounce of her fading strength, she pulled herself up sufficiently to slither untidily over the side, it was to collapse in a heap in the cockpit.

It was wonderful to lie there and rest, to be away from the pounding waves, to feel the hard boards under her body and know that the high deck forward concealed her from the island. But she could not afford to rest. She must leave the safety of the *Stella* for the exposed jetty, she must unhitch the rope and jump back into the heaving water and let the dinghy carry her away. Joe was waiting, and she must not fail him.

It was the thought of Joe that spurred her. She got to her knees, and her eyes dwelt longingly on the comfortable bunks inside the cabin. So much of her life had been spent in that cabin. She had slept in it, lazed in it, eaten in it. She had made the curtains, there were . . .

Eaten in it!

She dragged herself to her feet and went into the cabin, pulling out the cutlery drawer. The knives were table knives, and blunt; but they were knives, they would cut, and she tried several with her finger, selecting the sharpest. As she left the cabin and moved to the windward side of the cockpit the wheel caught her eye, and she touched it wistfully. If only she could take the *Stella* instead of the dinghy! It occurred to her that she ought to do something to prevent Bull from using the *Stella*; but she was no mechanic, and she could not bring herself wilfully to damage it. It would be like maiming an old friend. She slipped over the side, shuddering as the water gripped her, and struck out for the dinghy.

The rain was heavier now. As she sawed frantically at the rope it merged with the spray and beat into her eyes, so that she had to turn her head aside and work blindly. When the rope was jerked away from the knife by the tugging dinghy she could not find the cut she had started and had to begin afresh. Twice she was forced to let go of the gunwale and sink back into the water to rest her aching right arm. She had almost forgotten what she was doing and why she was doing it, when the rope finally parted, and the dinghy began to drift slowly away from the jetty.

With a sigh of relief she dropped the knife into the boat and hung on with both hands. But she could not relax for long. Travelling stern first, the dinghy swung sluggishly from side to side. If she were to control it later — and she would have to — somehow she must turn it round. She grabbed the trailing painter, lay on her back, and struck out with her feet away from the island. The waves slapped at the bows, fighting her, and she jerked sharply on the rope, hoping to gain the necessary momentum to bring the dinghy bows on to the wind. If she could do that it would need only one more tug and the wind would be fighting for her, not against her.

She succeeded sooner than she had expected. For a few seconds she saw the island clearly as the dinghy began to swing. Then it was round, and she let go of the painter and grabbed the gunwale, moving along it hand over hand until she was near the stern, her legs threshing the water to keep the boat on its course. As she drew opposite the wood she saw Kay come out from the trees and stagger across the lawn, one hand to her head, her body thrust forward against the wind and the rain. Janet wondered again what had happened in the cave. Where was Bull? Where were Donald and Fred? At any moment she expected to see one of them emerge from the wood. But they did not come; and presently her view was blocked by the trees, and she ceased to wonder about them.

The cold and the wet were taking their toll of her, and she felt desperately tired; at times her arms seemed about to come out of their sockets. But there was not far to go now, she had only to hang on for a little longer. Ahead of her she could see the Rudery (she had dubbed it the Rudery when she was a schoolgirl, and the name had stuck), a little tongue of land surrounded by teeth of jagged rock. Once she was clear of that . . .

The Rudery! With alarm she realized that from the windward side she should not be able to see it; the dinghy must be too close in to the shore. If it were to hit the rocks . . . those sharp teeth could damage the bottom . . .

Her hands were so numb that they no longer seemed to belong to her, and she watched them as they moved slowly and apparently of their own volition along the gunwale to the bows and snatched at the painter. But whereas the rope had seemed as thick as her arm when she had tried to cut through it, now it seemed too thin. When she tried to hold it it slipped through her fingers, and she had to swim after it and try again.

They were very near the rocks when she finally got a grip and kicked out away from the shore. But she had the wind against her; she brought the bows round, but her failing strength was not enough, and the dinghy sidled crabwise towards the rocks. There was a bump as the stern hit, and the bows swung round sharply, snatching the rope out of her hands. As she caught at the stern she saw with relief that the boat had merely grazed one of the outer ring of rocks and was now clear of them, that it was moving slowly in to where Joe would be waiting.

But that final effort exhausted her completely. She sank lower in the water, her arms at full stretch. Her head hung forward, so that with each wave she was completely submerged and found herself gasping for air as it left her. Her legs, stiff with the cold, trailed woodenly behind; she could no longer steer with them, she could not lift her body out of the water to see if Joe was there. She could only hang on grimly and hope that he was, that he would be able to reach the dinghy and stop it. She could do nothing to help him.

The dinghy bumped and tilted away from her, dragging her partly out of the water; she sank back again as it righted itself. Then strong hands gripped her wrists. She felt herself being hauled up and over the side, and then she was curled in a heap on the floorboards, with Joe kneeling beside her, chafing her hands and arms, inquiring anxiously if she was all right, telling her again that he loved her.

For a little while she lay there; then she sat up, smiling at him thinly. It seemed even colder out of the water, and she crossed her arms over her breast, tucking her hands into her armpits to try to bring life back to them, hugging her shivering body closely. 'Don't worry about me, darling,' she said, her teeth chattering.

'Get the motor started. I'll be all right. I'm just cold, that's all.'

He took off his jacket and put it round her, and then turned to the motor. There was a plug spanner in the tiny locker, and he worked swiftly, pausing only to push the dinghy away from the bank. Janet watched him wind the rope round the pulley, and prayed fervently that the motor would start. When it did she thought that its high-pitched whine was one of the most beautiful sounds she had ever heard.

They headed south, away from the island. The wind came at them over the stern, and the dinghy rose and fell, smacking heavily into the waves as the bows came down, the screw racing wildly as it cleared the water. At times they stayed poised uneasily on top of a wave, the bows tilted alarmingly upward, so that it seemed that the following wave must pour over the stern and swamp them. Huddled in the bows, Janet realized that the wiser course would have been to head due east, taking advantage of what protection from the wind the island might give them, and then to hug the shore south to their destination. But it was too late to change course now; to do so would serve only to lengthen their journey, for already they were too far south for the island to afford them effective shelter. She consoled herself with the thought that the direct course was the quicker — and unless Bull were dead or seriously wounded speed might prove essential to their safety.

She looked back at the island. Against the dark background of the Malloch Hills and the lowering sky it did not stand out clearly. She wondered when and under what conditions she would be going back to it. Joe caught her eye and grinned. He was almost as wet as herself now, but it had not damped his spirits. She knew he was exulting in the violent motion of the boat, in the sense of freedom it gave him. Freedom? Did he think at all of what lay ahead?

'Doing all right, eh?' he shouted.

Janet did not answer. She was staring past him at the island.

'All right may not be enough,' she said,

and pointed over his shoulder.

Joe turned. Rounding the Rudery, almost hidden in the cloud of spray that enveloped her, came the *Stella*.

★ ★ ★

Bull reached the foot of the hill, breathing noisily through his mouth; he had been up and down that hill twice, and he was beginning to feel tired. There was no sign of the dinghy as he crossed the lawn, but the *Stella* still rode at her moorings; he made for it at a trot, the rifle bumping against his back. If Fred were right and the girl had taken the money, then he supposed that she or Joe was responsible for the dinghy's disappearance. He could not understand why they should have taken it — they both knew that the engine would not work — but whatever their reason, it seemed to Bull that they were playing right into his hands. If they had concealed themselves on the island he could not have stayed to look for them; time was pressing. Adrift in the dinghy they would be easy to find. They had no choice but to go down wind. He could not miss them.

He had not realized it was raining so heavily, and he shielded his eyes as he lurched down the exposed jetty. As he came abreast of the *Stella* he looked over at the mainland; there was no sign of the launch, and with a grunt of satisfaction he turned to the *Stella*, tugging at the stern-rope to pull her closer to the jetty.

It was then that he saw Kay. She was in the cockpit, crouched under the wheel, apparently unaware of his presence. For a moment he stared at her in astonishment; then, with a bellow of rage as he saw what she was trying to do, he took a flying leap into the cockpit. The *Stella* was already drifting out again as he leapt, and his impact caused her to heel over sharply. Bull lost his balance and went sprawling on top of Kay.

Clumsily he got to his feet and stood swaying; he was not used to boats, and in that rough water he had difficulty in keeping his balance. He hung on to the deck rail and stared down at the woman. She lay in a crumpled heap, a trickle of blood oozing from her blonde head where the rifle had caught her as he fell. A look of reluctant admiration came over his face. He had not believed that a woman could show such determination, such courage — that she could dedicate herself to hate so completely, regardless of pain or personal safety.

He did not look at her for long. He picked her up and staggered to the cabin, forcing his bulk and his burden through the narrow door, and threw her roughly on to the port bunk.

Then he went aft to the engine.

When Kay recovered consciousness the *Stella* was rolling and pitching down the loch. For a moment or two she could not think what she was doing there; then she remembered and sat up slowly, flinching at the pain in her head. The exaggerated movement of the boat made it worse; the *Stella* came down into the troughs with a jarring thud, shuddering almost to a standstill, her timbers creaking and groaning at the strain imposed on them. Water was everywhere. It streamed down the portholes, it swept through the cabin door in a cloud of spray and rain, it trickled down from the cockpit to run riot on the floor.

Kay swung her legs over the bunk and sat up, bracing herself with her feet against the opposite bunk. From inside the cabin she could not see who was at the wheel, but she had no doubt that it was Bull. No one but Bull would be foolhardy enough to drive the *Stella* so hard in such weather; he would expect the boat to be as indestructible as himself. And he is indestructible, she thought resignedly. I can't touch him. Maybe no one can touch him — not even the elements. Angus McFee had thought that too. 'He hath no drowning mark upon him,' Angus had quoted. 'His complexion is perfect gallows.'

Her belief in this conception was rudely shaken as the *Stella* listed alarmingly to starboard, yawing drunkenly. Kay was thrown forward on to the opposite bunk. Through the submerged porthole she could see dimly the green waters of the loch, and she pushed herself back, convinced that the *Stella* was going down.

But slowly it righted itself and began to surge forward, and, looking back through the open door, Kay could see waves piling up behind and knew that they were once more running down wind.

But she had had enough of the cabin. She staggered to the door and stepped up into the cockpit, bending her head against the driven rain.

'Wet, ain't it?' Bull greeted her. 'Well, you would come, lady. Never seen such a dame for chasing a man. Must be me charm what gets you.'

Kay leant against the cabin and stared at him curiously, heedless of the rain that stung her face. His bald crown shone wetly. Water clung in glistening beads to the hair on his face, trickled down his beard, and dripped on to his chest in an almost continuous stream. The wind that flattened her against the cabin made no impression on him. Feet splayed wide for balance, he gripped the wheel with firm hands, peering ahead into the murk. He was confidence personified. Kay knew that his knowledge of boats and seamanship was almost nil, yet as he stood there he looked as though he had been born to them.

'Where are we going?' she asked.

He nodded ahead, water spraying from his beard. Kay turned her back on the wind and peered over the deck. They were running parallel to the island coastline, well out from it. Every now and again Bull spun the wheel slightly to port, following the line of the shore. If there was any purpose to their course she could not discern it.

Once more the *Stella* slid over a crest and plunged forward into the trough ahead. Kay ducked as water sprayed over and past her. Bull did not move. 'Bucking like a ruddy mule,' he said, and sucked in the water from his moustache.

She stood up, keeping her back to the cabin. 'You're going too fast,' she told him. She had to shout the words at him a second time before he heard her. But he did not touch the throttle.

'Lucky to be going at all,' he shouted back. 'You and your perishing spanner! Didn't want me to leave you, eh?'

'I'm only sorry I didn't kill you when I

had the chance,' she said.

He grinned. 'With that popgun?'

'Didn't I even hit you?'

'Nicked me in the arm. But don't worry, I'll live.'

'That's what I'm afraid of,' she said.

She wondered why it was that she could discuss the incident so calmly, so dispassionately; she had been neither calm nor dispassionate at the time. She studied him afresh, trying to whip her hatred into action. During the past few days it had grown to possess her as no emotion had possessed her before. It had become the very driving force of her existence. Yet it was not driving her now. Perhaps it was his rough humour, the common danger (for she knew there was a danger) that made her dependent on him, the fact that she had failed in all her efforts to hurt and defeat him, that made her feel differently towards him. She still hated him; she was sure she still hated him. That had not changed. He was still her enemy. If she had been a man — if she had had his strength — she would have fought him now, using fists and feet as he used them. She would have shown him no mercy; she had not changed in that. But somehow . . .

'There they are!' Bull shouted.

She turned to see what had excited him. Some distance away, and straight ahead of them, was a small boat. In that sea, and with the horizon swinging madly, she did not at once identify the dinghy. Only when she recognized Joe as he turned to look over his shoulder did she understand.

'What are you going to do?' she asked curiously.

He did not answer. He was searching his pockets for the dinghy's sparking-plug. When he found it he looked from it to the boat ahead in bewilderment. 'They must have had a spare, blast 'em!' he muttered. 'Well, it won't help 'em any.'

The *Stella* veered suddenly to port, and Kay slid across the sloping cockpit, grabbing at the cabin door to prevent herself from falling. She looked at Bull anxiously, wondering what had happened. He had let go of the wheel, which was swinging free; the rifle was tucked between cheek and shoulder, and he was trying to steady it on the deck. She saw his finger on the trigger and let go of the door, completing her slide. As she cannoned into him she heard the crack as the rifle went off.

Pressed against the side, he pushed her furiously away, and she fell to the deck. 'You lousy bitch!' he shouted, dropping the rifle to rub his wounded arm. The *Stella* wallowed into a trough and slid sideways, and he grabbed the wheel as water poured over the port side. He brought the boat round too quickly, and Kay felt it shudder under the pressure. But luck was with them. The *Stella* responded slowly, but she did respond.

Kay picked herself up from the floor and staggered back to the starboard side. She did not look at Bull. Presently he said, his good humour apparently restored, 'Never stop trying, do you? Lucky for you I got a nice nature; you'd be in the drink else.' Kay said nothing, and he went on, 'Come to think of it, maybe you was right to stop me. I don't want to sink the bastards. Not with three thousand smackers on board.'

'What will you do when you catch up with them?' she asked.

'Do?' He paused, thinking it out. How could he stop the dinghy without ramming and sinking it? The rifle lay at his feet, and he stooped to pick it up. Water dripped from it. 'I won't do nothing. Not if they do as they're told.'

'And if they don't?'

'They will,' he said confidently, patting the bulge at his hip. 'Lead ain't comfortable in the stomach; they know that. And if they don't . . . ' He shrugged. 'Well, that'll be just too bad for 'em, won't it?'

Kay started to laugh, and then stopped, shocked at the sound. How could she laugh now — and with him? But she wasn't laughing with him, she was laughing at him.

'And after you've shot them, what then? You jump down into the dinghy, I suppose, and collect the money — leaving me to handle the *Stella*?' She looked at him scornfully. 'Do you think I'd wait for you, you fool?'

He had not thought of that. He thought of it now.

'No,' he said, 'I guess you wouldn't. Okay. You can go overboard, lady. I'll stay in the *Stella*.'

★ ★ ★

'Bull, eh?' Joe said.

'Must be.' Janet looked anxiously at the cloud of spray behind them. The *Stella*'s course was erratic, but there was no doubt about its purpose. 'Did you hear that? I think he's shooting at us.'

'Let him. He ain't likely to hit us. Not in this sea — and at that distance.'

'He won't be at that distance for long.' Janet looked round at the shore, still agonizingly distant, and then back at the *Stella*. 'How well can he handle her, Joe?'

'He can't,' Joe said disdainfully. 'He don't know the first thing about it. We'll dodge him, don't you worry.'

That was their only hope — to dodge him. If they held to their present course Bull must catch them, there would be no hope of escape. To twist and turn in that sea and in such a light craft might be dangerous, but it was the lesser danger of the two. And if Bull wanted to catch them he would have to follow, to take the same risks. Janet had no doubt that he would try. But had he the skill to succeed?

'Look, Joe.' She pointed across the heaving water to a light patch in the dark coastline. 'Make for that gap in the trees. The rocks there come well out into the loch. It won't be easy to pick a way through them in this weather, but it can be done. But not in the *Stella*. Not even when it's dead calm. I've tried. If we can get in there he won't be able to reach us.' She wondered whether she should suggest taking the tiller herself; she knew the loch, Joe didn't. But he might feel hurt at her lack of confidence in him: and anyway she was cold and stiff and tired, she did not feel equal to the task. She had made her effort; now it was up to Joe. 'Take it steady, darling. I don't like the look of those waves.'

He mouthed a grimace at her. 'Me neither. I can't swim.'

As the next wave lifted them he eased

the tiller gently to port, straightened out as they slid down into the trough so that the following wave came at them from the starboard quarter, and then repeated the manœuvre. Worn out as she was, her nerves on edge, Janet had been terrified that she had asked too much of his skill, that he would not make it, that the dinghy would never stand up to the test. But her fears died as she saw how surely he handled the boat. His keen eyes followed each wave until it was past, he was never caught in two minds. A cross-wave came at them from the starboard beam, slapping angrily at the dinghy and drenching them with spray; but there was no real power behind it. Joe laughed, shaking the water from his fair hair.

'How's the enemy?' he asked, raising his voice above the wind. 'Sunk without trace?'

'Not yet.' The smile she gave him was a measure of her confidence in him. Had she been at the tiller she would have taken a more direct course; without the *Stella* in pursuit Joe, she thought, would have taken it too. But he was trying to puzzle Bull, to make it more difficult for him to pick a course and keep to it. The greater the skill that was required of Bull, the more errors he was likely to make. And with the wind blowing the way it was an error could be disastrous.

They were shipping a fair amount of water, and Janet busied herself with the baler. The *Stella* was bearing down on them fast. Bull had altered his course slightly to port, but he still had the wind mainly on his stern. She looked at the shore again, trying to gauge the distance, wondering whether they could reach the shelter of the rocks in time or whether they would be swept past them. The rain had eased a little, but not the wind; it was blowing as hard as ever. Lucky for us it's blowing diagonally, she thought, and not straight down the loch. But even so . . .

'I don't think we'll make it, Joe,' she called to him anxiously. 'We're drifting too far south.'

He glanced quickly over his shoulder at the *Stella*, looked at the shore, and nodded. He could just see the rocks now;

they were low in the water, seeming to bob up and down as the waves swept over them. His hand touched the throttle. As a wave lifted them and bore them on, 'Hang on,' he shouted, and swung the tiller over.

She knew what he was trying to do; to start each tack to port a little earlier, to end it a little later. It meant taking chances and shipping water. It meant that a slight error of judgment could bring disaster. But she did not try to dissuade him. She nodded, smiling at him wanly, and hung on.

During the next few minutes Janet knew all the anxiety and fear and pride of a lifetime. The dinghy creaked and groaned, shuddering as the racing screw came partly out of the water, careening wildly down the long green slopes to a jarring thud at the bottom, sidling crabwise up the next slope, away from the white-capped, menacing crest that chased it so closely. Water swirled round Janet's feet, racing away from her as the dinghy stood on its stern, and then flowing back. With each successive wave she was drenched afresh, her ears were deafened with the noise.

Yet through it all Joe sat crouched in the stern, seemingly unperturbed, the haversack still slung round his shoulders, his hand sure and steady on the tiller. Janet knew the strain on his arm, on his nerves. He may have shown weakness once, she thought, but he's strong now. She thanked God for that strength.

Joe eased the throttle back, steadying the dinghy as it threatened to spin out of control. 'We're shipping too much loch,' he shouted. 'How about putting some of it back?' He glanced towards the shore, trying to pick out the rocks. A round grey pillar seemed to leap out of the water as a wave left it, and he jerked his thumb up in a gesture of triumph. 'Looks like we've made it, eh?'

Janet nodded. She was watching the *Stella*, now less than fifty yards away and coming up fast, her white bow-wave curling to the high deck. If Bull held her on that course he would pass well to starboard of the dinghy. What was he up to? Why didn't he go to port?

She picked up the baler. Before she could use it she saw the *Stella* veer suddenly and fall away, her starboard side almost flat on the water. A wave caught her and lifted her, and swept her down into the trough. Janet thought she had gone; but she came up slowly, a little more erect, the water pouring from her deck. Janet saw the screw racing wildly as her head came round, caught a glimpse of Bull at the wheel, saw . . .

'Joe! There's some one with him! He's not alone!'

'Fred come along for the ride,' Joe said. 'Fred'll do anything for money. Even swim.'

'I think he'll have to,' she said.

But the *Stella* was once more on an even keel. She came charging madly down on the dinghy; Janet thought Bull intended to ram them, and called a frantic warning to Joe. But even as Joe pulled the dinghy round the *Stella* veered again, less suddenly this time, but drunkenly enough to send her listing dangerously, to enable Janet to see clearly the two people aboard — one still grimly clutching the wheel, the other clinging to the rail, her blonde head close to the water.

'It's Kay!' she cried. 'It isn't Fred, it's Kay!'

Joe had temporarily lost interest in the *Stella*. They were among the rocks now. But this was only the outer fringe, and in that heavy sea all but the bigger rocks were completely submerged. They reared up momentarily on either side of the dinghy as a wave passed over and left them — some round, some flat, some jagged and menacing. Ahead, a wall of water blocked Joe's view. He had to watch for the wave that rose a little higher than its fellows, its top creaming, its spray flung more wildly into the air. Even that was no sure guide. There were rocks that did not disturb the crests, that sprang at him suddenly as the dinghy slid down into the troughs, that only a last-second swing of the tiller could avoid.

Janet's eyes never left the *Stella*. Now it was less than thirty yards off their port quarter, racing to intercept them, spray flying high over the deck. She could see the frightened look on Kay's face as they stared at each other across the water, the white wake of the *Stella* swirling and frothing as the screw slashed at the waves. Above the wind came the noise of the engine, the surge and hiss of the bow-wave as it curled gracefully along the hull and was lost in the turmoil astern.

The dinghy bumped, checked, and spun crazily. Janet glanced quickly at Joe, saw him fighting the tiller. A grey object slid away on their starboard quarter; Janet stared at it blankly, her thoughts still with the *Stella*. Then, as realization came to her, she gripped the gunwales and half rose.

'The rocks, Kay!' she screamed. 'You're heading for the rocks!'

If Kay heard she gave no acknowledgment; she did not move, she made no attempt to warn Bull of the danger. The *Stella* held her course. She was level with them now, gradually narrowing the gap, forging rapidly ahead. Janet followed her with her eyes, fascinated. It seemed incredible that the *Stella* could plough blindly on, unscathed, through that forest of rocks and submerged reefs. At any moment now, thought Janet, Bull will bring her round, either to cut us off or to ram us. And if even the rocks can't stop him, how can we . . .

And then the *Stella* struck.

Bull could not have seen the reef that held her. She went surging forward on the crest of a wave; the watchers in the dinghy saw her check suddenly, so that the wave swept on without her, and it seemed that she slid backward into the trough behind. The following wave broke over her in a creaming lather of foam; her stern swung round, and she took the next wave on her starboard beam, rolling sluggishly. Through the welter of spray Janet caught a glimpse of her occupants. Bull had left the wheel; he stood beside Kay, clinging to the side, staring across the water at the dinghy. Another wave broke over them. It threw the *Stella* still farther on to her port side, left her a little lower in the water. The deck partially obscured Janet's view of the cockpit, but she could see Bull. He had moved back to the wheel — perhaps that last wave had swept him there — and was staring fixedly down wind.

There was no sign of Kay.

'She's held by the bows,' Joe shouted. They were the first words either had spoken since the *Stella* had struck. And a moment later, 'I think she's sliding off.'

Janet was not listening. Her eyes were searching the water to leeward, looking for Kay's blonde head amid that expanse of green and grey and white. Kay was a strong swimmer; but if, as Janet suspected, she had been swept overboard, she would not live long in that rough water. But it was Joe who saw her first. He shouted, pointing, and swung the tiller hard to port.

Kay was dazed but conscious when they reached her. The water was smoother here, its main force spent on the larger rocks to windward, but the dinghy swung and rocked dangerously as Joe left the tiller for the time it took him to help Janet drag Kay aboard. Back in the stern again, he looked over his shoulder at the *Stella*.

She went down like a lady; smoothly, without fuss or bother or noise. She did not break up. Her bows tilted acutely, swinging-round to take a last farewell of the loch, exposing the dark slime that coated the bottom of her hull. Bull was still in the cockpit, clinging to the wheel; Joe thought he saw his arm come up in a mock salutation, but at that distance he could not be sure. Then a wave caught the *Stella* and smothered her, and when it had passed only her bows and part of the deck remained above water. She did not wait for the next wave. Slowly and quietly she slid backward into the loch, and when the wave came it swept on and over her in a smooth, untroubled surge of green.

There was no sign of Bull. They raked the water with their eyes, but there was no bobbing head, no flailing arms. Bull had gone as quietly and as finally as the *Stella*.

Joe blinked, and turned to look at Janet. She was crouched by the recumbent Kay, staring over his shoulder. Then she shook her head quickly, as though to rid her mind of the scene, and looked at Joe.

'Bull?' She only mouthed the word, but he understood.

'Not a chance. We can't go back, and it wouldn't be no use if we could.'

She nodded. Her eyes slid away from him, searching the water astern. He could not see the tears mingling with the rain on her cheeks, but he knew they were there. He knew, too, that it was for the *Stella* she wept, not for Bull.

They had to help Kay across the shallows to the shore. The rushes that fringed it seemed never-ending, but at last they were on dry ground, with grass and heather under their feet. Joe went back to the dinghy and pulled it farther out of the water, giving it a valedictory pat as he left it. It had served them well.

He found the two women perched on a broad slab of granite, shielded from the wind by the trees. The rain had ceased. Kay sat leaning forward, her elbows resting on her knees, her head bowed in her hands. A wild spasm of sobbing shook her body. Janet had an arm about her, trying to comfort her; when Joe came up she looked at him in helpless appeal. But Joe had little help to give her; he needed help himself now. The strength that had supported him out on the loch was gone; he felt tired and weak and hungry. He could fight the elements; they were something he understood, he had fought them before. That which lay ahead of him was outside his experience, it was the bogey which had haunted him since childhood. Now it had caught up with him, and he was afraid.

Janet recognized the fear in his eyes and understood; she knew that despite what they had just been through together his greatest ordeal was yet to come. She held out her free hand to him. 'Thank you, darling,' she said softly. 'You were wonderful.'

Her praise cheered him; he was not used to praise. He bent and kissed her upturned lips. They were cold and stiff, as were his own, and he eyed her with concern, immediately forgetful of his own troubles.

'You ought to get out of them wet clothes quick,' he said.

Kay sat up suddenly, startling them. Her eyes glittered through the tears. 'I didn't want him to die,' she said fiercely, as though they had accused her. 'I hated him, but I didn't want him to die.'

'Of course you didn't.' Janet spoke soothingly, as though to a child. 'What happened, Kay?'

'You saw what happened, didn't you?' She sounded irritable, but her voice was calmer.

'Yes, of course. But why didn't Bull jump overboard with you?'

'I didn't jump. He told me to, that you'd pick me up — but somehow I couldn't. I was too frightened, I think. I said I'd jump if he would; it was then he told me he couldn't swim, that it wouldn't be any use. He — he said it was the captain's duty to go down with his ship, and since he had to die anyway he might as well die — doing — his d-duty.' Sobs punctuated the end of the sentence. She gripped Janet's wrist and peered into her face. 'And he laughed when he said it, Janet. He laughed!'

Janet nodded. She could believe that. Bull was crooked and brutal, but he was no coward. 'But you did jump eventually, didn't you?' she asked.

Kay shook her head. 'I think he pushed me as that last wave hit us. But I don't know. Maybe it was just the force of the wave itself that made me let go. All I remember is that one second I was there with him, and the next I was in the water.'

Presently Janet said, 'Are you all right now, Kay? There's a nasty bump on your head.'

'It feels as though it's all bumps. But I'm all right. Just cold and wet and — and miserable.'

Janet shivered, suddenly realizing that she too was cold and wet. In her anxiety over Kay she had forgotten her own worries. But Joe was watching her, and he said quietly, 'I'd best go now, Janet. I can send help.'

She hesitated, and looked at Kay. But Kay was still gazing at the loch, and she took Joe's hand and walked with him a little way across the heather.

'I'll come with you, Joe.'

'No. I'd rather go alone, I think. I wouldn't like you to see me — well, you know. Which way do I go?'

'There's a village a mile down the road.

They'll send a car for us if you ask them. But, Joe — are you sure you want to go alone?'

He wasn't sure, but he would not admit it. 'I'd rather say good-bye to you here. Less public, for one thing.' He drew her to him, holding her wet body close. 'I love you, Janet. You won't never forget that, will you?'

'Never. Never, never, never. Darling, shall I visit you when — well, shall I?'

'No.' At least he was sure of that. 'Go back to Garra and wait for me. I can picture you there. And maybe — well, you could write, couldn't you? When you know where I am?'

'Of course.' She smiled at him through her tears, brushing her wet hair away from her forehead. 'I hope you won't picture me like this. I look awful.'

'Not to me you don't.'

She turned in his arms and looked across the loch to the island. Thin lines of blue streaked the sky to the west, but cloud still hung over Garra. 'Poor Daddy,' she said softly. 'He's lost the *Stella* and he's lost me. I wonder which he'll miss most. The *Stella*, I expect.'

'He can get another boat, but not another daughter,' Joe said. He looked puzzled and faintly alarmed. 'Only — well, he hasn't lost you, has he? You're going back — you just said so.'

'Oh, yes, I'm going back. But I won't be the same person, will I? I'll be — well, some one else. I belong to you now, darling, not to him.'

He stroked her upturned face gently with his fingers. 'It'll be all right, won't it?' he asked anxiously. 'About me, I mean? He won't make you give me up?'

'He couldn't,' she said firmly. 'No one could. Perhaps in time he'll even give up trying.' And there'll be plenty of time, she thought sadly. 'He's a kind person really, you see. It's just that he's so used to running our lives — Mummy's and mine — that he thinks he can go on running them for ever. Well, he can't. Not mine, anyway.'

'But he'll make it tough for you, won't he?'

She shook her head. 'Not when he sees how much I love you. And I do love you,

Joe darling. You know that, don't you?'

'I wouldn't be here else,' he said.

She put her arms round his neck and drew his head down to hers, kissing him tenderly. They were cold and wet, but the fusing of their bodies gradually warmed them, and they clung together passionately, trying to crowd into that brief moment all the love that would be missing from the months, perhaps years, that lay ahead. Then, very gently, he pushed her away. He knew that he must go now, at once, before he lost the courage and the strength that her love had given him.

'You know I'm on the level, don't you?' he said, clumsy in his earnestness. He patted the haversack. 'About the money, I mean. You're not worried I might hang on to it?'

Janet shook her head. 'I love you, Joe,' she said, squeezing his hand. 'And one can't love without trust.'

For a few seconds he looked at her intently, trying to impress on his memory every feature of her face; memory would be all he would have of her for some time to come. Then he kissed her gently and turned abruptly away.

Janet watched him go. He walked purposefully, almost jauntily, aware that she was watching and proud of her faith in him. When he reached the road he turned and waved. Janet waved back, blowing him a kiss. There were tears in her eyes.

'Are you in love with him?' Kay said.

Janet turned, startled. She had not realized Kay was beside her.

'Yes,' she said.

Together they watched Joe's tall figure striding down the road, the haversack bumping at his hip. Just before he disappeared behind the trees he turned to wave again. Then he was gone.

'I've never really loved any man,' Kay said. 'Not even Donald. Not completely. I don't think I'm capable of it. But perhaps hate isn't all that different from love. Either can be the most important thing in one's life, and when you lose it there's a gap inside you that nothing else can fill. Or you think it can't.' She paused. 'That's why I didn't want Bull to die. He's robbed me of something I can't replace. One can't hate a dead man.'

Janet was shocked. 'You've got Donald,' she said. 'And Bobby.'

'Yes, I've got them. But they're not quite enough.' She sighed. 'I suppose I'm not a very nice person; hate seems more real to me than love. Hating Bull was the first completely satisfying and intense emotion I've ever experienced. And now it's gone. For ever.'

Joe had gone too, thought Janet. But he had not gone for ever. For them nothing was finished, they were just waiting for it to begin.

'He shouldn't have died like that,' Kay said. She had turned again to the loch, and was staring at the spot where the *Stella* had gone down. 'Bull was a fighter. He ought to have fought death, not accepted it so calmly.' She sighed. 'Angus was wrong, wasn't he? Bull must have had that drowning mark on him, after all. Angus just didn't see it.'

We do hope that you have enjoyed reading this large print book.

Did you know that all of our titles are available for purchase?

We publish a wide range of high quality large print books including:
Romances, Mysteries, Classics
General Fiction
Non Fiction and Westerns

Special interest titles available in large print are:
The Little Oxford Dictionary
Music Book, Song Book
Hymn Book, Service Book

Also available from us courtesy of Oxford University Press:
Young Readers' Dictionary
(large print edition)
Young Readers' Thesaurus
(large print edition)

For further information or a free brochure, please contact us at:

Other titles in the Linford Mystery Library:

THE RESURRECTED MAN

E. C. Tubb

After abandoning his ship, space pilot Captain Baron dies in space, his body frozen and perfectly preserved. Five years later, doctors Le Maitre and Whitney, restore him to life using an experimental surgical technique. However, returning to Earth, Baron realises that now being legally dead, his only asset is the novelty of being a Resurrected Man. And, being ruthlessly exploited as such, he commits murder — but Inspector McMillan and his team discover that Baron is no longer quite human . . .

THE UNDEAD

John Glasby

On the lonely moor stood five ancient headstones, where a church pointed a spectral finger at the sky. There were those who'd been buried there for three centuries, people who had mingled with inexplicable things of the Dark. People like the de Ruys family, the last of whom had died three hundred years ago leaving the manor house deserted. Until Angela de Ruys came from America, claiming to be a descendant of the old family. Then the horror began . . .

CARLA'S REVENGE

Sydney J. Bounds

Society girl Carla Bowman is young, beautiful — and wild. She is the honey of King Logan, a gangster running a protection racket on New York's East Side, and she becomes caught up in violence and bloodshed. Carla double-crosses Logan and joins his rival, Sylvester Shapirro, only to become his captive in a sanatorium. She escapes, but when she learns that Shapirro has killed her father, Carla's only desire is to revenge her father's death — whatever the cost to herself . . .

I SPY . . .

John Russell Fearn

Television experimenter Curtis Drew sets out to combine the X-ray with television to aid surgery. However, he discovers instead 'pure' television — invisible 'Z-rays' which have the potential to receive and record any situation — anywhere. Nothing is private any more. Immoral acts, and hidden crimes can all be exposed. The 'Z-ray' could benefit humanity, yet to Drew it opens up more lucrative possibilities. He becomes a scientific 'Peeping Tom' and blackmailer, but when murder results, Scotland Yard becomes interested . . .